QUARRY

JANE WHITE

Quarry

HARCOURT, BRACE & WORLD, INC.
New York

TO MY MOTHER

With Gratitude and Affection

Todd saw him first. He was standing still among the hot blackberry bushes, his head bent a little forward and his arms hanging loosely at his sides. He seemed to be looking at the ground, and they could not see his face because it was shadowed by a drop of thick hair. He was wearing a white short-sleeved shirt which was open at the neck and hung out over blue shorts. His thin childish legs were bare, and the grass curled over his brown sandals as if it had grown over them. He looked as if he had been there a long time.

Todd, Randy and Carter stood on the slope in the full sun and looked down at him. They could feel the heat pulsing over them like water. Todd and Carter had large dark patches under their arms and between their shoulder blades. Only Randy still looked cool. His thin black hair showed the careful lines of comb marks. Carter's brown hair stood up in damp tufts, and Todd's lay in thick blond bands across his forehead and neck. It was five o'clock in the afternoon and the sun still seemed as high and hot as midday. The air hummed with flies, and butterflies hung like motionless shreds of coloured paper over the gorse bushes. Below them, the boy stood motionless in the glare.

Todd said,

'He'll do.'

The others did not answer him. They went on looking down the slope of sun at the boy.

Todd said again,

'He'll do.'

He shifted his feet in the hot grass and looked over his shoulder at Randy and Carter.

'Well?' he said.

5

Carter gave his little high-pitched giggle.

'O.K., if you say so.'

'Call him.'

'You call him, Todd,' said Randy. He, too, shifted his weight and looked obliquely at the others. He had his hands in the pockets of his trousers, and now he clenched them into fists so that they looked like two balls resting against his thighs. The material stretched tight and then ran away into little creases as he flexed and unflexed his fingers. 'You call him, Todd,' he repeated.

Todd looked away from the other two. He stood still for a little while longer, slightly in advance of them, as if smelling the air. They could hear nothing except the flies and the distant drone as an aeroplane cruised through the hot sky. Todd stiffened his neck and they saw the muscles bulge as he opened his mouth and called softly to the boy.

'Hi! You!'

There was no response. The boy went on standing quite still as if he had not heard.

Randy said, with an edge of malice,

'Speak up – what are you afraid of, Todd?'

Todd tightened himself again and called, more loudly.

'Hi! You! Can't you hear me?'

His voice was still soft, but it seemed to carry down the slope. The boy turned towards them without lifting his head, merely swivelled his feet that had seemed rooted in the grass, and faced towards them without actually looking up.

'Can't you hear me? I'm calling you. Come on up.'

The boy did not move.

Randy said,

'Come up. There are three of us. You had better come up.'

Still without lifting his face the boy began to walk up the slope towards them. He moved his feet slowly and carefully through the rough grass, pushing the brambles out of his way with his hands. When he was about six feet away from Todd

6

he stopped walking and stood still again, in exactly the same posture as before.

The three of them looked at him. He was smaller than they had thought, yet Todd, at least, felt that, seen at close quarters, he was older than he had seemed at first. Eleven, perhaps, or twelve. Not more. Carter, who was fifteen, was infinitely weightier; there were years between Todd and Randy and this seeming child. Yet, now he was standing there, he contrived to confuse them by his silence, his hidden face, his lack of resistance. There seemed to be nothing in his appearance that they could grasp and make use of – certainly not fear.

Todd said,

'You are coming with us. If you don't want to, and if you try to fight or run away, we shall knock you out and carry you.' The threat, uttered in a voice tentative with nervousness, was incongruous. But he was too intent to notice it. 'Are you coming?'

Behind him, Randy said,

'Better knock him out anyway. He looks as if he could run if he tried.' For some reason he was breathing faster. He moved forward, nearer to the boy. 'We'd better knock him out.'

Todd put out a hand as if to ward him off – a gesture at once protective and angry. The boy looked up at them and said,

'I'll come.'

They all started a little on an intake of breath. It was as if they were surprised that he could speak at all – a repetition of the surprise they had felt when he had moved his feet to walk up the slope towards them.

Todd dropped his arm.

'All right. You follow us.'

'Someone should go behind him,' Carter volunteered in his breathy whisper. 'I mean – there's no knowing. He might try to run for it. He looks as if he could run, like Randy said.'

The boy looked up again, from one to the other of their faces. Presently he settled on Todd.

'I'll follow you. I won't run away.'

'Right,' said Todd. 'Come on then.'

They all turned and walked away up the slope between the bushes, to the quarry.

It was quite a long way, and they moved quickly; but every time Todd turned to look over his shoulder the boy was close behind them. He climbed intently and quietly, with the economy of a small animal. Todd swung his body along easily because it was a well-cared-for machine, and Randy made his intelligence do the work for his body. Carter merely poured out his energy with reckless prodigality and covered twice as much ground as the rest of them. The boy followed with well-organised movements, keeping up with no apparent effort. Soon they left the narrow path and went more steeply upwards through bushes to the mouth of the quarry. The soil was thin, the rock bared in many places, like flesh under the skin. It was yellow, and there were curiously shaped pebbles which slipped and turned under the hand. They came out of the soil and bounced away past the line of climbing boys to clink on to the flatter ground below them, or to disappear among the bushes. Towards the top they went almost on their hands and knees, and grasped and tore at the rough grass or at dry spiny roots which arched themselves out of the soil and then disappeared again beneath its surface like tendons. They pressed their chests, stomachs and knees against the earth and hauled themselves up the last few feet. One by one they appeared on the lip of the quarry, reared up for a moment, then flopped down again at full length. They pressed hot faces into the grass and rolled over with a tracery of lines pressed, like burns, into the flesh. The boy came last, silently pulling himself up beside Todd. He crouched on the hot soil, quite still. He hardly seemed out of breath. Presently he moved forward and began looking intently downwards into the quarry.

Randy pulled cigarettes and matches out of his breast pocket and blew out a stream of pale smoke. Propped on his elbow, he looked past Todd to the boy where he knelt, peering down.

'Yes, that's where we're going,' he said. He gestured out and down. 'You can't see it from here – in fact I doubt if anyone can see it from anywhere. But there's a cave. It's just underneath us. It goes right into the quarry face.' He drew on his cigarette and went on looking at the boy through the cloud of thin and motionless smoke. He looked menacing, thought Todd, glancing uneasily at him, and moved closer to the boy. Carter was throwing pebbles down, trying to hit a sheet of tin which glittered among the bushes at the bottom of the pit. Every now and again there was a faint clang as a stone hit the hard surface and bounced off into the grass, and each time Carter crowed with satisfaction and counted his score aloud.

'Six! I say, Todd, I hit it six times! I bet I get to ten this time.'

The boy drew back a little and looked at the faces surrounding him as if trying to calculate what he had to expect from them. Randy quietly went on smoking, his long pale face alert. Todd turned over on to his back and lay looking up at the endless height of the sky above him. It looked as if it had been peeled back, layer upon layer, until it was all heat, and stillness, and absence of colour. The smell of Randy's cigarette was acrid as incense in the air. When his eyes would not bear the light any more he rolled over again and got to his feet.

'Come on,' he said. 'Time we were going down.'

'Oh Todd! Wait a bit!' Carter protested noisily. 'I've got to nine this time. Just wait till I've done it once more.'

Todd went forward and, kneeling down, swung himself over the edge. He turned to look over the top for a moment before disappearing.

'You can stay and chuck your beastly stones if you want

9

to,' he said indifferently. 'We're going down. Come on, Randy.'

Carter flung a last despairing stone over the edge. It flew wide of its target and flopped into the bushes. Grumbling, he scrambled to his feet and followed Randy over the edge.

It was easier going down, though infinitely more dangerous. Also, by now the sun was off the slope and, abruptly, the coolness was as invigorating as immersion in cold water. They scrambled down in a slither of small stones. The boy came last, cautiously letting his small body slip down over the ground. He kept looking down over his shoulder to make sure that he was using exactly the same track as the others. When they had been going down for what seemed a very short time he saw that Todd was no longer on the slope below him. The next time he looked Randy, too, had disappeared. He gripped the roots near his hands and twisted his head back and down to watch Carter. The odd, foreshortened body stopped, edged sideways, then, seemingly, melted into the face of the quarry. He released his hold on the roots and let himself slide down a few feet until he came to rest on some flat surface which was just wide enough to support him. He imitated Carter – edged sideways, put out his left hand and felt nothing. He edged further left until his whole body had lost contact with the earth, and then walked forward into the face of the quarry.

To Todd, entering the cave, it seemed, as usual, that he had walked into total darkness. But in a moment his eyes adjusted to the glare of seeming blackness, and he stopped moving forward and looked about him. There was only a dark hollow surrounding him – walls, presumably, somewhere, but they were not seen, only felt in a sense of confinement, of boundaries. Above, undoubtedly, there was a roof. Indeed, as his eyes steadied, he fancied that he could see it as a rough arch, grey, and somewhat irregular. The ground under his feet felt uneven, but fairly smooth. It was not the smoothness of stone, nor that which is beaten out by much passage of feet. It felt like earth which had been pressed by a great weight, first resting upon it, then lifting – to form the arch above his head? He turned to face the direction from which he had come and saw the light – an irregular, flattened circle of gold, patterned by the thin figure of the boy standing against it.

He turned to look out of the cave and away to the opposite slope. Nothing moved, and there was no sound except that of the aeroplane, still beating the air in its idle flight. Beside him, he heard Randy blow out his breath in a little gasp of achievement.

'Well, we got him here.'

Todd did not answer. Randy, mistaking his silence for irresolution, said irritably,

'And what do we do now?'

Todd said, surprised,

'What we said.'

'Keep him here?'

'Yes, of course.'

Behind them, they felt the boy listening. They moved closer together.

'That's all very well, Todd, but how? We can't tie him up – in the first place we haven't even brought anything to tie him up with. It's all your beastly fault – you were in such a hurry you didn't bother to work out what we'd do when we actually got him here.'

'He climbs jolly well,' said Carter admiringly. 'He'd be out like a shot if we left him to it.'

'And we can't stay here with him to make sure he doesn't get away. It's a bloody stupid situation,' Randy hunched his shoulders morosely. 'Fat lot of good you are as a leader.'

'Oh, shut up!' said Todd irritably. 'I'm trying to think. The pair of you jabbering doesn't help, you know.'

Behind them, the boy sat down on the floor and leaned his back against the wall. The sunshine slid quietly down the slope, and they began to hear a bird calling tentatively from the trees. Todd seemed to come to a decision.

'Stand up,' he said.

There was a moment's silence, and then they all heard the faint sounds of movement as the boy got to his feet.

'Come here,' said Todd.

He came, and stood impassively in front of them.

'We're going to leave you here,' said Todd slowly. 'You won't go away, will you?'

'No,' the boy said indifferently.

Todd repeated,

'You won't go away, will you?'

Again the boy said,

'No.'

'We'll come back tomorrow with food and things; you won't be cold – the nights are almost as hot as the days at the moment. If you're thirsty you'll find some bottles of pop at the back of the cave. But you mustn't try to get away. Do you understand?'

The boy looked at each of them in turn. For a moment they saw something like contempt flicker in his eyes. Then he repeated indifferently,

'I won't go away.'

They stood still, watching him, Todd with urgency, Randy with something like disbelief mixed with submission, Carter with bright unconcern. After a moment the boy turned away and walked to the back of the cave. There he unbuttoned his shorts and urinated amply against the wall. While he did so he watched them over his shoulder. When he had finished he did himself up again and sat down on the floor. He leaned his back against the wall, closed his eyes, and appeared to go immediately to sleep.

'Good God!' Randy exploded violently. 'Of all the filthy little buggers—'

Carter burst out laughing.

Todd said,

'Well, I don't quite know what else he could have done. But he can't just pee all over the place whenever he feels like it. We'll have to bring a spade and dig a hole and make him throw in some earth each time.'

'After all, it won't be for that long,' said Carter cheerfully. 'Come on, you chaps, I'm starving. Let's bugger off.'

Todd looked at his watch.

'Getting on for half past six. Come on, Randy.'

Randy looked at the small body curled like a shadow against the wall.

'Do you really think he'll stay?' he asked Todd.

'He'll stay all right.' Todd was already half way out of the cave. 'For God's sake get a move on.'

But Randy, moving forward, still lingered, uncertain. To Todd, out in the warm air with the grass under his hands, his voice sounded far away and detached, as if he were still far underground.

'Who do you think he is?' came the voice. And again, 'Todd, who do you think he is?'

Todd, who was already climbing swiftly up the cliff face, was anxious only to get into the sun, and home, and so, not hearing this question, was unable to answer it. Randy came out of the cave and also began to propel himself up and up into the light. Behind them, and below in the ground, the boy sat coiled against the wall in the shadows, and slept.

Todd wheeled his bicycle into the garage and dumped it against the wall; then he went round the side of the house through the shrubbery and on to the lawn. The garden, after the arid heat of the waste land surrounding the quarry, looked all green and gold, full of flowers and abundant foliage. With its neat borders, its trim grass, it looked precisely what it was – a well-cared-for English garden in the height of summer. The sun still lay across the grass and the sprinkler was on. It sent a fine and gradually revolving cascade of water drops

13

over the grass. It looked cool and clean. Todd kicked off his shoes and raced across the grass, struggling out of his shirt as he went. The water hit his hot skin like little needles and exploded on his face and neck. It ran over him and trickled in erratic rivulets down his arms and over his feet. As he danced in it he felt it penetrate his hair and tickle his scalp. He opened his mouth and stooped down and tilted his head back so that it dripped on to his tongue and down his throat. It was not really cold, and the jets were not powerful enough to wet him thoroughly, but it gave him a feeling of exhilaration and cleanliness.

Behind him he heard his mother's voice calling, and he turned under the water so that he saw her through a fine wall of spray.

'Todd! Todd!' she was calling. She stood on the terrace in front of the long open windows and waved her bare arm so that the bright orange sleeve fell away to her shoulder like a wing.

'Todd! Come away from that water! You'll catch cold if you get wet after all this heat.'

'Catch cold? In this weather?' he shouted back, but he went through the water and walked to her across the grass laughing, and shaking the fine drops out of his hair. She waited for him on the terrace, shading her eyes against the sun. Her thin orange blouse glowed against the darkness between the windows. He ran up the steps and bent to kiss her cheek. She pushed him away, her hands cool on his wet skin.

'Pouf! You're soaking! For goodness sake go and put on something dry. You can't sit in the drawing-room like that. And find some shoes. I'm not having you paddling around on my carpet in your bare feet.'

When he came down in a clean shirt and trousers, his damp hair sleek with water, she was lying in one of the long basket chairs just inside the window holding a glass in her hands. With her long pale face against the cushions in a spread of dark hair and her narrow feet neatly crossed in thong sandals, she looked like a recumbent Madonna, and he said so, perching on the chair at her feet.

'A Madonna?' she arched her eyebrows at him. 'Compliment?'

'In a way.' He stretched, and sighed. 'Hot.'

'Bloody hot,' she agreed languidly, and moved her head restlessly against the cushions. 'It's extraordinary – the end of June, and it's been like this for three weeks already. Everything's ruined in the garden. The grass would be too, if it weren't for the sprinkler. Personally, I loathe it.'

'Do you? I don't.'

'I know – you soak it up like some awful dago. It suits you, though.'

'Suits me?'

'The tan, and the bleached hair. I just go yellow. That's why I stay out of it.'

'Vain.'

'I know – aren't I?'

He got up and went over to the sideboard. She watched him as he mixed a drink in a long glass and came back to the window swirling the cool amber liquid between his hands.

'What is it?'

He told her.

'Todd, should you? I mean, still at school and all that – you're quite a little boozer, aren't you?'

'Not always. Only on special occasions,' he said with satisfaction, and took a long drink from the glass, wiping his mouth on the inside of his arm and smiling at her. 'Why not? I like it. Don't you?'

'Me? That's different.'

'Nonsense.'

They sat in silence and looked out at the garden. The trees were throwing longer shadows on the grass and birds moved quietly among the leaves with small rustling sounds. There was the sudden noise of a car starting up, a woman's voice called to a child, an aeroplane droned. Todd leaned forward

15

to watch it as it crossed the sky, a remote dot labouring across the blue. His mother seemed to be asleep. He got up and carried his drink to the open window. Leaning against the frame and easing his shoulders into a comfortable position, he felt the first breeze pass his face and trickle down his arms. Behind him, Clare sighed and stretched. The room was so still that he heard the faint tinkle of ice in her glass as she set it down. He sensed her eyes on him, but did not turn to her, although he knew that she was tensing herself to some kind of approach.

'Todd, when does your term end?'

'In about four weeks.'

'And the exam?'

'Just before the end of term.'

'That dreadful school – I still don't see why—'

'For God's sake, Mother. Not that again. Anyway it's not that bad.'

'I still think a public school—'

'Mother dear, if you remember, at the time it would have been a pretty third rate public school on Daddy's screw. He did the right thing, for once. I'm pretty safe for an Oxbridge scholarship, you know.'

'Yes, I suppose so. Todd, when you've finished your exams and all that, let's go away together. For a holiday. We could manage a week in Spain and then go on to Italy, or somewhere, just us.' She lay and watched him, holding her glass tightly against her breast. 'Shall we? Would you like to?'

He thought about it.

'I wouldn't want to go immediately term ends,' he said slowly, working it out.

'Why not?'

'I couldn't go straight away,' he persisted quietly.

'But why not?'

He gestured vaguely, shaking his drying hair away from his forehead.

'Oh – just things. Things to do.'

16

'With Randy? And that dreadful little Carter?'

He turned to look at her.

'Yes, as a matter of fact. We've got one or two things planned.'

'Those two—' she said. 'I can't think why they always come first.'

'They don't come first,' he said patiently. 'It's just that we've arranged one or two things and I can't let them down.'

'I suppose you were with them today, and that's why you were so late this evening.'

'Yes.'

'Whatever do you find to do with them?' she burst out angrily. 'Chasing girls with Randy? Or playing games with Carter?'

'No, not exactly.'

'I must say it sounds unlikely.'

He smiled across at her.

'I'm really not going to tell you, you know.'

'I can see you're not.'

After a moment he said softly,

'Jealous?'

'Yes,' she said instantly.

'Silly,' he said. He came away from the window and sat facing her on the side of her chair. 'Silly old Clare.'

She lay still, looking up at him.

'You can't talk me out of it,' she said, but the edge had left her voice. She put out her hand and began playing with one of the buttons of his shirt, turning and twisting it between her fine, thin fingers. 'But you will come, won't you? When you've finished whatever it is?'

'Yes.'

'Promise?'

'Promise, hope to die.'

She left go of the button and ran her forefinger over the skin of his chest where it showed, furred with fine fair hair, between the open edges of his shirt.

17

'Nice boy,' she said. 'There's a nice good boy. Give Clare a kiss?'

He stooped slowly forward and touched her cheek beside the mouth with his lips.

'Better?' he said without moving.

They ate a cold meal off trays, still sitting at the open window as a thin luminous twilight crept over the garden. Clare drank a lot more, and Todd assiduously filled her glass for her. They hardly spoke, just sat smoking together in the cooling air which thickened imperceptibly until they were almost invisible to each other except as a cigarette end pulsed red and lit up a mouth, a cheek, part of a hand. When it was completely dark they went upstairs. Todd stayed behind to bolt the windows and to drop the latches on the doors. When he went into Clare's room she was stretched motionless on the top of the great double bed, as slight as a child. Her face was waxy among her loosened hair.

Todd went to the windows and threw them wide. A pungent smell came to him from the garden as he leaned out, a mixture of flowers, of cut grass, and an indefinable, moist decay. Behind him Clare said,

'Thank God, at least I've got the bed to myself. Guy slept disgustingly. He used to keep me awake just by being asleep.'

'Never mind – now you've got your nights all to yourself.'

'I didn't necessarily mean thank God I'm by myself,' said Clare dryly. 'I meant, thank God I'm not with Guy.'

'I know.'

She drew in her breath.

'You know a bloody sight too much sometimes, Todd.'

He laughed, lounging in the open window.

'I do, don't I?'

Her white nightdress, almost luminous in the light summer darkness, looked to Todd like a shroud. When he kissed her she opened her greedy mouth on him like a sea-anemone, and long after he was lying on his own bed, flat as a corpse in the darkness, he heard her next door, tossing restlessly – whether

18

asleep or awake he did not know. He lay quiet, waiting for coolness and for sleep, and thought of Carter, and Randy, and of the boy – and of his own reasons, which were deep, and tortuous, and inexplicable.

When Carter arrived home his tea was drying in the oven and his mother was sitting at the kitchen table waiting for him.

'So there you are! I was just going to eat your bit of fish myself if you didn't come soon. The heat makes me hungry – funny, it takes away most people's appetites, but it suits me. I always put on in a hot summer. It's in the oven. Anyway, where've you been?'

Carter opened the oven door and took out his plate of fish and chips. It looked rather dry and a lot of the batter seemed to have fallen off the fish. But he was, as usual, extremely hungry, and was not, in any case, a person of refined tastes. He cleared himself a space at the table, fetched a knife and fork, and sat down opposite his mother.

'Well? Where've you been?'

'Up at the quarry.'

'Oh, the quarry again.' She lost interest immediately, and sat back in her chair, fanning herself with the newspaper. 'Beats me what you find to do with yourselves up there – and in this heat too! It half kills me getting round the corner to the shops.'

Carter, methodically munching chips, said indistinctly,

'Went up there with Todd and Randy after school.'

'Oh, those two. Not that I've anything against Todd. He's a nice boy, even if he is a bit uppish because his mother's got money and they live in one of those posh houses up the hill. But that Randy! I don't know how you can stick him. He gives me the creeps, with that great long face – and always so tidy! It's just not natural, a boy of that age being as clean as all that. And always after the girls, I've heard. He's clever,

I can see that, and he's always polite, and he speaks nicely and all that, but he's just not normal. I don't know how a nice lad like Todd Gascoigne, with all his fancy ways, can stick having him around.'

Carter had finished his chips and now turned his attention, with rather less enthusiasm, to the fish.

'Randy's all right,' he said.

'Well, I don't know. I just don't like him, and that's that.' Having disposed of Randy, she inquired,

'Anyway, what do you do all the time up at that old quarry? Miles from anywhere, and not that safe after all this time, I shouldn't imagine. Don't you go climbing about and breaking your neck, young man, or I'll have something to say to you.'

Carter said nothing. As if stirred to a lazy kind of curiosity by his silence, she persisted,

'But what do you do up there?'

'Oh, just muck around. Do things.'

'What things?' she inquired suspiciously.

'Oh, just things.' He pushed his plate away, and looked up, to find her really curious. 'There's a cave,' he volunteered cautiously. 'Quite a big one. We've got some bottles of pop and stuff up there, and we go and talk and muck around –you know.'

'I can't say I do.' Only half satisfied, she got heavily to her feet and began piling up the dishes and taking them over to the sink. 'Still, I can't see Todd Gascoigne getting himself mixed up in anything, so I suppose it's all right. There's a bit of jelly and some fruit on the side there. I saved it for you. Take it over by the window while I clear up. It's like an oven in here, and if you open the window the flies are terrible. Switch on the radio, there's a good boy.'

'Where're the others?'

'Daphne and Anne went to the pictures. Gordon's cleaning his bike out at the back. He's going on one of his rallies to-morrow. Dead keen on that bike, he is. Gives him an interest,

I say, even if the neighbours do complain about the noise. Anyway, it's not all that noisy, only when he's starting it up or doing something to the engine. He's ever so careful with it. I don't mind admitting I was nervous about it at the beginning. He seemed so young to be messing about with a dangerous thing like that, but I must say he's been really good about it. I thought he'd get mixed up with a gang of rough lads and go rushing around doing ton-ups, like they're always going on about in the papers, but he's not like that a bit. Seems to like going off on his own into the country. Sounds a bit dull to me, but he likes it, and at least he's safe out there.'

Carter licked the last bits of jelly off his spoon. A distant burst of engine noise rose upon the hot air and then settled down to a quiet throbbing hum. Carter listened critically.

'Sounds healthy enough,' he remarked, and took his plate over to the sink. 'I'll dry. Give us a cloth.'

'Thanks. I won't deny I'm looking forward to a good sit down with my feet up. It's been a day – that hot, and one thing and another. We could do with some rain. Watching telly tonight?'

'No thanks, Mum. I think I'll go out and see how Gordon's getting on and see if he'll take me out for a spin.'

'Well, mind how you go. If there is a smash, it's always the one on the back who catches it.'

Carter found Gordon lying underneath his motorbike in the middle of the small lawn. Next door two small children peered silently over the fence. Their father sat in a deck chair reading a newspaper. There was a smell of cooking, and of hot machinery, which hung agreeably in the evening air. Carter squatted down and chewed a piece of dry grass as he watched operations.

'Take me for a spin? he inquired presently.

'Haven't you got any homework to do?' replied the voice from beneath the machine. Carter kicked amiably at the leg nearest to him.

'It's Friday, you ass. Who ever does homework on a Friday?'

'O.K. Give me ten minutes to put it together again.'

'What's wrong with it, anyway?'

'Nothing, now. I fixed it.'

Carter surveyed the debris of tools and bits of motorcycle surrounding his prostrate brother.

'I believe you only take the bloody thing to bits because you can't think of anything better to do,' he remarked offensively.

'Well, what about it? It's a darn sight better than messing around with a girl in the back row of the flicks like your friend Randy. Or lording it over the local peasantry in Mama's expensive car like your friend Todd Gascoigne.'

'Shut up!' said Carter. He got to his feet. 'Just leave them out of it, will you?'

'O.K. – O.K.! No offence meant.' Gordon put a somewhat startled face out from beneath his machine and regarded his brother in mild surprise.

'Just shut up about them, that's all,' repeated Carter. 'They're no business of yours.'

'Too true.' Gordon withdrew his head and began screwing away at something underneath the motorcycle. 'For goodness sake calm down! It's too jolly hot for rows. I won't be a jiffy. Give me five minutes and she'll be ready for anything.'

Carter withdrew to the other end of the lawn and waited until Gordon and his machine were ready to go.

They cruised slowly through the quiet streets, empty except for an occasional girl flouncing along in full skirts and high heels or a car cruising sedately home with windows wide and radio sounding thinly above the engine. When they were free of the last houses, strung out along the road in their identical pebble-dash and red brick, Gordon let out the engine, and they began to move fast through the stifling air until a real breeze was blowing into their faces. Hot as it was, and laden with stinging dust which gritted on their lips and made them gulp sideways at it as if trying to sift it free of dirt, it was welcome, and gradually it cooled and exhilarated them. Carter undid his shirt to the waist and bounced on the pillion with his hands clasped behind him. It was marvellous, it was exciting, it was speed, he thought, the body unprotected, and the rushing air free to break on the skin like spray. They rode past fields and fences, bursting out from arches of trees into the thick dusty sunlight, dazzled and swept by the gritty wind which did not really exist except in their own motion. Carter thought, as he gripped and swayed on his knees, that it must feel rather like this to be drunk, and he began to shout, 'Faster! Faster! Go faster!' above the contented roar of the engine, although he knew that the words would be snatched from his mouth and flung away behind him long before his brother could hear them.

When he was in bed that night, tossing like a puppy in the heat of his bedroom, his mind, half asleep, continually revolved with the images of speed; of skimming along the darkness on a cliff top; and of the cave where the boy slept underground, like a mole enclosed by its burrow.

Randy got home very late. It was almost midnight and the street lamps abruptly went out in a dazzle of darkness as he turned into the tunnel of the drive leading up to the house. He cursed morosely as he stumbled over unidentifiable objects which lay in his path and shied away from branches which hung down and ensnared him as he walked. The whole place was rank with overgrowth – even in the dark it stank to Randy of a misplaced and arid fecundity. The house had been a vicarage of some size and dignity in the old days, but now it was decaying fast, and nothing was being done to arrest the process. Mr and Mrs Johns, deserving and retired, had bought it, prudently as they thought at the time, for next to nothing, and, having done so, had found themselves dismayed and impotent in the face of so much structural collapse and vegetable growth. Randy, a nephew taken in a moment of much regretted compassion to live with them on the death of his parents, had lived in this place for ten of his seventeen years, and had seen it gaining the upper hand with a kind of sour satisfaction which did not endear him to his uncle and aunt. Mr Johns was a clergyman, retired from the active pursuit of his profession by reason of a mysterious complaint to which no name was given, but which was referred to by his wife, formerly his housekeeper, as a 'burden', presumably sent by the Lord, which they must all, including Randy, bear with patience and fortitude. Mrs Johns had prevailed upon Randy during his early days in their care to address her as 'Mother'. Having no child of her own this had seemed a suitable appellation. Later, however, this was dropped by mutual consent. He now called her by no name at all if he could help it; when driven, he achieved an occasional 'Aunt Elspeth', which, said as he said it, alienated the pair of them still further. She was tall and very thin, and she wore a pair of round pink-rimmed spectacles which went ill with her long face and sallow skin. Mr Johns was also tall and thin, but as he sat down a good deal of the time this was not so noticeable in his case. Randy, when he thought about them at all, which was as rarely as possible, loathed and despised them both with equal force.

Fortunately, they both went to bed very early, and Mr Johns, at least, got up very late, so they did not have to spend much time in each other's company. Randy, coming home very late on most nights, always turned the last corner of the dark drive where the house stood on its sweep of what had once been gravel, to find all the windows dark and the front door blankly shut against him. However dark the night, its aspect was so familiar to him as he crossed the small plot of grass and climbed the five steps to the door that he always felt as if he could actually see it standing there, waiting for him.

When he opened the front door and went inside, he smelt the same smell, winter and summer – of brown paint, of damp mackintoshes, and of food which had been cooked and eaten some hours before and still hung like an odorous malaise about the stairs and hall. This evening it seemed to be mainly compounded of fish, for Randy, to the intense disapprobation of his uncle and aunt, was a Roman Catholic. This was a bitter trial to him, and he believed with a kind of loveless obstinacy which had its roots mainly in fear. He felt his life to be hedged in by sanctions; the inevitable result of such an action was such a penalty, the loss of a faith which he longed to discard would bring down upon him a penalty which he could not contemplate.

His aunt, taking the child into her house without love, and with many misgivings, had nevertheless been sure that his Catholicism, at least, would raise no problems. It would imperceptibly slip from him, unnoticed and unregretted. That it had failed to do so was entirely due to the fact that the child, barely seven on his arrival, had taken in hand the organisation of his life as a Catholic and had arranged it for himself with complete efficiency. It was a success so unexpected and so swiftly achieved that Mrs Johns, defeated, she scarcely knew how, almost found herself respecting him for it.

However, this turned out to be the only matter on which Randy and his uncle and aunt came into open collision. In everything else he seemed docile enough – naturally tidy, quiet in his manner, polite when his own concerns were not brought into question, he fitted well enough into the life he found he was expected to lead. He did well at his primary school – indeed, he turned out to be more than ordinarily clever. His mind was quick, his sensibilities seemed acute, and he was painstaking and methodical in all he did. Indeed, the only criticism his teachers could find to make was one that was not easy to express – a lack of spontaneity, a watchfulness, an eye continually open for the main chance, which made him generally disliked and distrusted by the staff. Also by many of the boys, although when he duly got his scholarship and went on to the Grammar School he made one or two friendships which persevered as he moved up the school, and which disconcerted the few people who were interested enough to remark upon them.

By the time he was seventeen and in the sixth form he had discarded all but two of these, and these two were the most unlikely of all; Richard Carter, the friendly, ordinary fifteen-year-old from the 'Estate', with just enough brain to get into the Grammar School and no more; and 'Todd' Gascoigne, brilliant, handsome, arrogant. They were an odd, alarming trio. No one knew what drew, or kept them together, and no one was allowed far enough into their confidence to inquire. The combination was formidable – physical energy, intellectual brilliance, low cunning were its components, although few people went so far as to define them as such. Their teachers taught them, respected them, especially Todd, and left them alone. They were no trouble in class, not even the ebullient Carter. Their fellows did not attempt to break in on the circle, perhaps realising such a thing to be impossible. By the time Todd and Randy were taking their Advanced levels, and Carter, though lower in the school, was in his last term, they were virtually untouchable, and recognised as such.

To Randy, the thing was a triumph, most bitterly fought for. The fact that it had been difficult of achievement made it worth clinging to, worth cherishing in a way which Todd and Carter, each in their different ways, merely accepting it, could not have begun to understand. But Randy felt that the impetus of it all sprang from him. If he were to withdraw his support, to check the flow of his very life blood into it, it would collapse into its component parts and into meaninglessness. Leading his solitary, haunted life, in which he felt himself driven by a guilt which he could not exorcise, it was the thing which, so to speak, kept him warm, made him cohere.

But all the same, Todd was the leader. Without effort, and without conscious will, that was inevitable. Todd was the beautiful, the blessed one; he was tall, splendidly fair, effortlessly achieving everything which he attempted. Randy took these achievements to himself without jealousy, almost without pain, as if they did not belong to Todd, but to himself. He felt himself to be the creator. Nevertheless, and inevitably, Todd was the leader.

At night, when he came home, it was from the three of them that Randy took his life. Every night, as tonight, he went into the kitchen, snapped on the light, took a cup from the shelf and stood it on a saucer; poured milk into a pan, lit the gas under it, and while it boiled put two spoonsful of cocoa in the cup, added the sugar, then poured the hot milk on top, stirring vigorously to disperse the lumps. He drank from the cup held gingerly between his palms and turned his head, the cup at his lips, to look at the uncurtained window where nothing ever broke the blankness of the glass, not the moon, not a star, certainly not a face looking in at his modest carousing. The house was absolutely quiet. Upstairs, side by side in their blameless bed, Mr and Mrs Johns slept together like two planks under the blankets. Mr Johns slept upon his back because of his 'burden'. Mrs Johns lay sharp edge uppermost because to lie on her back even in her sleep might invite unchaste thoughts. Randy's room awaited him, and in time, his cup washed and neatly replaced on its hook, he padded quietly up in his socks and crept past the conjugal chamber thinking of the two bodies lying so close together and yet generating no warmth, and thus, inevitably, leading himself to think of other, imagined bodies pressed close to his.

Here the clumsy touchings and fumblings with breasts and between thighs became triumphant and assured; here there was no dribble of saliva down his chin, no girl to giggle or to push his hand away just as he was getting it right at last. Instead, in the darkness, there was the tiger-skin, the white body spread on it like a flower, the huge eyes, violet and

27

adoring, the red lips to murmur 'Master!' as he stood over her, bronze torso bared, magnificent legs astraddle, and possibly a barbaric ring or two flashing on his fingers as he stooped to take her. The image was tawdry, the setting lurid. But it never failed. Something immature in him responded to the shilling-shocker stimulus of it; the trappings of old-fashioned sin roused him as more sophisticated images could not. And so, again, the white bosom heaved, the smooth thighs opened, wound round his, and again he mastered and subdued her to his will. The childish innocence of this fantasy had long established itself with him. It was vastly more effective than any more realistic, more adult image could be. He abandoned himself to it with a clear conscience as a licence, a luxury which he must allow himself in order that he might exorcise the inconveniences of real lust, actual sin.

On Saturday afternoon it was as hot as ever. To Todd, who had arrived first, and who lay flat in the sun, his eyes shut behind dark glasses, it seemed, if anything, even hotter. There was absolutely no movement in the air and the few birds above him in the great hot spaces of the sky seemed to move heavily as if made languid even in flight. There was no sound either, and Todd felt as if he had come to the edge of the world and was poised above an immense and motionless sea. Presently, he heard the sounds of someone moving painfully upwards among the bushes below him and, supine on the grass, contemplated with pleasure the sounds of effort which floated up to him. Presently Carter, panting like a dog, hauled himself up the last few feet and plumped down beside Todd.

'Phew! It's even hotter today. I don't know why we chose this place. It nearly kills me getting up that blasted hill. Why couldn't we have found somewhere on the flat?'

'Because there isn't anywhere on the flat,' said Todd amiably. 'Seen Randy?'

'No. Probably still confessing his sins.' Carter giggled.

' "Please, Father, I tried to fuck a girl last night, but she wouldn't let me. What shall I do?" "Persevere, my son, persevere".'

'Shut up,' said Todd lazily. 'He can't help it.'

'Can't help what? Not being able to fuck a girl? Silly sod.'

There was a pause during which Carter continued to giggle to himself. Presently he said,

'I say, Todd, is he still there?'

'I don't know. How should I know?'

'Haven't you been to see?'

'I've only just got here, you ass. Have you brought anything?'

'Some sausage rolls and a chocolate cake. It's melted a bit because I sort of sat on it on the way up. What've you got?'

'Oh – a loaf, some butter, tins of stuff, lots of chocolate, and some soap. And some bottles of pop.'

'Soap?'

'Well, he's got to wash, hasn't he? Pretty beastly for us if he doesn't.'

'Oh, I see. What about water?'

'There's a stream at the bottom of the gully. We shall have to go down with buckets. I'll bring a bucket next time.'

'Oh. I say, Todd, it's not going to be easy, is it? I mean, there's all sorts of things.'

Todd rolled over on to his face and began to chew a withered blade of grass.

'Oh, I don't know. It'll work out.'

'Let's hope so.'

There was a pause while they lay still and felt the heat pulsing through their clothes. Presently Carter said, slapping irritably at a fly which had settled on his bare scratched leg,

'I say, Todd, who do you suppose he is?'

'Who?'

'Him – down there. I mean, he must come from somewhere. He must have parents or something. They're probably rushing around ringing up the police or something. A fat lot of idiots we'll look if they find out we've got him.'

Todd turned his head to regard Carter in mild surprise. 'Well! Well! Signs of intelligence from the egregious Carter!'

But Carter persisted, with the tenacity of one to whom, although not outstandingly bright, an idea has occurred.

'Don't be an ass. I'm serious. Kids of his age don't just appear from nowhere. He must belong to someone.'

'I have no doubt he does. All the same, he hasn't so far shown any signs of wishing to be reunited with the sorrowing parents you conjure up so vividly.'

'Well,' said Carter doggedly, 'I think it's jolly odd. And dangerous. If anyone finds out—'

'They won't,' said Todd with sudden and surprising violence. 'He just turned up, didn't he? It was what we wanted, wasn't it? We've waited long enough. If you want to rat, you can. But I'm not going back on it. If you do want to get out, though, I should do it now. We don't want you if you're not going to pull your weight. It was always the three of us, but Randy and I can manage it on our own, you know. You're not exactly indispensable. So just say, if you're getting cold feet. We won't stop you.'

'I'm not getting out – of course I'm not,' said Carter hurriedly. 'I didn't mean that. It's just that – well, I mean to say. You can't help wondering, you know.'

'If that's all that's bothering you, wonder away.' Todd rolled over again and cocked his arms up behind his head. 'It doesn't bother me,' he said sleepily. 'I don't bother about things until they happen, and nothing's happened yet. Also, I don't give a damn who he is, or where he came from. We wanted him. He was there. That ought to be enough to be going on with.'

His eyes behind the dark glasses might have been closed – in any case they were invisible. Carter asked no more questions.

Randy appeared noiselessly beside them and squatted down

on the short grass, pulling out his cigarettes. He tossed one over to Todd and they smoked silently for a while in the hot air. Presently Randy began taking various neat parcels and packets out of a large rucksack and ranged them on the ground. He had brought a quantity of tinned food, cans of fruit juice, a tin opener, a child's metal spade, a pair of underpants and a vest. Carter eyed these offerings with respect.

'How did you get the money for that little lot?' he said enviously. 'It must have cost a couple of quid!'

'Pinched it – if it's any of your business,' said Randy, smoking impassively.

'Who from?'

'Old Ma Johns, of course. She's got a cocoa tin where she puts the odd bit. She's hidden it under her corsets in her chest of drawers.'

'But how did you know it was there?'

'Because I looked. When she goes out to her Evening Service, I always have a good look round to see if there's anything I can pinch.'

'Won't she notice it's gone?'

'Of course she will.'

'But I mean – I say, Randy, won't she be absolutely furious?'

'I expect so – and much good may it do her. She can't do a bloody thing about it. She can't very well hand me over to the police, not with her old man being a parson, and she won't say anything to me about it.'

'Why not?'

Randy dug a small hole in the hard ground and buried his cigarette end, meticulously covering it over and smoothing the earth flat again.

'Because she daren't,' he said contemptuously. 'She's dead scared of me.' He stared insolently at Carter, who turned his head away, and looked past Todd at the food spread neatly on the ground. 'Any more questions?' he inquired.

'It's a good haul,' said Todd, who had been sitting up hugging his knees and smiling to himself during this exchange. 'A jolly good haul. It should keep him going for quite a while. What's the spade for, Randy?'

'Latrines,' said Randy succinctly. 'Teach the little blighter to dig himself a hole at the back of the cave where the ground's soft and throw in some earth on top of his shit. I've got some disinfectant too. The place will stink like a sewer if we don't break him of his filthy habits.' Immaculately clean and orderly, he had been offended in all his instincts by the urination against the wall. 'Nasty little blighter,' he repeated.

Todd began to put the supplies into three equal heaps.

'One each,' he said. 'Damn – no bucket. That means he can't wash.'

'I'll bring one tomorrow. There's a plastic one in old Ma Johns's boiler house. I'll pinch that.' Randy seemed to be anxious to make himself responsible for the sanitary aspects of the enterprise. 'We'd better get down there. You go first, Todd. And for God's sake don't go blundering down like a sack of potatoes, Carter. You'll bring the whole cliff face down on top of us one of these days.' Slight, and as sure-footed as a cat himself, he was always irritated by Carter's unrestrained method of progression.

They found the boy sitting cross-legged on the ground where they had left him. He looked as if he had not moved, but they saw his eyes, bright and alert, flicker as they approached. Beside him, and a little towards the back of the cave, was a small heap of excrement on which flies clustered heavily. They rose in a languid cloud as the three came nearer, then settled again. The noise they made was considerable, and the stench was intolerable on the motionless air of the cave. Randy stopped abruptly, and slung his rucksack to the floor. His body hunched itself tight, and Todd, standing beside him, could feel anger like heat off his skin.

'You filthy, sodding little bastard!' he said. 'You foul little tick!'

The boy did not get up. He uncrossed his legs and stretched

them out in front of him, but otherwise he did not move.

'Steady,' said Todd quietly to Randy. 'That won't get you anywhere.' He moved a step forward and said to the boy, 'Get up'.

Unhurriedly, the boy unfolded his long thin body and got to his feet. Todd stooped and picked up the child's spade with its bright red handle and tin blade. He threw it across the ground so that it clattered down at the boy's feet.

'Pick it up,' he said. The boy did so, and stood holding it between his hands. He looked, in his brief shorts and sandals, as if he were at the seaside, making castles in the sand.

'Go to the back of the cave,' said Todd, 'and dig a hole. You will find the ground is soft. Then scrape up that unpleasant little offering, put it in the hole, and cover it with earth. Then wipe the spade thoroughly and stand it in the corner.'

The three of them stood and watched him as he performed these actions. He made a good job of the hole, putting his weight well over the spade; carefully he scraped every remnant of dirt off the ground before replacing the earth and stamping it down. He then cleaned the spade by rubbing it with earth and stood it upright against the wall.

'Good,' said Todd when he had finished. 'That's the last time we'll have any of that sort of thing. You will dig a trench with that spade and pile the earth beside it. When you've used the trench you can throw in some disinfectant and then put some of the earth on top. Make sure you use enough – we don't want flies all over the place. Do you understand all that?'

The boy came away from the back of the cave and stood in front of Todd with his arms hanging loosely by his sides.

'Yes, thank you,' he said politely.

'And why you couldn't think of it for yourself—' exploded Randy.

'Well, you see, I hadn't got anything to dig with,' said the boy. 'I thought you'd probably bring something with you, so I left it until you came.'

'Oh, you did, did you?' said Todd scornfully.

Carter went off into his high pitched giggle.

'Shut up!' Randy rounded on him savagely.

The boy looked interestedly from one to the other of the faces surrounding him.

'I'm hungry,' he said. 'I drank the pop, but there wasn't anything to eat.'

Todd squatted down and began arranging the food in two neat rows against the wall of the cave where the shadow was deepest and where the rock felt cool and almost damp. The boy watched him with bright eyes.

'I'll eat the sausage rolls first,' he said. 'They'll go bad in this heat.'

He picked one of them up and examined it, then took an experimental nibble from the end of it and turned it round on his tongue as if he were tasting wine.

'Not bad,' he said.

He put the rest of it into his mouth and squatted down beside Todd, curling his legs under him with the effortless ease of a small child. He began to eat quickly and with concentration while they watched him. Presently he paused in the middle of a mouthful and said politely,

'Would you like some?' He gestured towards the chocolate cake, which did indeed look as if Carter had sat on it. 'I should have some of that cake – it doesn't look as if it's going to keep very long.'

Randy had turned away to the mouth of the cave and stood smoking against the light, his back straight and taut under his blue shirt. Todd shook his head, but Carter said,

'I say, can I have a bit? I'm sorry it got rather squashed, but I fell over it coming up the hill.'

He crouched down beside the boy and broke off a large piece of the brown sticky cake. They ate together in silence, Carter furtively watching the boy, the boy seeming to be entirely concentrated on the food. When he had had enough he sighed, licked his fingers, and wiped them on his shirt. Then he sat back on his haunches and said,

'May I have a drink, please?'

Todd opened a can of fruit juice and he drank it down, tilting his head and swallowing rhythmically so that Todd could see the tender brownish skin under his jaw pulsing and relaxing like a heart beat. He lowered the can, peered into it to make sure that it was empty, and then set it down beside the crumbled ruins of the cake. He looked brightly up at Todd and smiled.

'That's better,' he said.

There was a pause. Randy, still smoking in the entrance, did not move. Todd tidied up what was left of the food and Carter got up and wandered round the cave, tapping the walls and kicking at the packed earth with his heels. No one seemed to know what to do next. Only the boy was at his ease. He sat still and relaxed and watched them with the alert eyes which were so disconcertingly bright in his thin face.

Presently he began searching for something which seemed to have become lodged in a fissure in the wall beside him. He scrabbled at the hole for a minute or two with his fingers, got a grip on whatever it was he was looking for, and fished it out in his thin grimy hand.

'Look what I found this morning,' he said. He held it up with the air of a clever dog who has performed some action which he hopes will please. Todd, squatting beside the row of tins with his hands hanging loosely down between his knees, looked at it with indifference.

'What is it?'

The boy turned it over between his palms, his head with its thick sweep of hair bent over it.

'It's an old tennis ball.'

Carter came hurrying from the back of the cave.

'I say! How on earth did that get there?'

'I don't know. It looks pretty old,' said the boy. 'I should think it's been there a long time.' He bounced it gently on the ground beside him. A small puff of yellowish dust spurted from the contact, and it rose sweetly back to his hand. He bounced it again. He looked up at Carter, pleased. 'It's still got plenty of spring in it,' he said.

Suddenly, without warning, and with a quick agile turn of the wrist, he flung it straight upwards at Carter. Carter, startled, instinctively darted aside, and the ball flew past him and struck the opposite wall with a small thud. The boy laughed aloud, showing all his strong white teeth.

'Missed!' he said; and then, as Carter stood still, stupidly watching the ball roll gently back to rest at the boy's feet, 'Butter fingers! Can't catch for toffee!'

He leaned forward to pick up the ball, and began flicking it up so that it turned over and over in the air and fell back again into his cupped hands. As he did this he watched Carter.

'Can't catch for toffee! Can't catch for toffee!' he chanted in his high small boy's voice.

Carter suddenly lunged forward and snatched the ball out of the air.

'Who can't catch for toffee now?'

He moved backwards away from the boy, and in his turn began throwing the ball high in the dark air above his head and flinging himself to and fro to catch it as it fell to left or right of him.

'You're not the only one who can play ball,' he panted, throwing out his right arm and snatching at the almost invisible grey sphere.

The boy let out a sort of gasping laugh and scrambled up. He rushed at Carter and leapt high up beside him trying to reach the ball before Carter could get to it. Carter threw the ball higher and higher and more wildly, so that they both had to dash about under its flight in their efforts to catch it. The boy was much the shorter of the two but he was incredibly swift on his feet, and he jumped like a spring uncoiling, high and neat, so that he compensated for his lack of reach. They

36

both laughed and panted as they leapt round each other like puppies. Above their heads the ball flew and swooped like a bird. First Carter had it, then the boy seemed to launch himself upwards like a diver in reverse to grab it from a seemingly impossible height. Their feet kicked up little flowers of dust and Carter began to sweat, the moisture breaking out in little spurts under his arms and on his face.

Todd, rocking gently on his heels, watched them. Every now and again the boy turned his body in one of its prodigious leaps and looked back at him over his shoulder. Under the shadow of the heavy flopping hair Todd could see his white teeth splitting the almost invisible face. His white shirt was the other point of vision in the dim swirl of the two bodies. It had come out of his shorts and flung round his moving body like a pair of wings.

Suddenly the boy snatched the ball down and, holding it against his chest like a prize, ran stooping with it across the cave straight at Todd. Half way across the intervening space he faltered, stumbled, and sprawled down in a flailing heap of body and limbs. The ball jerked from his grasp and rolled gently towards Todd, slowed, turned once or twice, and bumped gently against his foot. The boy lay still. Behind him, Carter slowly doubled his body over his hands in an agony of breathlessness. Randy turned slowly in the entrance to see what was happening.

'Oh, get up,' said Todd to the boy.

He leaned forward to peer at the face turned into the crook of a bent arm.

'Have you hurt yourself?' he said sharply.

Behind him Randy said with deliberation,

'I hope he's broken his bloody neck.'

Todd went over and knelt beside the boy. He crouched down, and without touching him, looked closely at the face. The eyes were shut. He sat back, his hands on his knees, and said,

'It looks as if that's exactly what he has done.'

37

'Serve him right,' said Randy. He turned away.

Todd looked down at his hands. Then he bent forward and slid them under the shoulders and knees and picked up the light limp body. It lay against him, not as though dead, rather as if deeply and comfortably asleep. For the first time he saw the face closely. The hair of the eyebrows was fine and fair, but the lashes were strong, sandy, and blunt at the ends as if they had recently been singed. The skin was superficially fair, but it looked as if the flesh beneath were unexpectedly darker and showed through with a faintly dusky tinge. The lips were firmly outlined with a little ridge of colour, and the whole face looked flat, as if a strong corrosive wind had blown across it and levelled it off like a desert landscape. The effect was one of beauty, but it also alarmed. It was disquieting at close quarters – or so it seemed to Todd, stooping so closely above it.

He laid the body down near the mouth of the cave and began to examine it for possible injuries. He lifted the arms and turned them on the joints. They moved flaccidly, with complete fluidity and ease. The legs, bony and brown, lay loosely apart with the feet turned out. Todd opened the shirt and put his head down to listen for the heart. He put his ear against the skin and instantly felt it warm. It was soft and smooth and tightly stretched over the delicate cage of bone beneath. There seemed to be no intervening structure of flesh or fat, merely the curious dusky skin and the tender bone which it so perfectly encased. Todd knelt still, his hands flat on the ground one on each side of the narrow body, and felt the heart pulsing with frail and regular strength against his ear. It seemed to be his own heart, beating a little faster.

He lifted his head and straightened up. The boy lay perfectly still between his hands, but his eyes were wide open. Between the straight light lines of the lashes they were almost green, with a pitchy black pupil surrounded by a strong black line. His mouth was slightly open and Todd could see the teeth, again startlingly white and regular. They were parted so that the tongue just showed like a furtive little animal hiding in his hole.

Relief, and something else – shame? – suddenly made Todd extremely angry. He got quickly to his feet and stood back, dusting his hands down the sides of his trousers.

'What the hell did you do that for?' he demanded furiously.

'Do what?'

'Fall down and pretend to be in a faint, or whatever you were playing at. You gave me a hell of a fright.'

'I wasn't pretending.' The boy sat up and shook himself. 'I fell over and hurt myself.'

Todd was shaking.

'It's your own bloody fault, rushing about like that. You could have broken your neck.'

'Pity he didn't,' said Randy.

'You shut up,' said Todd, still furious. 'Get up, and behave yourself,' he said to the boy.

Carter came slowly forward, still panting.

'Phew! You can't half jump!' he said admiringly. 'Did you see him jump, Todd?'

'I did, and I don't want to see it again.'

Glaring at both of them, he went on rubbing his hands up and down on the material of his trousers. The boy went on sitting on the ground, watching him with his childish half smile. As he did so he slowly did up the front of his shirt and tucked it into his shorts. All the time he watched Todd, and Todd, standing a little away from him, looked back at him, breathing fast.

It was almost dark when they left the quarry and walked back towards the town – at least, as dark as the light summer night would ever be. Everything seemed to smell very strongly. The plants in the gardens they passed, the exhausts of passing cars, the hot surface of the pavement itself, all seemed to assail them as if with nausea. Randy and Todd were silent. Only Carter was garrulous, but they did not listen to him and even he stopped talking in the end, discouraged by their inattention. When they turned into the main street and began walking past the shops, closed, but brightly lit behind their glass, Todd stopped, and said,

'I'm hungry. Let's get something at the coffee-bar.'

'Mum'll wonder what's happened if I don't go back,' Carter began doubtfully, but Randy broke in contemptuously,

'Who's a Mummy's darling, then? Come on, don't be an ass. She's probably gawping at the telly – old Ma Johns will be tucked up with the Burden and sleeping the sleep of the unjust. What about your doting Mama, Todd?'

Todd shrugged.

'She'll have given me up by now. Come on, let's get a move on before the bloody place shuts.'

They turned down the narrow alley between the neat half-timbered shop fronts and heard the sound of the juke box, mellowed and made almost melancholy by the filter of thick air. When they pushed open the door and went down the three shallow steps into the light, faces like fish swam up and goggled at them through the smoke. Todd wedged himself in his narrow seat and drank thin black coffee in scalding gulps. Carter, eating doughnuts, shouted to him above the din, but although he heard the words he could not make them into sense. The faces of two girls opposite him at the table swam towards him and receded again like objects seen through moving water. Their black eyebrows and whitish mouths made triangles which he formed and re-formed into endless shifting patterns. Turning his head, he saw Randy hitched on a high stool at the counter between two girls. Their faces, too, as they swayed together and away again, made triangles in the smoke. It was unendurably hot. The door behind him swung open and more people came in. They let in air which eddied round him, but which seemed hotter and more sluggish than ever. He saw Randy put out his hand and lay it on the thigh of one of the girls. She pushed it away, but Randy put it back again, higher up, under her short skirt. Todd could see his thumb moving on her nylon thigh. This time she did not push him away.

Todd drank what was left of his coffee and got up to push past Carter.

'I'm going home,' he bawled. 'See you there – about four o'clock tomorrow.'

Carter nodded and grinned at him like a clown through the smoke and shouted something back which he did not hear. He stumbled out, past Randy, whose hand was now completely concealed under the girl's skirt.

'Four tomorrow,' he mouthed, and Randy, too, nodded and mouthed something back which Todd could not hear. He noticed that the girl sitting, flushed and giggling, beside Randy was Carter's sister, Daphne.

The silence of the street was an intense relief. He walked slowly along, up the high street, and turned away from the town, under the huge trees and up the hill. He passed neat white gates and houses which were widely separated by their surrounding gardens. There were a few lighted windows; once he saw a dim figure standing alone in one of the gardens, a pallid patch of face raised to the sky. A dog ran busily past him and a voice called it back, but dreamily, as if not really caring whether it came or not. Todd walked on, looking up at the trees which filtered the thin darkness down to him like dust. He passed a group of people standing at an open gate. They talked quietly together, their heads close, and one of them moved so that the gravel shifted and rustled. He came to his own house and turned in, up the short drive between stumpy laurels which looked humped and black in the dark.

There were no lights at the windows and he let himself into the quiet hall, closing the door behind him. The air smelt of flowers, and of scent, almost too faint to be recognisable, except to Todd, who had smelt it on his mother on innumerable warm evenings. The drawing-room door was ajar and he went quietly over and pushed it open, looking into the

41

room as if he expected to find someone there, perhaps sitting at the open window, the sleek dark head turned away from him against the wicker back of the chair. The room was empty, as he had known it would be.

He went along the hall to the kitchen and saw his face for a moment, looking back at him like a furtive ghost from among the gilt curlicues of the mirror opposite the stairs. He opened the fridge and drank almost a whole pint of milk straight from the bottle. Then, still without turning on any lights, he went back into the hall and began to climb the stairs. He moved with infinite stealth, and had actually put out his hand to push open his own door when she called out to him.

'Todd? Is that you?'

He stood still, absolutely quiet, to see if she would call again.

'Todd? Is that you, darling?'

He turned away from his own door and went into her room. It smelt of the same scent, and the windows were wide open so that it also smelt of the hot night air. She lay in the middle of the great bed, dimly discernible as a slight ridge under a single sheet.

'Todd darling, wherever have you been? I've been worried about you. I couldn't sleep until I knew you were back. You might have let me know.'

He went over to the bed and looked down at her. In the dimness her face was washed clean of lines and looked very young. She turned her head fretfully on the pillow and put out her hand to the clock beside the bed.

'Oh Todd, you are naughty. It's terribly late. What ever have you been doing?'

He sat on the edge of the bed. She drew the sheet up under her chin and wrinkled her nose.

'You smell horrible – smoke and sweat. Don't pull the bed about. I haven't got anything on.' Her eyes were as bright as a small child's as she peered at him over the sheet. 'Well? Where have you been?'

42

'With the others. I'm sorry I'm so late. We stopped for a coffee. I didn't realise the time.'

'You could at least have rung me. I've been on my own all day. Anyway since you left after lunch. And it's still so terribly hot. You might have come back, Todd.'

'I know. I'm sorry.'

'You're not. You always say that, as if you've only got to say it and it makes everything all right again. It's not fair, spending the whole week-end with those two instead of with me. I hardly even see you nowadays. You treat the house like an hotel. I'm getting sick of it, absolutely sick of it.'

He heard the rising note in her voice with resignation. It was the eternal thing between them, the worse for being unresolved. He saw her still beautiful flawed face with pity, and set himself to his task of appeasement, of reconciliation.

'Clare darling,' he said, 'I'm sorry, truly I am. Promise I won't leave you again without letting you know. But I can't just stay around here all day, can I? You know I love being with you, but—'

She was not listening, and she interrupted him with an abruptness which showed that she was forcing herself to bring out a long-standing preoccupation.

'Is it a girl?'

He stared back at her, answering her look of fierce concentration with one of total surprise. He noticed that she looked almost ugly in her intensity.

'A girl?' he repeated stupidly.

'Yes – a girl.' She mimicked him savagely. 'You say you spend all the time with Randy and Carter. I don't believe it. I think you've got a girl. I think you're spending the time with her and not telling me.' She stared at him, clenching and unclenching her fingers. 'Are you sleeping with her?'

Todd put his head back and laughed. It sounded like the laugh of purest spontaneous amusement.

'That, sweetest Clare, would be the least of my troubles! No, I haven't got a girl – I leave that to Randy, though

43

whether even he actually 'gets' them in the fullest sense of the word seems to be open to doubt.' He put his hand on his heart and leaned towards her in a kind of mock bow. 'Cross my heart and hope to die, no girls.'

He sat forward, half stooping over her, and felt the narrow body between his hands. Suddenly, he almost got up and walked out of the room, straight back to the cave where the boy, presumably, slept. The impulse passed, and he drew breath again. She was still looking up at him, but her expression had slackened.

'You know, I believe you.'

'So I should hope.'

'There's one thing about you, Todd, you never actually lie. You just shut up, and when you're like that I can't budge you. I've given up trying.'

'Very sensible.'

She pushed the sheet away from her shoulders and hitched herself higher on the pillows.

'Get me some water, darling, and one of my sleeping things. I shall look a hag in the morning, but I must get some sleep. This heat will kill me.'

She drank the water and sank back with a fretful sigh. The sheet fell away and Todd saw her breasts, full and beautiful like two white fruits. She turned her head sideways and crooked an arm under her dark hair.

'Good night, darling. Sleep well.'

She was asleep before Todd was out of the room. He pulled his clothes off and lay down naked on top of his bed. He was asleep almost before his eyes were closed.

Daphne Carter hit out at Randy in genuine alarm and rolled away from him in the grass.

'Here!' she said indignantly. 'What do you think you're up to?'

She pulled her skirt down over her knees and sat up. Randy,

44

left lying in the grass with the major part of his need unsatisfied, looked up at her with hatred.

'If you don't like it, what did you come with me for?'

'Not for what you seem to think,' she said virtuously; but she was frightened, and her knees trembled as she sat stiffly upright beside him in the warm darkness. If he had rushed her, she thought – but he had fumbled and had mauled her with clumsy hands, and fear had made her angry.

'Frightened?' he sniggered.

'Not of anything you could do,' she said, but she was.

He watched her.

'I don't believe you've ever done it,' he said softly.

She rounded on him, fright making her honest.

'And I don't believe you have either – messing me about like that – I don't believe you could do it if I asked you to!'

When she had said it she drew in her breath with a little gasp and pressed the back of her hand against her mouth. She looked furtively at him over her tensed fingers, but he made no move towards her. He got to his feet and stood looking down at her.

He was so angry that he felt sick. He looked at the soft skin of her neck and arms, luminous in the dusk, and wanted to smash her. She turned her head away from him with a stiff little movement and looked down at her knees hunched close up to her chest.

'So you don't believe I could?'

She could think of no reply that would not make him more angry – indeed, at that moment, she felt him to be genuinely dangerous.

'Please go away,' she said weakly. 'Leave me alone.' She made a little thrusting gesture at him as if to push him away. 'I'm sorry, leave me alone, please, Randy.'

She knew she would not be able to control him if he touched her. She sat still, clutching her knees. She could see him, out of the tail of her eye, as a dark shape looming above her.

'Leave me alone,' she repeated.

Without turning her head she tried to make out whether he had moved closer to her. The soft darkness made it almost impossible for her to judge distances. She heard his breathing. It was unsteady, like hers, and she sensed that, like her, he was rigidly trying to control it. This thought comforted her a little. She raised her head to look more directly at him.

'I really ought to go home now,' she said. 'I'm sorry, I didn't mean to upset you, Randy, but I can't help it.' She felt out with her hand for her bag. Its familiar surface on her skin comforted her, and she clutched it tightly against her. 'Don't bother to come with me, I can find my own way home.' She wanted to be rid of him, and since he made no move her courage was returning.

He said,

'You know what you are, don't you? You're a bloody little tart, that's what. You go around with all that stuff on your face, looking like a common little tart, and when it comes to the push you cry off. You're not that sort, thank you very much. Very virtuous, aren't you? It would serve you right if I held you down and gave it to you whether you wanted it or not.'

She began to tremble again.

'Don't you speak to me like that.' Her teeth were chattering so that her words came out in disjointed fragments. 'If you lay a finger on me I'll scream the place down.'

'Don't worry, you bloody little virgin– I wouldn't touch you if you paid me for it.'

He walked quickly away from her across the grass, under the trees and out on to the road. His legs trembled violently. After a while, when the trembling had stopped, he began to walk very fast. Then he began to run, faster and faster, panting and sobbing to himself as if he were being pursued by something which was bound, sooner or later, to overtake, to hurt, and finally to destroy him.

*　　*　　*

Carter made a detour on his way home. The estate on which he lived was being extended out into the country, and there were several houses at various stages of completion on the newly cleared land. Trees had been felled, hedges uprooted, and heavy machinery had churned the ground into a morass of ruts and holes. To Carter, cautiously inserting himself through a gap in the temporary fence which surrounded the area, it looked as he would imagine a landscape on the moon would look. One house was almost finished, but the thin wooden beams of the roof stood up bare and open like the ribs of a gigantic monster with a chimney for a single listening ear. Breeze blocks stood in huge heaps like listening animals, bricks were piled up into fantastic turrets and pinnacles. One house was merely a foundation with a few feet of brick in which the frame of a front door was set, keeping nothing out, letting nothing in. A shed for the workmen stood sturdily in the middle of the site. It was built of weathered wood and looked a good deal more solid and permanent than any of the buildings surrounding it. Here and there plastic sheeting was draped over a pile of bricks, or had been flung over a half finished wall. It looked glossy and gay, like some exotic substance evolved on another planet.

Carter got himself through the fence and stood still to listen; everything seemed to be absolutely quiet. There was no wind to move in the trees – in any case they had almost all been cut down, sawed into convenient lengths and driven away in lorries. As a child, Carter had played in the grass in this very field, and even then it had seemed to be another planet, though a very different one from the alien desecrated place it had become. None of this, however, occurred to him at the moment. He was merely listening, absorbed in the necessity of making sure that he was completely alone and unobserved.

When he had made sure that there was no one near and that the workmen's hut was empty, he moved cautiously forward to a pile of timber beside the wall of the almost completed house. Most of the planks were much too long and bulky for his purpose, but on an earlier reconnoitre of the site he had seen some smaller pieces underneath the longer ones and now he made for these. He made his way carefully over the pitted ground, using a small torch when he suspected that a stump or a considerable hole lay in his way. The heap of timber was protected by a large piece of sacking. He pulled this off and laid it cautiously to one side. Then he squatted down and began groping with his hands, feeling along the pieces of wood to find out how long and thick they were. He dared not use his torch; it was quite possible that someone in the neighbouring council houses would see the light and send the police along to find out who was raiding the building site. Most of the pieces were unsuitable but he found several planks which were only a foot or two in length. These he drew from the pile and laid on one side.

He spent some time in the warm darkness, crouching over the wood and feeling at it as if he were a blind man. It seemed a long time before he had collected enough, but eventually it was done. He stood up and carefully replaced the sacking over the timber that was left. Then he fished some string from his pocket and tied it round the pieces he had selected. When he picked up the bundle of wood it made a considerable load and was much heavier than he had expected. He had to clasp it to his chest as he made his way back to the gap in the fence, and he could not use his torch to avoid the obstacles in his path because both his hands were occupied in preventing the planks from slipping from the ill-tied bundle. Lurching and stumbling and sweating with fear at every sound he made, he eventually reached the fence, dropped the wood over and scrambled after it.

It was worse when he got out into the road. The going was easier, but he was in continual terror lest he should meet someone who would, not unnaturally, wonder what he was doing hurrying along with a load of timber half concealed under his jacket. Once he did meet a man who was walking swiftly towards him along the pavement, his head bent as if he were searching for something on the ground. Carter put the wood down and knelt over it as if he were doing up a shoelace, shielding it as much as he could with his body. The man went straight past, and Carter picked up his load and hurried on.

He got safely to his own gate at last and hurried up the path and round the side of the house. It was a relief to let the bundle of wood slip to the ground and to stretch his arms. The next problem confronting him was that of where to hide it until he could take it to the quarry the next afternoon. Eventually he decided to conceal it at the bottom of the garden among the bushes and long grass which grew rank under the one apple tree. It would not be easy to reclaim it without being seen, but at least he was fairly certain that no one would find it in the interval.

He pushed it well down into the rough grass and pulled a heap of sticks and grass cuttings over it. While he was doing this he felt as if he were, at the very least, disposing of a corpse. It was his first theft of public property and it made him feel elated, but also extremely, and probably disproportionately, guilty and frightened. When he had finished he dusted himself down, smelling his own fresh sweat as he did so. The garden felt airless. There was no wind, no movement of the air, and the sluggish darkness felt stifling. When he had cleaned himself up he stood still for a moment and listened. He heard the drone of a car a long way off and nearer a dog barked incessantly, as if made irritable by the heat. He went softly over the lawn to the house.

As he fumbled under the mat for the key he heard the front gate click. He froze in his stooped position and waited. Footsteps approached, coming round the side of the house and up behind him. He realised that they were made by high heels, and almost simultaneously that it was his sister Daphne. He straightened up.

'Dicky! Whatever are you doing out at this time of night?'

she hissed. She smelt reassuringly of hair laquer and cheap cosmetics.

'Same as you – courting,' he whispered back, and she slapped at his hand and giggled.

They went into the kitchen together and he snapped on the light. It showed her blinking and yawning, a long strand of fallen hair curling across her forehead. Carter filled a glass with cold water from the tap and drank it down. It tasted clean and wonderful. He filled the glass again.

'Want some?'

'No thanks – I'm going up. I'm dead beat.'

He drank the second glass more slowly, watching her over the rim.

'Who was it?' he inquired.

'Guess.'

'I don't know. Don't care either.'

'You will when you hear.'

He shrugged, and put the glass down on the draining-board.

'Will I? Come on then, tell me and see.'

She opened her mouth and yawned widely, showing her pink tongue between her lips.

'I said guess, didn't I?'

'O.K., I will then. Randy.'

She pulled the corners of her mouth down.

'You saw us at the coffee-bar.'

'I'll say I did. Having fun, weren't you?'

'If that's your idea of fun you can keep it.'

'What do you mean?'

'What I said. You can keep it – and your friend, Randy Randolph too.'

He looked at her with sudden interest.

'Why?'

She shrugged.

'Nothing really. I just don't like him, that's all.'

'I say,' inquired Carter, after looking closely at her, 'has something been going on? Did he try it on or something? You look a bit green.'

She avoided his eye.

'He didn't get very far – dirty beast,' she added morosely.

'So you managed to resist the irresistible Randy!' Carter blew out his lips in surprise.

'Not as irresistible as all that. A lot of talk and not much to show for it. I don't think he's ever even done it.'

Carter digested this piece of information in silence.

'I say, that's pretty interesting,' he remarked. 'I'd always imagined he was rather hot with the girls.'

She said flatly,

'Well, he's not. A bit of a cuddle in the back row of the flicks is about his limit, I'd say.'

They thought about Randy for a while. Daphne got up and fished about under the table for her shoes. She stood up with them in her hand and padded flat-footed to the door. There she turned to say,

'All the same, I don't like him. I was dead scared this evening. I thought he was going to hit me or have a fit or something. I'm sure he could be really nasty if he tried.' She shrugged, thinking it over, then added, 'Still, it's your business, not mine. After all, he's your friend, isn't he?'

Randy knelt at the Sanctus bell with the rest of the congregation and put his head between his hands. It was early and the church was still cool. It was moderately full and Randy knelt beside a girl with bare brown arms and a yellow scarf tied over her hair. When she put her elbows on the bench her forearm lay beside his, and he looked at it sideways without turning his head, distracted by the smooth taut skin, sprinkled with shiny gold hairs. He could not see her face, and for a moment or two he amused himself by imagining the profile – turned-up nose, long lashes, the bloom on the full line of the cheek. When she leaned forward to put her prayer-

51

book down on the bench in front of her and he did see her face, it was something of a shock, being pale, with slightly protruding teeth and spectacles. Chastened, Randy applied himself to his prayers. 'Oh Lord,' he improvised, 'I believe in you, I hope in your Grace, I love you,' and he looked up to the high roof and saw the early sun falling on stone, and thought of Todd, and found that he was not praying, but reciting the familiar, consoling rigmaroles while his mind was given away to pictures – the Quarry, the hair on the girl's arm, the weight of Daphne's breasts in his hands. That last, he thought, hurriedly, was certainly blasphemy at this particular moment, and he started his recitation again. 'Oh Lord, I believe in you, I hope for your Salvation, I trust in your goodness and mercy—'

The first of the Consecration bells was rung. Beside him, the girl put her face in her hands. Randy did the same, then lifted it at the second bell to look at the tiny white disc held high by the priest and said in his mind 'My Lord and my God', and ducked his head again. My Lord and my God, he thought, that fragment of wafer which was put into one's mouth, which one swallowed as reverently as possible without desecrating it at all with tooth or tongue, unless it became stuck to the inside of a dry mouth when, agonisingly, it had to be dislodged, peeled off, swallowed with the help of saliva collected from beneath the tongue – and then? Down the oesophagus, into the stomach, through the intestine, the usual process of digestion, until it arrived in the bowels and was excreted with whatever other nourishment of a more homely nature might be passing along the same route at the time – impossible, he thought violently. Somewhere, as soon as possible, it must become merely bread. Immediately after ingestion the Godhead must depart – where? The God he knew, the God of pursuit, of retribution, could never travel such a path.

The bell rang again and the chalice rose and twinkled in the sun and was lowered again to the Altar. 'The blood of my Saviour,' said Randy in his mind, and again the images started coming, of blood, warm and sticky in the chalice. It was wine, of course, cheap red altar wine, but it was changed into blood by the words, a barbaric miracle which made his senses tingle as if it were in fact being offered to his lips so that he could drink the freshly shed blood of a butchered God. 'Do this in commemoration of Me.' Then why the actual deed done again? Why the killing done again and again, times innumerable all over the world at this moment alone, not to mention the times in the past and in the future? The thought of all the millions of deaths died again was insupportable. He took his hands down from his face and stared over the bent heads up to the altar and the figure moving in its slow ritual over the bread and the wine.

The words at least were familiar and soothing. 'Domine non sum dignus,' – 'Lord, I am not worthy,' he dutifully repeated, and softly struck his breast three times and bent his head again. There was the complete silence of reverence and of prayer around him, then the sound, like a sigh, of people moving, getting up, climbing past one another out into the aisle to go up to receive Communion. He knelt in his place and watched them file slowly up, kneel, raise their heads over the Communion plate, lower them again, rise, then walk back to their places. He watched their faces as they came back, some bent over clasped hands in piety, some preoccupied with finding the right bench, some blank, some smirking with self-consciousness – as usual he did not join them. He had rolled with Daphne in the warm grass, and although the encounter had come to nothing he had wanted, and still wanted, to commit fornication with her, or with some other girl. He was in mortal sin, and if he should die now he would go to Hell. He felt as if he were walking a precarious tightrope. It was as if he were condemned to carry a load of dynamite which might at any moment explode and blow him into an eternity of just retribution. His petty sins, amounting in reality to no more than the usual impulses towards lust and self-gratification, loomed enormously before him. He knelt still, and felt the cold strike up at him from the stone floor.

'Oh Lord,' he prayed again without hope, 'free me from my sins, make me love you more.' There seemed to be no love anywhere in the whole affair, but he went on saying the words as if they might bring him comfort.

Carter drove the last peg into the wall of the cave and stood back to admire the effect.

'Not bad,' said Todd, sitting in the entrance with his legs stretched out in front of him, and squinting up at the row of wooden pegs. 'A bit crooked, but they'll do.'

'They're perfectly straight,' said Carter indignantly. He took a couple of paces back and put his head on one side. 'Well, almost. The one at the end's a bit low, but I struck a hard bit so I had to move it down. Anyway, they won't come out. I've banged them in as hard as I can.'

Randy began hammering again. He had finished the table and it stood beside him, a sturdy contraption of planks nailed together and covered with a checked cloth. It stood about four feet off the ground and was strongly and neatly made. Now Randy was making a stool. The top was done, and he was driving nails through it to attach it to the planking legs. He hammered in the nails with strong methodical strokes which seemed to make an appallingly loud noise in the confined space of the cave, and then laid down the hammer and began sawing a piece of planking in half to make bars for the legs. He held the piece of wood across his knees and sawed at it with complete absorption. Carter watched him with grudging admiration.

'You're making a good job of that, Randy,' he said.

'I like doing it,' said Randy without looking up. 'I like making things. Rotten wood, though. Full of knots. It keeps splitting.'

'It was the best I could get, and it wasn't easy in the pitch

54

dark. I couldn't see what it was like – I just had to take anything I could find that seemed the right length.' Carter
sounded hurt. 'You ought to be glad to have it at all.'

'Oh, I am. I'm not complaining.' Randy put down the saw
and bent the wood across his knees. It broke with a clean
sharp crack, and he picked the pieces up and weighed them
in his hands, examining the broken ends. 'Not bad,' he said.

'Not bad! I'd like to have seen you crawling about on that
beastly building site in the middle of the night, and then lugging the stuff home and hiding it without getting nabbed.
Not to mention getting it up here today. It weighed a ton
in this heat.'

Randy grunted, and bent over his work, juggling the pieces
into the best position. Carter flung down his hammer with as
much noise as possible and stumped over to Todd.

'Honestly, Todd, he's the ruddy limit! Just because he's
the only one of us who's any good at knocking bits of wood
together—'

'Oh, shut up!' said Todd lazily. 'You're like a couple of
old women. What do you want him to do? Go down on his
knees in gratitude to you for a few bits of old planking you
pinched from a building site? All right, all right, it was a
jolly good effort, and we all appreciate it. But we're not going
to give you a signed testimonial to that effect. Cool off, for
goodness sake. It's too hot for fighting. Have a drink.'

He pushed an open bottle of beer across and Carter sat
down beside him and put it to his mouth. It was warm and
flat, but at least it was wet. Randy began hammering again.

'Bloody racket,' grumbled Carter. 'I don't believe he really
needs to make all that noise. I think he enjoys it.'

'What are the pegs for?' asked Todd, tactfully changing
the subject.

'Hanging the bucket and spade on – and the clothes and
stuff. Anything you like. I thought it would tidy the place
up a bit.'

'Good idea. Looks a lot more like home.'

55

A hot triangle of sun inched its way across the floor and moved stealthily towards Todd's sandalled feet. He hitched himself sideways out of its path as if it were an unwelcome animal. Outside the landscape blazed in the sun. As Carter looked at it the trees and bushes seemed to sway in the heat as if they were in some kind of stately ritual dance. They no longer looked green; they seemed to have given up all their colour to the sun and to have become a uniform grey. When Carter had scrambled down to the bottom of the quarry he had found that the small stream which meandered between these bushes had halved itself. It still trickled out from a rough mouth of rock half-way up the opposite slope and ran down its slimy grooves and flat grey stones to the sandy bed below. But the stream was thin and moved slowly. It no longer splashed and leapt as it did after rain. Carter filled his bucket from the deep pool below the mouth of rock and scrambled back, spilling a lot of the water as he struggled up.

'I wonder if it's ever completely dry,' he said, rubbing the sweat out of his eyes.

'God knows. I wouldn't be surprised in this heat. There hasn't been a summer like this that I can remember. We haven't been coming here that long, so we don't really know.'

Randy said,

'We could ask someone.'

'Who?'

'I don't know. There must be someone who used to work here when it was still a quarry.'

Todd thought it over.

'Better not bother. It might attract attention to the place. Not worth it.'

Randy nodded and turned away.

'But does it matter?'

'Of course it matters, idiot. Do you really think we can bring buckets of water out from the town and drag them up here?'

'We could bring bottles,' said Carter. 'It would be just too bad about the washing.'

Todd grunted and turned away.

Now they sat and watched the motionless trees and the flat colourless stretch of sky which was drawn up before them until it was cut off by the roof of the cave. Since their arrival after lunch they had worked hard and the place was now as neat and orderly as even Randy could wish. The store of food was arranged on the floor against the wall which the sun never reached, and the floor itself had been swept clean. Carter had done this with a small brush, going over it foot by foot and sweeping the dust in front of him as he moved forward until he brushed it out of the mouth of the cave. This performance had enveloped everyone and everything in clouds of yellowish choking dust, and when it settled they all felt grit on their mouths and inside their clothes. Todd had brought two large blankets with him and out of them he had made a sort of bed; the boy was so small that they could be folded over many times, and the nights were so warm that no covering was needed. He had laid some of Carter's planks on a ground sheet underneath them. The rock floor, though dusty, held a curious chill which struck upwards to the body after a time. It was perfectly dry, since no rain ever fell upon it, and the walls for two-thirds of the way back were clean non-porous rock. But the chill was there, and the body in prolonged contact with it needed protection.

Randy, meanwhile, had taken the wood and immediately started to make furniture out of it. The objects he produced were unorthodox, but they were sturdy and well made and curiously pleasing to the eye. He loved the clean wood in his hands, and he worked it well. The other two knew this and left him to it.

All this time the boy sat and watched them. As soon as Todd had finished his bed he went and sat down on it. He sat still for a moment or two as if considering its comfort. Then he lay down and curled his arm under his head in the position of sleep. He then sat up again, crossed his legs and leaned back against the wall to survey them from this improvised throne.

'It's very nice,' he said, and then politely, to Todd: 'Thank you very much.'

They stood in an awkward row in front of him, almost as if soliciting his approval.

'I hope you'll be comfortable,' said Randy sarcastically.

'Oh, I'm sure I shall – though I would have liked something under my head. I don't like sleeping so flat. Do you think you could manage a pillow?'

'No, I don't think we could,' said Todd coldly, speaking for them all. 'Shove a couple of bottles under the blankets. I'm not lugging a pillow all the way up here.'

'All right, I'll try that. Thank you very much.'

He had remained in this position, sitting cross-legged and immobile while they worked at tidying the cave as though he were directing operations. Todd found his interested gaze disconcerting and Carter grew irritable. Randy alone, working away in his corner, seemed oblivious, and impervious to it. When they had finished and flopped themselves down to rest and sweat amid the dust they had raised the boy remained sitting there, seemingly quite at his ease.

Todd lit a cigarette and inhaled the smoke deeply. Carter finished the warm beer and leaned forward to throw the bottle into the depths of the quarry below. It arched and spun in the air and then landed with a distant splintering of glass on the sheet of corrugated iron among the bushes.

'Got it!' he shouted. 'I say, Todd, I hit it! Did you hear?' He jumped up and ran to peer down the slope of the hillside. 'I hit it! Jolly good shot, wasn't it?' he exulted.

'Considering you weren't even aiming at it, an extremely good shot,' said Todd. 'And don't do it again, you messy little beast. Broken glass can cause a fire in this heat. You'd better go down later and pick it up.'

Carter came back and sat down again.

'O.K., O.K.,' he said sullenly. He scooped up a handful of small stones and hard pieces of earth and began lobbing them out into the sunshine. 'I presume you don't object to stones?'

'Oh, stones are all right,' said Todd cheerfully. 'Heave away.'

The boy said,

'What day is it, please?'

'What day?' asked Todd, startled.

'Yes. I mean, what day of the week?'

'Sunday.'

'Oh. Thank you.' He seemed to be doing some calculations in his head. 'That means I've been here two days, doesn't it?'

'Yes – since Friday,' said Todd curiously. 'Why?'

'I just wondered.' His calculation complete, he seemed satisfied.

Todd said cautiously, feeling his way,

'Do you live near here?'

'Oh no.' The boy shook his head. 'A long way away.'

'Then how did you get here?'

'Oh – I just came, you know.'

'What were you doing?'

'When?'

'When we saw you.'

'You mean, when you found me?'

'Yes, if you like.'

'Oh, I don't know. The same as you, I expect. Just waiting.'

'Waiting? What for?'

'Anything. I mean, it was so hot, there wasn't really much to do. I was just sort of hanging around. What were you doing?'

Todd laughed softly.

'The same as you. Just waiting.'

'You didn't look as if you were,' said the boy, as if accusing him. 'You looked as if you were looking for someone.'

'Well,' said Todd, considering this, 'I suppose we were in a way.'

'Well then—' said the boy, still accusingly, as if to say, 'Why can't you be more accurate?'

Todd tried another tack.

'Won't they miss you?'

'Miss me? Who?'

'Your parents. The people you were living with. The people wherever it is you come from.'

'Oh them,' said the boy, dismissing them, whoever they were, with a wave of the hand which was positively airy.

'Well, won't they?' Todd persisted, though he was beginning to feel increasingly befuddled as the solid ground beneath him dissolved into insubstantiality.

'Oh no,' the boy said vaguely. 'I'm sure they won't.'

'But won't they try to find you? Don't they care what becomes of you? Won't they wonder where you are?'

The boy thought about this. Then he said, as if he had come to a considered decision,

'No, I don't expect so.'

Seeing Todd retreating as if in despair, Carter took over.

'But who are you?'

'You know who I am. Anyway, who are you? I mean, I know your names because I've heard you talking to each other. But I don't know anything else.'

'What do you want us to tell you?'

The boy leaned his head back against the wall.

'Anything you like,' he smiled.

Put like that, thought Todd, there seemed nothing to lay hold of, and nowhere in particular to begin.

'Suppose you tell us your name, since you seem to know ours,' suggested Carter.

'What do you call me?'

'How do you mean? We don't call you anything.'

'But you must. When you talk about me when I'm not there you must call me something.'

Todd said,

'We don't talk about you when you're not there.'

'All right – suppose you did. What would you call me then?'

'I don't know. The boy, I suppose,' said Todd lamely.

The boy described another of his wide airy gestures. With the thin brown arm raised he looked, sitting cross-legged on the coloured blankets as if on a throne, like a young Rajah holding court.

'Well, then,' he said triumphantly, 'you'd better call me that.'

'It sounds bloody daft,' said Carter. He giggled. 'The Boy! Like one of those books about India where they call the servants "boy" even when they're about seventy. Kipling, or something.'

'Don't call me anything then. You haven't so far and it's worked perfectly well.'

With an effort, Carter went back to the beginning. He, like Todd, was beginning to feel that he was walking in circles.

'But we still don't know your name.'

'Fred.'

'Fred?' said Carter, startled.

'Or Bert. Or Jim. Anything will do – I really don't mind.'

Todd looked hard at the boy.

'This,' he said, 'is becoming ridiculous.'

The strong white teeth showed themselves below the upper lip in a smile.

'Yes, I suppose it is. But you did ask, you know.'

'Right,' said Todd patiently. 'Let's try something else. How old are you? And for God's sake,' he added hastily, 'don't say "How old do you think I am?"'

'What do you want me to say?'

'I want you to tell me,' said Todd in a kind of ecstasy of self-control, 'how old you are.'

'Well,' said the boy, thinking it over, 'you and Randy must be about eighteen. And you—' he transferred his grave contemplative gaze to Carter, 'you look about fifteen. Which would mean I am – twelve?' he suggested.

'You know best,' said Todd politely, and the boy bent his body forward in a grave little bow.

'But why should it make you anything?' said Carter, puzzled. 'It doesn't affect you, how old we are. How can it make any difference? You're either twelve or you're not. After all, you must know.'

The boy merely looked from one face to another, bewildered.

'But you must. I mean, everyone knows how old they are,' persisted the unfortunate Carter.

'Do they? Well yes, I suppose they do. But it doesn't really matter, does it, so long as we all agree.'

'We'll settle for twelve,' said Todd, and again came the little bow and the polite, white smile.

Carter looked from the boy to Todd, and back again to the boy. They were looking at each other with a long, curious gaze, the boy watchful, Todd guarded and somehow apprehensive. Their long looking at each other, this wary mutual contact bothered Carter. He felt baffled and excluded.

Randy stopped hammering and stood up, holding the completed stool and turning it over in his hands to examine the workmanship. Apparently he was satisfied with it because he brought it forward to the front of the cave and set it, with the table, at the head of the improvised bed.

'There you are,' he said. 'Now you won't have any excuse for pigging it on the floor.'

The boy turned.

'They're very nice,' he said, having looked them over. 'Thank you very much.' He then spoilt the effect by adding, with a faintly patronising note of surprise in his voice, 'How clever you are.'

'It doesn't take much intelligence to knock a few pieces of wood together,' said Randy.

'I think it's very clever of you all the same,' persisted the boy. 'I couldn't have done it. I'm not at all clever with my hands.'

This phrase seemed peculiarly offensive to Randy.

'Indeed?' he said, turning slowly on his heels to look directly at the boy. 'And in what particular direction would you say your talents lie?'

The boy merely looked puzzled. He wrinkled his brows for a moment at Randy, then turned to Todd as if asking him to translate.

'He's asking you,' said Todd helpfully, 'what you are good at if you're not good at woodwork.'

'Oh, I see. Nothing much, I'm afraid.'

Randy looked him up and down with a long cool stare, a scrutiny which the boy bore with complete impassivity.

'I thought not,' he said, and went to sit down beside Todd.

'I think you're very clever, too,' said Carter. He was feeling the need to take things out of someone, and he achieved a very respectable imitation of the boy's unbroken childish treble. 'Being so good at woodwork,' he added.

Todd kicked out at him.

'Shut up. Don't be an ass, Carter.'

Randy's sallow face flushed.

'At least I haven't spent the whole afternoon knocking in a few pegs which will fall down as soon as you hang anything on them; anyway, they're so bloody crooked that you must have a squint if you think they're in anything like a straight line.'

'They are not crooked,' said Carter angrily.

'They bloody well are.'

'They're not.'

'They are. Just look at them. They'll fall out as soon as anyone tries to hang anything on them.'

'Oh no, they won't. They're in as far as I can get them.'

'Oh yes – all of half an inch. Fat lot of good you are – you can't do a damn thing without making a mess of it.'

'And who got you the wood in the first place?'

63

'You did. And pretty rotten wood it is too. I could have bought some twice as good for practically nothing.'

'Just because I don't happen to have much money—' Carter began dangerously.

'Oh for God's sake spare us the sob stuff,' said Randy wearily, watching Carter to see the effect of his words. 'We all know – born on a council estate, got to the Grammar School by sheer hard work and guts, son of a widowed mother – or is she a widow? You've never told us about that, Carter. Is your old man really dead? Or couldn't he stand the sight of your mother any more? I must say that if I'd had the misfortune to be old man Carter faced with eighteen stone of your old Mum, I'd have dropped dead with exhaustion or fled the country long ago. Which is it? Dead, or fled?'

Todd, sitting between them, felt the inexplicable violence flare up like the heath fires which seemed to generate themselves in the fierce heat of that extraordinary weather. He saw the boy watching them, his unsurprised gaze moving from one to the other. He felt his own skin tense and prickle.

'Shut up, you two!' He turned to appeal to Randy as being possibly the more susceptible to reason. 'For God's sake, Randy, stop it, can't you? It's too hot for squabbling.'

To his intense alarm he saw that Randy was enjoying himself. He was deliberately baiting Carter, as if driven to it by some urge towards violence which must be satisfied.

Carter was so angry that he was almost unable to speak. He began to stutter at Randy as if he had developed an impediment in his speech.

'You – you—' he stuttered, 'you foul beast, talking like that about my mother. I'll kill you, I swear I will.'

'Oh yes?' said Randy. 'Just let's see you try. And as for your mother, I'll say one thing for her. I bet even she could have knocked in a straighter row of pegs than that one!'

'All right! All right!' Carter was practically screaming. 'I'll tell you, then. What were you doing last night when I was crawling about in the dark getting your blasted wood for you? Come on, Randy Randolph, tell us, we're all waiting to hear.'

Randy went white instead of red.

'What do you mean?' He drew his knees up and half turned himself away from them. 'I don't know what you're talking about. I wasn't doing anything, if you really want to know.'

'Oh yes, you were. Come on Randy. If you've forgotten, would you like me to remind you?'

Todd could feel Randy's tense body almost touching his as it hunched away from Carter.

'Oh shut up,' he mumbled childishly. 'Don't be an ass.'

In the silence which momentarily followed this, during which Carter breathed through his mouth like a drunkard and Todd prickled with helpless apprehension, the boy said clearly, in an interested voice,

'I say, Randy, what were you doing? Do tell us. It must have been frightfully interesting.'

Randy uncoiled himself like a spring. For a moment it looked as if he were about to launch himself bodily at the boy. Carter, thinking the attack was about to be directed at him, scrambled to his feet. They glared at each other across Todd, who still sat stupidly between them.

'I'll tell you what you were doing,' Carter gabbled suddenly, as if determined to get it out before he were annihilated. 'You were trying to fuck my sister Daphne, and she says you don't know one end of a girl from the other. She says you couldn't fuck an old nanny-goat if it went down on its knees and asked you to!'

This last remark was a flight of fancy which Carter had invented on the spur of the moment, and which was not actually attributable to Daphne. It seemed, however, to be the last straw for Randy. Producing a noise like a train whistle, he threw himself forward at Carter, and hit him with all his strength on the side of the head.

Carter staggered, but did not fall. Randy stood back a little, and they glared at each other, breathing heavily. The boy,

65

sitting on his blankets like a ring-side spectator, cried out enthusiastically,

'Oh, jolly good shot! That was a good one, Randy!'

As if maddened beyond endurance by the remark, they now began to fight in earnest. Although the younger of the two, Carter was the more heavily built, and there was power behind the lunging blows which he aimed at his opponent. Randy, although lighter and more spare, was extremely nimble on his feet and was able to dodge most of these blows, while darting in and getting in some of his own. To Todd, helplessly watching them as they grunted and circled on the dusty floor, it soon became apparent that while Carter was inspired by a sort of glorious animal anger, Randy was fighting with real viciousness. After that first furious blow he had become very cool. He was watching Carter to find the weak spots in his guard, and when he found them he darted in and hit out savagely. He got several hard blows to his own head and shoulders in the process, and after a few of these he abandoned all pretence of fair fighting. He began to use his feet as well, kicking viciously upwards whenever he could at Carter's crutch and stomach. Fortunately none of these blows fell where they were intended – had they done so, the battle would have come to an abrupt and bloody conclusion. As it was, Carter's whirling arms served as a kind of unorthodox protection for his more vulnerable parts.

After they had been fighting for about five minutes, Randy was struck hard on the face. He moved back and put his hand up to his nose and mouth. It came away covered with blood. He stared at it, while Carter crowed and panted, exhorting the enemy to come on and take some more. The boy jumped up and down among his blankets and shouted impartial encouragement at both sides. For the first time, thought Todd, he looked like a real, ordinary, twelve-year-old boy.

Randy wiped his hands on his trousers and looked uncertainly at Carter. For a moment Todd wondered if he were going to give in and walk away. Then suddenly, without any kind of warning, he threw himself at Carter and kicked and struck savagely at him, while Carter stood and panted with his arms down. Carter lurched backwards, wavered, bent forwards at the waist, and toppled with his face in the dust at Randy's feet. The fight, brief and inglorious, was over.

The boy sat still, wide-eyed, and stared at the prostrate and retching Carter. Randy stood trembling and breathing loudly for a moment, then turned away and walked unsteadily to the mouth of the cave. Here he sat down and put his head between his hands.

Todd went over and knelt beside Carter. After a moment the boy got off the bed and came and knelt on the other side of the heaving, groaning body. They looked at each other with complicity. Todd felt as if he had been fighting too. His blood beat in his head and his hands shook.

'Help me turn him over,' he said.

Together they heaved Carter on to his back. His eyes were closed and his face was grey. It was streaked with blood and sweat; a trickle of blood outlined his jaw and ran down inside his filthy shirt. He looked terrible.

'Get some water,' said Todd. 'He seems to be coming round.'

Carter opened his eyes, moaned, and closed them again. The boy brought the bucket of water and set it down beside Todd. They poured some of the water over Carter's face and Todd tried to wipe off some of the blood and dirt with his handkerchief. Carter groaned again, opened his eyes, and made a convulsive effort to sit up.

'Stay where you are for a bit,' said Todd quietly. His relief was enormous. 'You've been winded. Don't try to sit up yet.'

Carter put his hand above his face and looked at it. The knuckles were split and bleeding.

'The sodding bastard,' he whispered. 'He kicked me. I could have beat him if he'd played fair. You saw him, Todd.

He kicked me.' He turned his head feebly and saw the boy's face, anxiously close to his. 'And as for you—' he said weakly.

'All right – just shut up and get your breath back,' said Todd grimly. He sat back on his heels and surveyed the body. 'You'll survive,' he said.

'He looks terrible, doesn't he?' the boy whispered in awe. He looked at Carter and then across at Todd. His eyes were gleaming.

'I feel terrible,' groaned Carter.

Todd said,

'Lie there for a bit. You're only winded, you'll be all right. Serves you right for trying the toss with Randy.'

'I could have beat him if he'd played fair,' whispered Carter. Surprisingly, tears came into his eyes and trickled down among the blood and dirt on his face. He looked up at the boy. 'Get out of the way. It's all your fault.'

The boy knelt still.

'All my fault? But how could it be? I didn't do anything.'

'Butting in,' said Carter weakly. He put up a filthy hand and brushed his face with it. 'It wouldn't have happened if you hadn't butted in.'

'But I didn't. I didn't say anything.'

From behind them Randy said,

'Oh yes, you did, you little tick. Keep your mouth shut in future or you'll find you'll get a bloody nose as well.'

'But I only asked—'

'We all know what you asked. I'm just warning you – keep out of it next time.'

Still on his knees, the boy flinched away from them. He looked down at his hands, clenched between his bare knees.

'We've had arguments before,' whispered Carter, 'but we never came to blows. Not before you came. Randy and I are always squabbling and it doesn't mean anything. You know it doesn't mean anything, don't you, Todd?'

Todd got to his feet and dusted the knees of his trousers.

'There's no need to blame the boy,' he said. 'Anyway, it

serves both of you right, fighting like a pair of silly kids.'

The boy looked up. He smiled gratefully at Todd. Todd looked away.

'And next time, Randy, if you must have a fight, leave out the dirty stuff. Kicking's a mug's game. You could have done some real damage. Stick to your fists next time – and above the belt.'

'Quite the honourable little British gentleman, aren't we?' sneered Randy. He turned round to face them. 'We'll have to appoint you as referee next time – just to make sure no one breaks the rules.'

'Oh, shut up,' said Todd irritably. 'Don't let's start all over again.'

Carter sat up with a groan and shook himself.

'Get me a drink, Todd. I still feel as if I've got a mouth full of dust.'

The boy crept back to his bed and sat there watching while Carter and Randy drank bottled beer and surveyed each other in some dismay. Randy had a black eye coming up and a badly bruised cheek, while Carter's chin was swelling fast and continued to ooze blood in a steady trickle. Both of them looked pale and exhausted. The state of their clothes was deplorable. Carter's shirt was ripped from shoulder to waist and Randy's trousers were covered with brown streaks of blood where he had wiped his hands on them.

'You'd better come back to my place and tidy up,' said Todd. 'It's the nearest – let's hope we can sneak in at the back and upstairs without my mother hearing us.' He began to laugh. 'My God! I wish you could see yourselves – you look like a couple of prize-fighters.'

The boy, sitting behind them on the bed, began to laugh too. It was a high childish laugh of pure amusement, but they all stood still and watched him uneasily, as if afraid he was laughing at some private joke which he did not intend to share with them.

*   *   *

Their plan to creep in at the back door and upstairs to Todd's room without being detected was not a success. By the time they got to the house Carter was nearing collapse and had to lean heavily on Todd in order to keep going at all. The heat was extreme and they were all beaten down and exhausted by it. Their stumbling progress up the drive was not the silent approach they had intended, and when they rounded the last corner and came in sight of the house, they pulled up in disorder. A large and gleaming car was drawn up on the gravel, and Todd looked at it in dismay.

'Good Lord! Visitors!' he said disgustedly. 'What a moment to choose!'

'Will you be expected to go and do the only son stuff for them in the drawing-room?' asked Randy.

'I shall indeed – if she spots us. Come on, round the back. I hoped she'd be out in the garden. We'll have to creep up and hope for the best.'

They went round the side of the house and through the back door into the kitchen. It struck blessedly cool after the inferno outside. Carter subsided into a chair while Todd quietly opened the door into the passage and listened. They could hear voices in the drawing-room. A man's voice spoke and a woman answered him with soft laughter. It sounded intimate and remote. Todd looked back at the others and motioned them to follow him. They were almost across the hall – indeed Todd had his foot on the bottom stair – when the door opened behind them and Clare spoke sharply.

'Todd? Is that you?'

Drearily they turned to face her. She stood in the doorway, cool and immaculate in navy and white linen, and looked them up and down in turn. Carter went red and shuffled his feet, Randy stiffened his body and looked past her at the great bowl of flowers which stood on a small polished table just inside the drawing-room door. Todd alone met her eyes with a sort of resigned smirk. When she had finished looking at them and had taken in every detail of their exhaustion and dishevelment, she said smilingly,

'Well! Well! Todd and his young friends. I was wondering when you'd be back, Todd – and whether you would bring your friends with you. We have a visitor. You must all come and meet him. Come along, Todd, and you Carter, and Randy. Do come and have a drink.'

'If you don't mind, Mama,' said Todd politely, 'I think we'd rather go up and have a bit of a wash and brush up first. We're not feeling very – er – presentable at the moment – particularly as you have a visitor. We won't be a minute.'

'Nonsense, Todd dear. Come along in. We've waited quite long enough already. You can go and tidy up later. Come along, all of you.'

Todd hesitated, and Carter shuffled towards the stairs trying to hold his shirt together with a grimy hand. But Randy, who had gone white round the nostrils, said in a high voice,

'Certainly, Mrs Gascoigne. Come along, Carter. We mustn't keep Mrs Gascoigne waiting, must we?'

He swept into the drawing-room as if he were taking possession of some piece of disputed territory. The others, defeated, slunk after him.

A tall thin figure uncoiled itself from a deep chair by the window and stood up.

'This is Mark Savory,' said Todd's mother. 'Mark, this is my son Edward – known as Todd – and this is Randolph, and this is Carter, two friends of his. They seem to have been involved in some kind of accident. Do please excuse their appearance.'

Mark Savory came forward to meet them. As he picked his way round the furniture and put out a formal hand to each of them in turn Todd received an impression of height, of pallor, and of heavily horn-rimmed spectacles behind which gleamed a pair of bright grey and very intelligent eyes.

'How do you do – how do you do!' he said genially. He shook hands with each of them, doing it at length and with extreme deliberation. He came to Todd last, and his hand felt

71

like a bundle of bones too thinly clothed in flesh. The skin was cool and dry and belied the geniality of the voice. When he had finished shaking hands he stood back a little and beamed at them.

'My goodness!' he said. 'Did you say an accident?'

He leaned forward a trifle on his toes as if to get a better view of Randy's eye. Carter furtively put up a hand to conceal his chin. Savory transferred his chilly beam to Mrs Gascoigne. In transit it acquired an element of knowingness which irritated Todd beyond measure.

'You know,' he said, rocking gently on his toes, 'I would hazard a guess that these two,' a precisely airy gesture towards Randy and Carter, 'have been involved in a fight. Whether a fight with each other I would hardly like to say. But – undoubtedly – a fight.'

'Your guess would be correct, sir,' said Randy, who alone of the three seemed to be rising to the occasion. 'We have been fighting – and with each other. Todd looks so clean because he was the referee,' he added.

'Dear me!' said Savory. 'I hope you have now made your peace?' But he was looking at Randy with new respect. 'What a curious pastime for an exceedingly hot Sunday afternoon. And who, if one may ask, got the better of this curious encounter?'

'He did,' said Carter, finding his tongue in pure self-defence. 'But only by kicking me.'

'It all sounds most alarming,' said Savory. 'And you,' he gestured towards Todd, 'I gather, refereed the battle? You certainly look less battle-scarred than your friends.'

'Involuntarily,' said Todd. 'Three is not a good number for a fight.' They eyed each other. Mentally, they were circling as if preparing to engage in some conflict of their own. Todd looked at the high structure of the face and at the two bony wings of the eyebrows and felt himself forced to respect what he saw. There was will and intelligence behind the manner.

His mother said,

'It sounds to me as if you've all been very silly. Still, boys will be boys. Todd, get something to drink. You must all be dying of thirst if you've walked all the way back from the quarry.'

Carter, startled, said,

'The quarry? How did you know—' and stopped.

She smirked at Todd, triumphant.

'But you always go to the quarry, don't you, dear?'

Mixing drinks at the sideboard, Todd said over his shoulder,

'Quite a lot of the time.'

Mark Savory had sat down on the sofa beside Mrs Gascoigne. He cocked one immensely long leg over the other and dangled a glossy shoe.

'Indeed? And what is there that is so fascinating about this quarry? No – don't tell me – a gang!' He gleamed at them through his immense spectacles. 'Now don't tell me I'm wrong!' He appealed to Todd. 'It is a gang, isn't it. It must be!'

Todd came back with the drinks and perched on a small stool beside Randy.

'It is indeed a gang,' he said gravely. 'We have fearful initiation rites and a terrible oath of secrecy, and we leave our sign on walls in public places. So if the next time you visit a public lavatory you see among the graffiti a scrawl of four fingers and a thumb in black ink surmounted by a dagger dripping blood, you will know that the Black Hand has struck again.'

He drank from his glass and watched Savory being shaken with a kind of saturnine mirth.

'Oh, my dear boy! Most amusing!' He beamed at them. 'And may I become a member of this delightful fraternity?'

'No,' said Todd gently. 'No outsiders.'

'Not even an honorary member?'

'No trespassers allowed,' said Randy. There was menace in his voice. He moved a little closer to Todd as if asserting their combined purpose.

'A pity. Still, never mind. Perhaps I would not, after all be an ornament to so – what shall I say? – so athletic a fraternity. I am getting a little old for fisticuffs.' He looked blandly at Carter who squirmed uncomfortably. 'And where is this quarry? I gather it is quite a long way from here.'

'Oh, it's an old deserted quarry on the edge of the town,' said Mrs Gascoigne impatiently. 'It's all too silly. I can't imagine what they find to do there. It's all overgrown with stunted bushes – I don't think it's really safe myself. One of these days it'll all come down round their ears. I've told Todd, but he doesn't take any notice.' Sitting gracefully upright in her brief navy dress, her dark hair drawn up from her face into a high crown on top of her small neat head, she looked very young and, Todd thought, very beautiful. She saw him looking at her and put her hand up to her long neck. 'I'm afraid he's quite out of my control,' she said indulgently.

She seemed to have got over her temper, and was prepared to be generous. 'I wouldn't let them drag you there even if they wanted to, Mark. It's most frightfully dreary, and no one ever goes there now – except these three lunatics, of course.'

So she calls him Mark, thought Todd. She had never spoken to him about this strange, disconcertingly intelligent man who was watching him with eyes which were both sleepy and alert.

'Still,' Savory was saying, 'in spite of the fact that it doesn't sound a very inviting spot, I shall have to pay it a visit sometime, if only to find out what attraction it can exert for three such redoubtable warriors. I say three – I have no doubt that you sometimes engage in pugilistic encounters with your friends, Todd? – I may call you that?'

'Certainly,' said Todd gravely, answering both questions together.

'Mark is thinking of buying a house and settling here,' said his mother suddenly, as if it were something which she could

74

no longer keep to herself. 'He wrote to me some time ago to say that he was considering it, and today he turned up to say that he's found one that he likes.'

'He wrote to you?' Todd could not help saying it.

'We knew each other years ago, didn't we, Mark. Before I met Guy.'

She turned to him with her vivid smile, and Todd, watching her, felt that she was explaining something, the importance of which only he would realise, although it was said to all of them.

'What house?' he asked.

Savory said, swinging his dangling shoe,

'It's called High Clere. Do you know it?'

'It's a beautiful place,' Randy said suddenly, before Todd could answer. 'It's been empty for more than a year. I've been over it.'

'Have you indeed?' said Savory politely. 'And how did you manage that?'

'I climbed in through the scullery window,' said Randy shortly.

'Indeed! Most enterprising!' Savory said, with an ironical little bend from the waist which Randy returned with complete equanimity. 'Well, I'm glad you approve, since I shall probably buy it within the next month or two.' He eyed them blandly.

Warily, Todd said,

'When would you move in, then?'

'There's a lot to be done – my flat in town has to be disposed of first. Certainly not until the end of August.' His fantastically quick eye caught the almost imperceptible movement of relief which came from Todd and communicated itself to Randy as a minute exhalation of breath, a tightening of the hand holding the glass. 'I hope this is not too early for you? That I shan't be spoiling any plans? Upsetting any apple-carts?'

It was Todd's turn to be bland.

'But how could your moving down here upset any of our plans, sir?' he asked innocently.

Savory's eye gleamed momentarily, as if in recognition of a checkmate.

'I think it will be wonderful!' said Clare. She leaned towards Savory with the peculiarly brilliant smile which was reserved for her really happy moments. 'It will be so nice to have a friend round here – everybody's so horribly suburban, you'll liven us up no end!'

I bet he will – and how! thought Todd. A really bright bird, this one.

The bright bird was talking to Clare about the house. Todd collected his friends' glasses and went to the sideboard to refill them. Outside the garden looked all green and gold. It must still be very hot, he thought, but the low sun over the trees and the velvety shadow of the privet hedge pushing out across the grass gave an illusion of coolness. Randy said something in a low voice to Carter. His mother stretched her arms above her head and laughed. She sounded warm and relaxed. I suppose she's going to marry him, thought Todd, and wondered about living in the same house with Savory, whichever house it might be. Alarming, he thought, but possible, once this business was over.

He took the glasses back to Randy and Carter and lounged on his stool enjoying the quiet and the coolness of the shaded room. Beside him Randy sat with arms linked loosely round his knees, smoking. It was like the cave before the boy came, he thought – or should he say, before they found the boy? A space between things happening.

Presently, after a whispered consultation, Randy and Carter stood up to take their leave. Mark Savory shook hands with them again with the same extreme deliberation, and said, with apparent sincerity, that he hoped to see them again soon. They thanked him politely, and departed with obvious relief.

Todd returned to the drawing-room with an uncomfortable sensation of support withdrawn. He was much on his guard, and so, he thought, was Savory. The two of them were standing by the long open windows, looking out at the garden. Savory looked immensely tall. His hair, hardly less dark than Clare's, was sleeked down over his long skull as if it had tended towards unruliness in youth and had been disciplined into extreme orderliness by years of ruthless brushing. He held his hands loosely linked behind his narrow back – strong, bony hands, thought Todd, looking at them with distaste. Clare was vivid beside him, even her back seemed to express life and warmth in its straight spring from the waist.

They heard his approach, and turned away from the window. Clare smiled at him with simple and extraordinary affection, Savory with a more guarded warmth.

'Clare's been telling me that you play a good game of golf,' he said. 'We must have a round together. I used to be a passable player, but I get little practice. The exercise would be good for me. I spend too much time indoors over my books. I write, you know – on matters of little importance connected with literature.' He spoke the word with distaste.

'He means that he writes book reviews and articles for the Sunday papers,' said Clare, laughing up at him. 'He's too conceited to admit that he enjoys it.'

Savory preened himself a little. Todd thought that being teased was a new experience for him, and that, in his solemn way, he rather enjoyed it.

'A good deal of money coming one's way too early in life is a great disincentive to creative endeavour. Since I find I can't write the books, I review them instead. I must admit I enjoy it.'

'Of course you do. Come along and eat. Do you mind a cold supper? We always have rather a scratch meal on Sundays, and since I didn't know you were coming—'

He bent over her in courtly deprecation.

'I am rebuked. I don't deserve anything at all, and I shall consider myself fortunate in whatever you set before me.'

As they went into the dining-room Todd could have sworn

that one of the large bright eyes slowly closed and opened at him in a solemn wink.

In spite of Clare's apologies the meal was excellent. They ate with the long windows on to the garden wide open, and the flames of the six tall candles on the table stood yellow and motionless. There was not a breath of wind to disturb them. Todd said little. He contented himself with watching Savory and listening to him talk. He talked well – with the air of one giving a performance, but also of knowing that it was a performance. Clare listened to him too, with an intensity of interest which Todd was convinced was not assumed. She sat opposite them, and her eyes rarely left Savory's face except to flicker sideways now and then to see if Todd had duly noted some flash of wit, some peculiar felicity of expression. She seemed to be drawing Savory out. Everything she said was designed to lead him into excelling himself. Hers, too, in a less perceptible way, was a good performance.

He talked of travel, of places he had visited, of people he had met. Gradually it became apparent to Todd that he was drawing Clare into his scheme for the future. It was subtly done – 'you will like him, Clare,' – 'you will love Venice, the grey will complement your looks,' – it was very flattering and, to Todd, disturbing. He began to feel that he was being cut out; not because he was hostile, or because he had shown himself unwilling to be drawn into this unknown scheme, but because he was an unknown quantity. After a while, Clare began to notice these small assumptions. At first she flushed and looked down, a little anxious, uncertain what her reaction should be. Todd thought that perhaps she was afraid of conceding too much ground too soon. Before long, however, she began to accept them, and to respond, timidly at first, then with enthusiasm. Glances of mutual understanding passed between them. Todd began positively to feel that he should leave the room so that they could come to an immediate understanding without the embarrassment of his presence.

They left the table and went into the drawing-room for

coffee. Clare served it very strong in tiny jade green cups. She made good coffee, and flushed with pleasure when Savory put down his cup after the first sip and said:

'I think this is the best coffee I have ever tasted. Most women make it too weak, or resort to that abomination, the percolator. It is excellent. I congratulate you.'

She perched herself on the arm of Todd's chair and crossed her legs. She had long slender legs, the flesh of which was brown and silky smooth, and unblemished by hairs. She knew this, and Todd saw that she was showing as much of them as possible to Savory. She, too, is bringing out her weapons, he thought. He stood up.

'Dear Mama, I hope you won't think it is very rude of me to go upstairs. I haven't done any work at all this week-end, and when it's so hot the only time I can concentrate is at night.'

'He's got exams coming up,' Clare explained. She slipped over the arm of his chair and sat down. 'Frightful in this weather, isn't it? Do please excuse him.'

Savory waved his long white hand at Todd in an airy gesture of dismissal. Sickeningly, it exactly reproduced the airy gesture when the boy was in what Todd privately called his 'rajah' mood.

Clare looked up at him.

'Dear Todd, don't stay up too long. You look so tired – quite drawn – or is it just the light?'

Indeed, Todd had felt his face pinch into pallor at that airy gesture of Savory's hand.

'Probably the light,' he said. 'I feel perfectly all right. Come in on your way up.' He went over to Savory and held out his hand. It was engulfed in that strong chilly grasp.

'Good night, sir.'

'Good night, dear boy, good night. I am delighted to have met you. I hope we shall soon get to know each other better.'

Todd felt the watchful, calculating gaze on him all the way to the door. Indeed, in a way he felt it all the way up the stairs, and it was still with him when he went into his room and switched on the reading lamp at the desk.

The room had been exposed to the full glare of the sun for most of the afternoon and was exceedingly hot. Todd immediately went into the bathroom next door and ran himself a cold bath, flinging off his clothes and stepping into the water as if into another element. He lay flat for some time with his eyes closed. Through the fringe of lashes he could see the blue-green water and his own legs, white as fish, motionless beneath its surface. His arms lay beside his pallid body and looked startingly brilliant in colour, a deep, rich honey. When he had dried himself he looked at his head and shoulders in the mirror. His face, and the deep V where his shirt opened were the same rich colour. His hair was dyed and bleached into a fine brittle thatch, almost white. He looked startling, almost a stranger to himself.

He went into his room and sat down at the desk. The impulse to go out, to go to the cave, was still with him, so strong that he wondered how he was able to resist it. He pulled his books towards him and started to work. When about ten minutes had passed he found that the urge was beginning to decrease, and before long it had totally disappeared.

Much later, he heard the subdued crunch of footsteps on the gravel underneath his window. Startled, he raised his head and sat listening. After a moment he heard their voices, first Savory's, then Clare answering him with that peculiar breathy little laugh which meant that she was excited and happy. He put his hand out to the light and switched it off. Then he went noiselessly to the window and leaned on the sill. The night air was so still that at first he thought he could actually make out their words. Then he realised that all he could really distinguish were the rhythms and inflections of their speech. What they were actually saying was inaudible. He put his hand out of the window on to the stone sill, and by craning forward at a perilous angle found that he could see them below him on the drive. They were standing close together, their heads bent. He was stooping over her, and for a moment Todd thought they were kissing. Then he realised that this must be an illusion caused by their foreshortening and by the illusory dimness of the light which caused stationary objects to look as if they were wavering and fluctuating when in reality they were motionless. He heard their voices going on. Savory seemed to be making some kind of speech which was punctuated by polite little noises of acquiescence from Clare. Todd wondered if he were making a declaration of love, but after a moment's thought dismissed this as improbable. He would hardly choose to do it in the drive when he had had all evening to do it in the comfort and seclusion of the drawing-room.

The speech drew to an end, and Clare made some short reply. The two figures moved together to the door of the car and Savory opened it. Its metallic click sounded shockingly loud and abrupt in the stillness, so much so that Todd jumped violently and almost pitched out of the window. That, he thought, as he steadied himself, would indeed have provided a dramatic conclusion to the evening. Savory half insinuated himself into the car, then climbed out again. This time, thought Todd, he really must be going to kiss her. This, indeed, he did. But it was only a chaste salute upon her hand. He was so tall that he had to bend his long body almost in half at the waist, and Todd could see the white flash of his shirt dip, disappear, and then come into view again as he straightened himself.

After this he really did get into the car. The engine started almost silently, the great car swished and circled on the gravel. Its lights sprang out and flashed round in a huge arc, illuminating Clare's gleaming head and bare arms, a row of bushes which leaped up in black and green, and a golden vista of ruffled gravel. Then the car moved off, its red tail lights rapidly diminishing like a couple of receding eyes. Todd heard the light sound of Clare's heels on the steps and the click as the front door shut behind her.

81

When she came into his room he was seated at his desk with the books open in front of him, and he blinked at her out of the light as if she had only just disturbed him. She came in and sat down on his bed, sliding her feet out of the narrow sandals and wriggling her toes with a sigh of relief.

'Gone?'

'Yes – gone. Didn't you hear the car?'

'I was working.'

'I thought you might have gone to bed, I didn't see the light.'

'I switched it off for a bit to rest my eyes.'

'It's terribly late. You're up early in the morning, you know. You ought to be in bed.'

'I don't call one o'clock late. Whatever time will he get back to town?'

She shrugged.

'God knows. Anyway, that's his business. I didn't ask him to stay so late. It wasn't my fault.'

'Wasn't it?'

'As a matter of fact, it wasn't.'

He swung his chair round to face her. She sat slightly hunched on the bed with her arms crooked above her head as she pulled the hairpins one by one out of her piled-up hair. As she took them out she put them into her mouth. At last the dark mass toppled down and spread itself heavily round her face and on to her shoulders. She took the pins out of her mouth and arranged them neatly on his bedside table.

'That's better.'

'I would have thought it was hotter with it hanging down like that.'

'It is in a way, but it's blasted uncomfortable with it pinned up. It's so heavy it seems to pull all the time and it gives me a foul headache. I really must get round to having it off.'

'Oh no – don't do that. It's beautiful. It would be a shame to cut it off.'

She grunted.

'That's what Guy used to say. "A woman's crowning glory!" Good old Victorian Guy. It's the sort of thing Mark might say.' She stopped fiddling with the hairpins and looked up at him. The dim light made her look vulnerable and anxious. 'Do you like him, Todd?'

'I don't really know. He's a funny sort of chap, isn't he? He's obviously very bright, and he's interesting to listen to, but he's a bit peculiar, isn't he?'

She clasped her hands between her knees and hunched herself forward over them.

'I don't know – I suppose he is in a way. I met him years ago, you know. Before I knew Guy. It was when I was working in London. We went around together for a while. He was older than me, and he was pretty dazzling, brilliantly clever and successful. He'd just published a book on Swinburne which had made quite a sensation. I never got down to reading it, but everyone was talking about it. It looked as if he was going to make quite a name for himself. It was funny – he just sort of fizzled out after that one book. He never wrote anything else, just contributed to magazines and papers and that sort of thing. He had money when I met him, but not on the scale he has now.' She brooded. 'He's awfully rich, Todd.'

'So I gather.'

'Anyway, I was still seeing quite a bit of him when I met Guy. It was always frightfully proper – I believe he only kissed me once, and that was a sort of accident. I egged him on to see if he ever would. I don't think he enjoyed it much. I can't say I did. Then I met Guy, and everyone and everything went by the board. I seem to remember seeing him a couple more times, and then he sort of dropped out. Neither of us actually said anything, but he must have guessed what had happened. Being young and silly at the time I daresay I made it pretty obvious. I don't think I've given him a thought since, except when I noticed his name in the papers when he'd written an article or something, until he wrote to me a couple of months ago. It gave me an odd feeling. Almost as if he's been keeping tabs on me all these years.'

'Maybe he has. He looks the sort of chap who'd enjoy that kind of thing – long-term planning,' said Todd.

She wasn't listening.

'So here he is. Coming to live almost next door.'

'Well? Aren't you pleased?'

'I suppose so. I should be. I do like him, Todd, honestly I do. I wasn't just putting it on.'

'I know you weren't. He's an interesting chap. But he's a bit older than you, isn't he?'

'Not that much older. I'm forty-three, you know. He can't be much more than fifty. He looks older than he is, and the way he talks and everything makes him seem old. He always used to put on a bit of a performance, and he does it now with a vengeance. I suppose it began as a fairly harmless pose and now he can't stop. It seems perfectly natural.' She giggled. 'All that "dear lady" stuff! It's incredibly Victorian. But somehow I don't mind. It's rather sweet really.'

Todd thought to himself that 'sweet' was hardly the word he would have chosen. However he did not say so.

'Why were you so awful to Randy and Carter, making them come in and meet him looking like that?'

'Oh, that dreadful pair!' She shrugged. 'I don't know – they irritate me – at least Carter does. He's such a lout. And Randy – I just can't stand him.'

'I know you can't. So does he. You make it pretty obvious.'

'Do I? I'm sorry, Todd. He just gets me down. He's so smooth and confident, and always so dreadfully tidy. I suppose I just wanted to catch him out.'

'You didn't succeed.'

'I know I didn't. He didn't turn a hair. You know, I get the feeling there's something wrong with him. I think he's vicious, almost dangerous. I wish you wouldn't spend so much time with him. I don't really mind about Carter, though he's

84

a dreadful lout and a bore, but Randy's different. He's no good, Todd. I wish you'd give up this business.'

'What business?'

'Whatever it is you're up to at the moment. I know you. You're up to something, and those two are in it with you. What is it, Todd?'

'It's nothing important, and anyway it'll soon be finished. By the end of term, I promise you. It's only a sort of game – a gang thing.'

'Aren't you getting a bit old for gangs?'

'Maybe.'

'Mark guessed, you know. He knew straight away.'

'Did he? How do you know?'

'By the way he talked. He knew at once it was something to do with that quarry. If it weren't so hot I'd come myself and find out what you're up to.'

'I wouldn't do that, you know.'

She looked up at him, startled.

'My goodness, Todd – it sounds almost as if you're threatening me!'

He laughed.

'Perhaps I am.'

'Well, you'd better finish whatever it is before Mark moves down here. He's not the sort to waste time asking questions.'

Todd had already realised this, and it made him uneasy. Clare opened her mouth and yawned, showing her teeth.

'I'm dead tired. I'm going to bed. Don't do any more now, Todd.'

'I shan't. I've finished.'

She picked up her shoes and got up off the bed. In her stockinged feet, with her hair hanging round her face, she looked like a little girl. Todd felt sudden affection for her as if she had touched some secret deep spring in him. He went over and put his arms round her. She felt bony and slight against him. She smelt of scent and of body warmth.

'Dear Clare, don't worry about me.'

85

She looked up at him, tilting her face back. In it, he saw himself in a twist of the mouth, a turn of the nostril.

'I can't help it. You don't tell me anything and sometimes I imagine awful things.'

He rubbed his cheek against her hair.

'Silly Clare. You mustn't worry. It's nothing to worry about, nothing at all. Just a silly game. It's not important.'

'Isn't it?'

He told his lie valiantly.

She went on looking doubtfully up at him, only half comforted.

Randy arrived home very late and very drunk. He had left Carter at the turning which led to the estate, and went straight to the nearest pub. Normally, he did not drink, because he hated and feared the loss of self-control which drink produced. On this occasion, however, he went into the pub with the explicit intention of getting, not completely drunk, but thoroughly tight. He sat alone at a table in the corner and got down to drinking quickly, without pleasure. He knew no one and no one took any notice of him. He smoked steadily and occasionally glanced at the clock over the bar to make sure he would have enough drinking time before the bar closed. Before long he noted with satisfaction the signs of intoxication – swimming vision, shaking legs, a tendency to giggle to himself when he burnt his fingers lighting a cigarette or dropped a coin in picking up his change. The landlord began to look rather closely at him and to pause before drawing his order. But in his week-end clothes he looked older than his age and if he were getting drunk, at least he was doing it quietly.

Randy knew how much he needed, and when he had drunk exactly this amount he stopped, and left the pub. The air outside, although extremely warm, was at least clear, and it had hit him like a blow to the head. But he had allowed for its effect, and he made his way safely, if somewhat unsteadily, back to the house. He had some difficulty in getting his key into the lock, but eventually he succeeded, and made his way noisily into the kitchen. Here he switched on the light, which hurt his eyes a good deal, and looked round for something cool to apply to the black eye which was now giving him a good deal of pain. He tried a cloth wrung out in cold water, but that only seemed to make the throbbing worse. Eventually he found a plate in the fridge with three chops on it, and with vague memories of raw beef as a remedy for black eyes he decided to apply the juciest one to see if it did any good. Although he held it patiently to the affected area for several minutes it did not seem to have much effect, so he put it back on the plate with the others and returned them to the fridge. He then decided that bed was the best place, and set off upstairs, falling over a kitchen chair on the way and making a good deal of noise on the stairs.

When he got to the top of the first flight and had started along the landing to the second which led up to his room, he heard a sudden and totally unexpected sound behind him. He stopped, and turned. Confronting him in the open door of their bedroom stood Mr and Mrs Johns, close together as if to yield to one another mutual support. Both wore wollen dressing-gowns which reached to their ankles. Mr Johns' was red, and Mrs Johns' was brown. In addition Mrs Johns wore a hair-net over a serried and bristling rank of curling-pins. It was an unprepossessing sight. Randy, momentarily bereft of speech, gaped at them in awed silence.

Mrs Johns spoke first, and she did not do so in her usual tone of long-suffering reasonableness.

'And what,' she inquired, 'is the meaning of this?'

'It's me,' said Randy unnecessarily.

'So I see. And why, may I ask, are you making so much noise? Of course, it's your own affair if you choose to use the house like an hotel, leaving immediately after breakfast and getting in at Heaven knows what time of the night, but you might at least do it quietly. You don't even try to be quiet. I never interfere with your comings and goings, but if you're going to come in at this time of night you must try to be quiet.'

They stood together in the doorway, looking, thought Randy, like a pair of animals making a stand in front of their burrow. He went a little towards them in the low, garish light, and together they retreated before him, giving ground with their eyes fixed on his face. Mrs Johns' gaze suddenly riveted on his eye. She shot out her arm and pointed at him.

'You've been fighting!' she crowed. 'You've got a black eye!'

Randy went up to them and stuck out his neck, bringing his face close to theirs.

'I have indeed,' he said. 'It was a splendid fight until I kicked him in the balls and winded him.'

They blinked at him. Mr Johns wrinkled his nose and sniffed.

'And you've been drinking – I can smell it on your breath. You're drunk.'

'I am,' said Randy. He leered at them. 'And what's more,' he added, 'it was your money I used to get drunk on. I pinched it out of your chest of drawers. You'll have to think of a better place next time.'

He then proceeded to suggest a place in terms of the utmost crudity. Mrs Johns went white.

'You are a bad, wicked boy,' she said, trembling. 'We have had enough of you in this house. I've done my best for you, but I can't do any more. You must go. I can't have you in my house any longer. Do you understand?'

'It's all right,' said Randy thickly. He put out a hand to grasp the bannister. 'Don't worry, I'm not staying in this place a moment longer than I have to. I shall go when my term finishes and when I've cleared up one or two little matters that I'm busy with at the moment. Then I shall clear out and leave you two love-birds to sing to each other in your little nest.'

Still with their wary gaze fixed on his face, they silently withdrew backwards into the room and slowly, still watching him, they closed the door. There was complete silence inside the room.

The brief outburst of violence had exhilarated Randy. He stepped forward and traced a large and elaborate cross on the door with many flourishes and airy gestures.

'Bring out your dead! Bring out your dead!' he chanted in a sepulchral voice, brushing his hands across the brown panels of the door with a dusty swishing sound. He could feel them listening to him, strung up and vibrating on the other side. He felt violent and powerful, as if he could kill them both with impunity.

He began to chant obscenities at them in the darkened passage. The light bulb on its long black cord hung bleakly over his head and cast few shadows on the walls with their bunches of brown flowers, and on the green, yellow and brown dado. Inside the room Mr and Mrs Johns sat side by side on their bed and looked at each other in terror. They truly thought they had brought a madman into the house to live with them.

Mrs Carter moved round the kitchen putting away the supper things. Her voice went on and on, enveloping Carter in a kind of protective balloon of sound.

'And what you want to go fighting that Randy for I shall never know. He's a nasty one and no mistake. You should have known he wouldn't fight fair. That sort never does. I knew his kind as soon as I saw him. "Randy, my lad," I said to myself, "I wouldn't trust you as far as I could throw you." It serves you right. I've always said you shouldn't go around with him. He's vicious, and that's a fact. What did he do? Kick you?'

89

'Kicked me and winded me,' said Carter moodily. He drank some more of his strong sweet tea. His stomach muscles still hurt and his head ached.

Mrs Carter sniffed.

'Kicked you where it hurts most, I'll be bound. Trust him. Anyway, what have you been doing?'

'Nothing. Just messing about.'

'At that old quarry again, I suppose?'

'Well, and what about it?' said Carter sullenly. 'Why shouldn't we bloody well go to the quarry? The way you go on anyone would think we were planning a murder, or something.' He stopped abruptly and looked down at his hands. They were trembling, and he thrust them quickly into his pockets.

'Now, now, none of that sort of language to me,' said Mrs Carter. She looked closely at him. 'Come on, Dicky, what's up?' she said in a different tone. 'There's something the matter. Have you got yourself into some kind of trouble with those two? Because if you're mixed up in anything you'd better tell me now, before anything serious happens. I don't want you getting into trouble with the police or anything. Come on now, Dicky, out with it. What have you been up to?'

'I haven't been up to anything,' said Carter furiously. He stood up, and knocked his chair backwards so that it fell with an appalling clatter on to the tiled floor. 'For God's sake, can't you let me alone? It's hot, and I'm tired, and I've got some work to do. I'm going upstairs.'

He walked towards the door, scarlet and trembling. As he tried to pass his mother she put out her hand and caught at his arm. Helpless, he stood still and looked past her upturned face at the wall, familiar with its stylised pattern of fruit and flowers.

'I'm not trying to find out anything about what you're doing,' she said pleadingly. He folded his lips tightly with his determination not to speak. 'Honestly, I'm not trying to bother you. It's just that I'm bound to be a bit worried. Those two have both got far more money than you have, and they're older and everything, and I don't trust Randy. Todd's all right, but I wouldn't put it past him to get into a bit of mischief. I've always trusted you up till now, but I get the feeling there's something going on, and I'm worried.'

'There's nothing going on,' he said, stiff-lipped. 'Honestly, Mum, there's nothing to worry about.'

He could feel her eyes upon his face.

'Are you sure?'

'Of course I'm sure.' He twitched his arm away from her fingers, and then relented a little. 'It's nothing important. It's only a game. If I told you about it even you'd only think it was silly.'

'Why don't you tell me about it, and see, then?'

'I will, some time. Promise I will. Only for goodness sake stop worrying.'

He hesitated, then stooped and kissed her awkwardly. She moved as he did so, and his lips touched her cheek and not, as he had intended, her hair. The skin was smooth and smelt of soap, and of something indefinable which brought back to him an awareness of his existence close to her when he had been a very small child. This awareness – too faint to be called memory – brought with it a rush of tenderness, but before he had even fully recognised it for what it was, it had evaporated and he was as far away from her as before. He straightened up, and she sighed, crossing her arms over her huge bosom.

'Well, I suppose I shall have to be satisfied with that.' She reached out and patted his forearm with her brownish scrubbed hand. 'You go up, dear. Don't do too much. You must be dead beat, and it's school tomorrow. I must say I shall be glad when term's over and you're not seeing so much of those two. Go on, up you go. Good night, love, sleep tight.'

Carter went slowly up the stairs and into his room. He sat on the edge of his bed and fingered his cut chin. He felt horribly tired, but at the same time elated in a remote, detached way. He felt as if he had narrowly escaped some kind of disaster and that he had gained for himself a breathing space. He kicked off his shoes and lay down. Instantly, he was asleep.

Todd and Randy made their separate ways to the senior library. It was a large shady room whose long windows looked out on to the playing fields. Thanks to a generous endowment from a former pupil it was extremely well stocked. The tables were equipped with reading lamps and bookstands and the deep chairs were comfortable. Todd, who arrived first, found it empty except for one other senior boy who had barricaded himself in behind a formidable pile of books. He seemed to be battling with some knotty problem which involved the use of an elaborate case of geometrical instruments in its solution, and he did not even look up as Todd made his way to the usual secluded corner. Here he sat down and spread himself in comfort to wait for Randy.

Below on the brownish grass a game of cricket was in progress. It looked very sluggish as the small white-trousered figures ambled up and down in the brilliant sunshine. The pavilion looked like a little white toy house sitting neatly on the edge of the pitch. After watching for a time Todd was able to make out the sturdy figure of Carter. He was batting, and the only outbursts of anything approaching activity seemed to come as a result of his efforts. Todd could see his bat flash and swing as he drove strongly between two fieldsmen to the boundary. A small figure set off in half-hearted pursuit of the ball and then slowed down to an amble as the almost invisible sphere bounced cheerfully past the white markers and rolled away into the long grass. Carter leaned on his bat and raised an arm to his face. It must be unbearably hot out there, thought Todd, and turned away from the window as Randy came up the room towards him.

'Watching our friend Carter?' he inquired with a gesture towards the window.

'Poor chap! He must be almost fried.' Todd put his feet up on the table and belched discreetly. 'After that lunch too. Bread and butter pudding! I ask you. It's uncivilised.'

'You don't mean to say you ate it?' asked Randy, sitting down.

'Of course I didn't. I swopped plates with Maclean when he'd polished his off and he ate mine as well. Revolting chap, Maclean. A human dustbin. He'll eat anything. That's why I make a point of sitting next to him. It's not for the sake of his conversation. His sole contribution today was "Bloody hot again". Then he got his nose down and concentrated on the trough.' Todd tilted his chair back and linked his arms behind his head. 'Still, not much longer, thank God.'

Randy said,

'I don't think I'm going to bother with Oxbridge.'

Todd did not betray any surprise.

'Oh?'

'I don't want to waste three good years mucking about up there – not to mention more exams into the bargain.'

'What'll you do then?'

'I don't know yet. Get a job. Something I like, for a change.'

'Row at home?'

Randy nodded and showed his teeth.

'I got back drunk last night, and Frankenstein and partner were waiting for me. We exchanged views on one another. Distinctly personal.'

'Good for you! Has she twigged about the money you pinched?'

'She has – among other things. I'm off, Todd. I've had enough.'

'They won't be particularly overjoyed here. I mean, so far as the scholarship goes you're a dead cert.'

'They can keep their fucking scholarship,' said Randy with considerable force.

'Well, I want that scholarship,' said Todd after a moment's silence. 'And I want those three years at Oxbridge.'

'What for?'

'I don't know. I just do.' Todd brought his feet down off the table and leaned towards Randy. 'I say, what do you think of Mark Savory?'

'Why?'

'I am interested. What do you think of him?'

'Too bloody curious,' said Randy succinctly.

Todd nodded, pleased.

'That's what I think. He's up to something.'

'He wants to marry your mother. Do you think he'll ask you to call him "Daddy"?'

'It won't get him far if he does. Except in the direction of a boot up the backside.'

Randy looked curiously at him.

'Do you mind?'

'If they get married, you mean? I don't know. I don't think I mind particularly either way. Except, as I say, if he gets too nosy.'

'He's not moving in for a bit yet.'

'I know. That's something. We shall just have to make bloody sure everything's settled before he does.'

'Surely it will be? I mean, we never meant it to be for more than a week or two.'

'I don't trust him. He's the sort of chap who'll come and settle in an hotel if he thinks he's on to something. He's too sharp for his own good.'

'Do you like him, Todd?'

Todd looked thoughtfully down at the table. A frown drew little puckers of white flesh across his forehead.

'No, I don't. I think he's affected and pompous – and a failure. But he's very clever, and ruthless, and he's interesting. He stimulates me and menaces me at the same time. I can't make out what he's up to. I feel as if he and Clare are up to something together, something concerning me. Almost as if they're trying to get hold of me.' He pushed his forefinger along a crack in the table and frowningly watched its progress. 'It's an odd feeling, and I don't like it. I can't even explain it,' he said sombrely.

Randy watched him.

'Are you thinking of going back on it?' he said. 'Because if you are I can do it on my own.'

Todd looked up at him in amazement.

'Don't be bloody daft!' he said crossly. 'Damn it all, we've been planning it for years.'

'Two years,' said Randy in his soft precise voice. 'It was your idea in the first place.'

'Not really – I think we thought of it together. And Carter, of course.'

'I can't think how he got into it.'

'Nor me really. But now he's there he fits. You and I on our own do not balance well. We need Carter for ballast. He prevents us from becoming top heavy.'

'He's ballast all right – thick as they come. Still, as you say, he fits.'

Todd swung idly round to the window and was in time to see Carter swing his bat in a prodigious sideways sweep. He sank on to one knee and all the small white figures turned together to watch the ball loop into the air and skim clear of the boundary.

'What are you looking at?' inquired Randy.

'Carter. He's just hit a six. An absolute beauty. Clear into the long grass. A lovely stroke.'

Randy grunted.

'That's about all he can do – hit balls about.'

Todd swung himself back to the table.

'Don't forget I'm pretty good at knocking a ball about too.'

'I know, but among other things. Football in the winter and cricket in the summer – it's all he lives for.'

'There are worse things.'

Randy flushed under his sallow tan.

'Meaning what?'

'Meaning nothing, you ass. Touchy, aren't you?'

'Maybe. Perhaps I'm getting a bit sick of you and Carter getting at me.'

'We don't get at you.'

'What about Carter yesterday, then?'

'He was angry. You were pretty foul about his wretched wood. He was only trying to do his bit.'

'I don't see why he had to go on about his sister. Silly cow.'

'Perhaps you should steer clear of his female relations.'

'Don't worry, I will. She was willing enough until it came to the point, stupid bitch. She cried off, and then said I couldn't do it.'

'Well, could you?'

'That's not the point. Anyway, I don't have to explain to you.'

'I didn't ask you to explain. You brought the subject up in the first place.'

'Pure as the driven snow, aren't you? Fight clean, and don't hit below the belt. Proper little English gentleman, in fact.'

'You've said that before,' remarked Todd peaceably, refusing to be drawn.

'And as for that little perisher—'

'What little perisher?'

'Who do you think? Him.'

'Oh. What about him?'

'Putting his oar in like that.'

'He didn't put his oar in.'

'He did. He said it deliberately. If he'd kept his mouth shut the whole thing would have blown over. Damn it all, we've had squabbles before, but they never came to blows.'

'It was nothing to do with him.'

'Oh yes it was. Even Carter noticed it, and he's a lot less bright than you are. It was his fault.'

'It wasn't. He didn't have anything to do with it.'

Randy put his elbows on the table and propped his chin

on his hands. He looked closely at Todd, who turned his head away.

'You certainly are on his side, aren't you?' he said curiously.

'Not particularly. I just think you're being unfair. Trying to shift the blame for your silly fight on to him. It's ridiculous. It was hot, and you were both spoiling for a fight. It's not a question of being on his side – or on anybody's, if it comes to that.'

'I still say you're on his side. I saw you looking at him. I didn't know you had a penchant for little boys. He certainly is pretty, isn't he?'

Todd put his hand up to the side of his mouth where a pulse had begun to beat.

'That's enough of that, Randy. You have got a filthy mind, and no mistake. Just because you can't keep your mind off sex you have to go lashing out at me. Shut up, and don't be more filthy than you must. You've had your little go at Carter and it's no use thinking you can provoke me into the same sort of thing. Let's drop it, shall we?'

They looked at each other across the table. The altercation had been conducted in low voices. There had been no overt signs of violence. But Todd was frightened. He did not understand the cause of the hostility which had sprung up between them any more than he had understood the eruption of violence between Randy and Carter the day before.

Randy was the first to drop his eyes.

'All right – sorry,' he said shortly. 'Forget it. No offence meant.'

'And none taken,' said Todd in what he intended to be a jocular cockney accent. But he still felt shaken and uncertain of himself.

'By the way,' said Randy after a short pause, 'I can't go this evening. I must get some work done.'

'So must I. And tomorrow we've got some people coming to dinner – I shall have to be there.'

'What shall we do, then?'

'We'd better make it Wednesday.'

'What about food and stuff? He won't last on what he's got.'

'We can send Carter. I'll catch him when he comes in from games. I'll give him some money and a list. He can get the things on his way home and take them after supper. It's easier for him – I don't suppose his family give a damn whether he's in or not.'

'Right. That's a good idea. I really ought to get a move on. What with one thing and another I've got a hell of a lot to do.'

They stood up. Randy hesitated for a moment, standing with his head bent, the palms of his hands pressed flat on the table.

'I say, Todd,' he said almost diffidently. 'Why do you suppose he stays there?'

Todd shrugged.

'I don't know. Perhaps he likes it. He may see it all as an adventure, just a sort of game, like being shipwrecked or something. After all, he's only a kid.'

Randy looked up with a troubled expression.

'That's just it. He's a funny sort of kid. For a twelve-year-old, I mean. Most of the time he seems half-witted, and then he says something more or less by mistake that hits the nail right on the head. Like when you and Carter were trying to get him to talk yesterday. He didn't half lead you a dance.'

'Oh, I don't know. Perhaps he really is half-witted, or he's lost his memory, and honestly doesn't know who he is!' said Todd lightly.

'It's not as simple as that,' said Randy. 'He's an odd fish, and I'd feel a lot happier if he did something a bit more normal, like raising merry hell and trying to run away.'

'Don't worry – perhaps he will,' said Todd, laughing. 'And then you really will have something to worry about!'

*   *   *

Carter stopped for a rest at the top of the quarry and spent a few minutes throwing pebbles down into the bushes in an attempt to hit the sheet of corrugated iron concealed among them. His aim, however, seemed even less accurate than usual. He only hit it twice in about twenty shots and soon gave up. Instead, he hitched his shoulders out of the strap of Todd's rucksack and lay on his stomach on the baked earth, scanning the opposite side of the quarry. There was nothing to see of any interest. The low bushes still seemed to lean and quiver in the heat, and the yellow earth showing between their scrawny stems looked drier and more thinly spread over the bare rock face than ever. He wondered if there was any water left in the stream at the bottom of the gully. Even when it was running full and strong it could not be seen from his present position. He propped his chin on his clenched fists and watched a bird making idle loops low in the blinding sky. When he looked down again the landscape tilted under his dazzled eyes, drained of colour, and speckled with little grainy spots like the print of an old film. He shut his eyes, and when he opened them the scene had readjusted itself and regained its colour.

He fumbled in the pocket of the rucksack and pulled out a block of chocolate. It was soft and pliable in its wrappings. When he pulled the silver paper open the chocolate was swimming in a pool of liquid. He licked it off the paper and found it pleasant, although almost immediately it made him extremely thirsty. He screwed the paper round a largish pebble and tossed it at random into the bushes below. It hit the corrugated iron and bounced once with a satisfying clinking sound. Carter struggled back into the rucksack, turned round to lower himself feet first over the ledge, and began the climb down.

The earth under his fingers felt hotter than he had ever known it. His feet kept slipping and starting little avalanches which fell away beneath him and rained into the gully below his descending body. The path he followed was well worn by their frequent passage and was now comparatively easy to negotiate. He wondered how visible it would be to anyone standing on the opposite edge; probably it would show as an irregular worn line down the cliff face. Fortunately, the entrance to the cave itself was masked by the outer edge of the great slab of rock which formed one of its walls. This slab described a sharp turn, and was a natural shield and concealment of the mouth. They had themselves passed and repassed it many times without realising its existence, until one day Todd, standing on the rock to rest, had casually moved on the rock face and had disappeared into the darkness, leaving the other two, appalled and terrified, to think that he had fallen through some hole or shaft to his death – until he had reappeared to them as they stood below, gazing silently up, and stood astride the narrow ledge of rock as if he had returned from the dead. It was a place which could really only be found by accident – unless someone should actually stand on the opposite slope and watch them go in and mark the exact spot among the rocks and ledges of thin earth where a narrow mouth of darkness showed.

They had waited for this to happen, patiently taking their turn in the opening day after day. But no one came. Indeed, no one seemed to know that the cave existed. Everyone seemed to assume that they spent their time, and played their games, whatever they were, among the bushes at the bottom of the gully. There was, indeed, a broken-down shed among the bushes. Carter's sheet of corrugated iron had once formed its roof. One wall and part of another still stood, and they had found an ancient kettle, some bits of broken china, and a few rotting sticks of furniture much overgrown with nettles and grass. Rebuilt, it might have made them a good place. As it was, they had found themselves something much better, and could afford to leave it alone to rot. They were glad to do so, for it smelt of must and damp decay, and none of them would willingly have spent time alone in it.

To Carter, the discovery of the cave was a source of simple

and uncomplicated delight. While Todd and Randy went solemnly over it, tapping the floor and testing the walls with their feet, discussing its advantages and demerits with the grave demeanour of two business men discussing a new proposition, Carter leapt upon it with the full enthusiasm of his fifteen years. He ran about inside it like a puppy, frisking up to the others with cries of happiness, calling upon them to join him in his enraptured gambollings. It was dimly evident to him that they were discussing the place in the light of some enterprise which they hoped it would serve. What this enterprise was he did not know, and did not, at the time, particularly care. It was a cave – a perfectly marvellous cave. It was absolutely super, he cried, and he ran round and jumped up at the roof and could not touch it with his hand however high he leapt. His joy in it had never abated, even when it became clearer to him what purpose the others had in mind for it. He left the working out of that intention to them. He merely loved it, because it was hidden away, and secret, and made such a perfect place to come to, either alone, or with the others. It gave him something which he found nowhere else – a share in importance, and a stake in something which no one else, except the other two, knew existed. Why they tolerated him he did not know and, again, did not inquire. He knew that he had almost nothing to contribute; only, occasionally, he dimly perceived that he fulfilled some purpose as an interpreter, a link between them, and his own world. This, while it alarmed, also pleased and obscurely flattered him.

He was glad when he got his feet squarely on to the ledge of rock and could rest for a bit. The straps of the rucksack made hot wet bands over his shoulders, and he flexed his fingers, trying to loosen the muscles made stiff by holding on to the scanty roots and outcrops of stone on the way down. He shook his damp hair out of his eyes and felt the heat of the rock through the front of his thin shirt. Below and opposite him as he half turned on the ledge, a fine greyish haze of sunshine softened the outlines of the bushes and made the sky above him look like water. It seemed to be filtered down on him through the accumulated heat of the recent weeks; as if, there having been no winds, no cool nights to disperse it, it had merely piled itself layer upon layer, until walking in it was like walking through warm water. It slowed the muscles, impeded movement, and even, at its height, clogged the mind with a desire for inactivity. It was alien and unaccustomed, like a new and vitiating atmosphere which was heavy in the lungs.

When Carter moved sideways on the rock and stepped into the cave the instant refreshment was delicious. He dumped the rucksack on the floor and blew out his breath, momentarily blinded by the sudden darkness. Slowly, as if it were building itself up around him, the floor, the walls, and lastly the irregular ceiling high above his head, took shape. He looked round him. The heap of blankets was neatly arranged against the wall. At the head of the bed stood Randy's table and chair. A mug, a white china plate, a knife, fork and spoon were neatly arranged on the checked cloth. On the hooks he himself had driven into the wall hung a jacket of Todd's; a shirt, and a vest and pants hung next to it, all clean, but unironed. Todd had washed these clothes through in successive buckets of water and had spread them out to dry in the sun on the rocks below the entrance to the cave. They had emerged moderately clean but much creased. Below the pegs stood a bucket, a broom, and a small spade. Tins of food and a plastic bread-bin containing perishable articles of food were ranged in a tidy row close to the wall. The place was exquisitely orderly, and seemed to be empty.

Carter took a step forward, his heart jumping. He peered into the depths of the cave, but could see no one. He cleared his throat, and called,

'Hey! Are you there?'

There was no answer. My God, he thought, he's done it.

He's cleared off. He did not attempt to analyse his feelings about this.

He tried again.

'Are you there? It's me – Carter. I've brought you some more grub.'

The cave was absolutely silent. He thought with relief, I'll just go and pretend I saw him when I left the stuff. I won't have to tell them he's gone. They'll never know. He stood irresolute, wondering whether to call once more.

Something struck his hand and fell on to the floor with a small thud. He jumped violently. Sweat started out all over his body and ran coldly down his forehead. Again something struck him, this time on the shoulder. He looked up and saw, as if suspended above him in the darkness, the boy's face. It was grinning down at him, all the teeth gleaming white in the open mouth. The whites of the eyes seemed completely to surround the pupils.

'My God!' Carter whispered shakily. 'What on earth are you doing up there?'

'Come up and see,' invited the face.

'Where are you?'

The face retreated, and showed itself to be attached to the boy's body, which was perched, seemingly on air, half-way up the wall of the cave.

'On a ledge. I found it this morning. I've been up here ever since. Actually, I'm not sure if I can get down.'

'How on earth did you get up there in the first place?'

'It's not difficult – there are some holes in the wall. It's a bit of a scramble, but you could manage it easily. What did you bring?'

'Some tinned meat and some more bread, and some biscuits and a pound of bananas. And drink. Are you hungry?'

'Yes. Bring it up with you. We can share it. What about the others?'

'They're not coming.'

'Oh.' The face retreated while the boy thought about this.

After a moment he stuck it out again. 'Why not?'

'They're busy.'

'What are they doing?'

'Homework. Prep.'

'Haven't you got some too?'

'A bit, but it doesn't matter. They've got their exams, in a couple of weeks.'

'Oh, I see. So you're not in a hurry?'

'Not particularly.'

'Good. Come up then. It's nice up here. Much cooler.'

Carter hesitated, wondering if he really wanted to. Then he wriggled himself back into the straps of the rucksack and advanced upon the wall. He found the holes, and began to haul himself up.

'That's it,' said the boy above him. 'You can get your hands over the edge now, and pull yourself up.'

He felt strong small fingers guiding his hands to the best holes. He gave a final heave, kicked out with his feet, and rolled over on to the ledge beside the boy.

When he sat up and examined his surroundings he found that he was not really on a ledge at all. It was more like a second, very small cave, hollowed into the wall of the larger one. It went back for a considerable distance. Indeed, it might have formed a passage running right back into the rock for all that they could tell; but the aperture soon became so narrow that even the boy, slight as he was, could go no further. The walls and roof were formed of hard, smooth rock. It was cold to the touch, and had none of the irregularity of surface which might have been expected. Carter sat beside the boy, hugging his knees and exulting.

'It's super!' he said joyfully. 'I thought I knew the place pretty well, but I never knew about this. How did you find it?'

'I didn't really. I found the holes in the wall and began climbing up, just for something to do really. And then I found this.'

Carter struggled out of the rucksack. Rummaging, he said,
'We can't eat the meat unless I go down again for the tin-opener, but we can have some bananas and biscuits. Will that do?'

'That's plenty. What sort of biscuits?'

'Chocolate digestives.'

'They're my favourite,' said the boy contentedly. He took two biscuits and a banana and began munching. Carter peeled a banana and dropped the skin on the ground beside him. The boy picked it up and put it tidily back in the bag with his own.

'Fussy, aren't you?' grunted Carter.

'I like things to be tidy,' the boy said primly. He ate his second biscuit and took a third from the packet. They munched happily side by side, dangling their legs.

'I'll show you something else,' said the boy presently when they had finished eating. 'Look at this.'

He went over to the wall and pressed himself against it, putting his cheek against the rock and tilting his head back so that he was looking straight up along the wall.

'Stand like this and look up.'

He moved away and Carter took his place. For some moments he could see nothing except blackness above him, and said so.

'Move your head around,' said the boy. 'You'll find it.'

Carter moved his cheek against the coolness of the rock. Not knowing what he was supposed to see, he was fully prepared to see nothing at all. But suddenly his eye caught a flash of light. Immediately he lost it, but after a bit more juggling with his position he found it again and was able to get a steady view of it. It looked like a golden coin with slightly irregular edges hanging above him in the darkness. It looked small and very dazzling, and at first he could not tell whether it really was extremely small, and was only a few feet above his head, or whether it was extremely large and was at such an immense distance that it merely looked small. He stared at it until he felt his eyes going out of focus and he had to look away.

'Whatever is it?' he asked stupidly.

'It's the sky,' said the boy in an awed voice. 'There's a hole right up through the roof and through the rock, or stone, or whatever it is. It goes up to the open air. It's probably quite big, really, only it's so high up that it looks small. You can see the sun shining up there and coming right down into the cave through the rock. Isn't it marvellous?'

Carter looked again. This time he found it quite soon. He felt he had only to put out his hand to be able to grasp it in his fingers. He thought of the hole going straight up to the hilltop above them, and realised how much earth there was above them. The thought oppressed him. He came away from the wall. The boy was grinning at him.

'I call it my crow's-nest,' he said shyly.

'Crow's-nest?' repeated Carter, puzzled.

'Yes, you know, that little barrel thing on top of the mast of a ship where the look-out used to stand and shout, "Land ho! Land ho!"'

'Oh, I know. You mean on sailing ships. Galleons, and that sort of thing. I once learnt a poem about a galleon,' said Carter gloomily. 'About a stately Spanish galleon sailing from a something-or-other, which had a cargo of apes and peacocks and gold moidores – whatever they may be,' he added.

'But this isn't a Spanish galleon,' said the boy eagerly. 'It's a pirate ship with black sails and a row of guns set low along her raking sides, and a skull and cross-bones flying from her mast. It's the sort of ship which would give chase to your Spanish galleon, and because she's low in the water, and light, she would crowd on sail and catch all the wind, and come up to her, and open fire.'

'And then there would be a splendid sea fight,' Carter interrupted excitedly. His imagination took unwonted flight. The boy's eyes glittering at him from the shadows inspired him. 'One after another her guns would fire low across the water, and shot would whistle through the rigging of the galleon, and cut away her masts so that they would come walloping down on the heads of her crew, and shot would rip into her sides and tear away the planks and the water would start rushing in; only not too much, because if she sank too fast the pirates would lose the gold what's-its-names.'

'The galleon's guns would be set too high,' said the boy eagerly, 'and her shot would just pass over the pirate ship and not do any damage at all. She's too heavy to manoeuvre properly, so she just sits helplessly on the water in a great pall of smoke and flame while the pirate ship runs round her, pumping shot into her, and with all the crew, guns between their flashing teeth, climbing up the rigging and swearing strange oaths and cheering like mad.'

'At last the pirate ship moves in for the kill.' Carter hunched his shoulders and glared at the boy. 'She sails in, right under the lee of the galleon, still belching fire and smoke from her guns. Her crew are all perched in the sheets, or whatever those bits of rope at the top are, waving their cutlasses and shouting as they get ready to leap down on to the deck of the galleon. The galleon's crew are ready for them. They are not going to give in without a fight. With a terrible shock the two ships crash into one another—'

'And the pirate crew leap on to the men below, waving their weapons and dealing death with every blow!' shouted the boy, jumping up and down on his stalky legs. 'The air resounds with the shouts of the boarders, the oaths of the wounded and the groans of the dying. There are terrific splashes as men fall into the sea, crashing as bits of rigging fall down on to their heads. The scuppers are running with blood – in every direction groups of men are engaged in desperate hand-to-hand battles, fighting for their lives!'

'And in the thickest of the fight, where the blows rain down the hardest, the pirate captain comes upon the captain of the galleon. "Have at thee!" he cries in whatever language he speaks.' Carter took up an offensive posture, then dropped his arm. 'Actually, I think you ought to be the pirate captain,' he said politely. 'After all, it's your ship.'

'Oh well – if you're sure you don't mind – thank you very much,' said the boy. He raised his imaginary sword and flung back his head, scowling horribly. 'Have at thee!' he cried fiercely.

'Defend thyself!' Carter raised his own sword above his head. 'Defend thyself, or die!' he cried, and lunged at the boy with his bloody blade.

Breathing heavily and occasionally grunting with effort, they circled and parried on the stone floor, watching each other through narrowed eyes. Twice the captain of the galleon drove the pirate back against the bulwarks, and twice the pirate dodged beneath his arm and sprang up to wield his trusty blade anew. They danced round each other, lunging and thrusting. Once the pirate captain staggered back with a hand clapped to a wound in the fleshy part of his right arm, but recovered instantly, changed his sword into his left hand, and fought on with renewed skill and valour.

After a while, he panted,

'I think I'd better kill you now, if you don't mind. Most of your crew are dead, and I want to save a few to walk the plank.'

'Oh, all right,' said the galleon's captain a trifle regretfully. 'Do you want to stab me through the body, or what?'

'I think I'll plunge my sword through your chest, and you can stagger about for a bit clutching it and then die at my feet in a pool of blood. Will that do?'

'That's fine. Come on.'

Carter lunged forward, and the pirate blade caught his sword and forced it up, then plunged home in his heart. The gallant captain dropped his sword and staggered. He clutched the handle of the blade protruding from his chest and tried to pull it forth. It was stuck in his breastbone, however, and would not budge. He abandoned the attempt and staggered about for a bit, groaning horribly. The pirate captain leaned on his sword and looked on admiringly. At last the stricken sea-dog did a final stagger and a final groan, and fell to the deck. He rolled to and fro, kicking his legs about and clutching himself, finally produced a most realistic death-rattle, and died.

'I say!' cried the boy, impressed. 'That was absolutely marvellous! Do people really die like that?'

Carter sat up and rubbed the back of his head where he had hit it rather too realistically upon the floor in his death-throes.

'I don't know – they do on the pictures. That was a super battle. What happens now?'

'Well, I thought perhaps the crew of the galleon who haven't been killed in the fight ought to walk the plank.'

'Jolly good,' Carter agreed, getting up and brushing some of the dirt off his clothes. 'Would you like to go on being the pirate captain, or would you like to walk the plank?'

'Oh, I don't mind – you choose.'

'Well, we could both have a go. We'll have to be blindfolded, of course, and then we can take it in turns to walk to our deaths in the watery main. What about jumping off the ledge?'

The boy went to the edge and cautiously peered over.

'I think it's a bit far,' he said dubiously. 'I mean, you could probably manage it, but I might break a leg or something. It's quite a long way down.'

Carter joined him and they peered over the edge together.

'It is a bit far,' he agreed. 'We'd better do it on the flat. Have you got a handkerchief?'

They searched their pockets. Neither of them had.

'Never mind – we'll pretend to blindfold each other,' said Carter. 'Come on, you do me first and I'll plunge to my death, and then you can have a go.'

He stood still while the boy reached up on tiptoe and tied an imaginary bandage round his eyes.

'Now my hands behind my back.'

He linked his hands behind him and the boy trussed him tight.

'Now! Go to thy death, thou scurvy knave!' he cried, and gave Carter a sturdy push in the small of the back. Carter teetered off along his imaginary plank.

'Mercy! Mercy!' he cried most piteously. 'Have mercy, masters! I have a wife and ten children at home. Spare me, I beseech you! Mercy! Mercy!'

'Never!' cried the boy. 'Die, coward, and a good riddance to thee and all thy kind!'

Carter reached the end of his plank, hesitated, felt forward with his foot, stepped off into thin air and plummeted like a stone to the sea below. Here, to the shrill accompaniment of the pirate's derisive cheers, he floundered, rose once, sank, rose again, and finally disappeared for ever beneath the waves.

The boy jumped up and down with excitement.

'My turn! My turn!' He hopped up and down on one leg. 'I'm going to be eaten by ravening sharks. Come on, blindfold me.'

He, too, executed a dramatic fall, and died, shrieking most horribly and threshing about in the water until torn to pieces by the sharks. Their performances pleased them so much that they repeated them several times with increasing realism, embellishing them with subtle variations until they were both so exhausted that they had to stop and sit on the floor to giggle at each other. They were both streaked with grime, and so out of breath that they could hardly speak.

'Phew! I'm thirsty,' said Carter.

'Yo ho ho and a bottle of rum,' said the boy feebly. He rolled on to his back and kicked his legs in the air, giggling. 'Bags you go down and get something to drink.'

'I don't think I shall ever get up again,' protested Carter. 'It's not much use me going – I can't even get down!'

In the end Carter went, grumbling, and painfully hauled himself up again with the bottles clinking in the rucksack.

They propped their backs against the wall and absorbed warm ginger beer in complete happiness.

When they had had enough the boy belched, and heaved a long, satisfied sigh.

'I'm glad you came,' he said. He smiled sideways at Carter, a little shy. His soft child's hair hung heavily on his forehead, and his thin brown legs in their scuffed sandals stuck straight out in front of him in complete relaxation. 'How's your face now?'

'My face?' Carter was momentarily at a loss.

'Where Randy hit you.'

'Oh that!' Carter had forgotten the fight. It seemed a long time ago and of little importance. 'It's perfectly all right.'

'I'm sorry Randy and you had the fight.' The boy spoke after a small hesitation. He peered sideways again. 'Everyone seemed to think it was my fault, but I didn't mean it to be.'

'Oh, I didn't think it was your fault,' said Carter carelessly. He felt sleepy and comfortable.

'You did at the time,' the boy said with curious persistence. 'When you came round after Randy knocked you down.'

'He did not knock me down,' Carter interrupted indignantly. 'He kicked me and I was winded.'

'I'm sorry. I mean, after Randy kicked you and you were winded, you said something about it all being my fault. The others thought so too.'

'Todd didn't.'

'Well, no. But you and Randy.'

'Did we? Oh well – I suppose I was just annoyed. It wasn't a fair fight and I felt like picking on someone. I didn't mean it.'

'Promise?'

Carter turned to look at him.

'All right, I promise. Here, what's up? Why's it so important?'

The boy looked away, dropping his eyes as if embarrassed.

'Oh, it's not. I'm glad you didn't mean it, though. Even if Randy did.'

'Oh well – Randy! I mean, why bother about him? It doesn't matter what he thinks. He always thinks the worst of everyone. He was just trying to put the blame on someone else. He's always doing that – usually it's me. This time he picked on you.'

'Oh, I see. You don't think it was what I said, then?'

Carter, who could not even remember what it was the boy had said, except that, whatever it was it had undoubtedly infuriated Randy beyond breaking point, yawned, and then laughed.

'For God's sake forget it! It's all over now. It was only a silly scrap.'

'You said it was the first time you'd actually hit each other.'

'What if it was? It was time someone hit Randy. He's got a gorgeous black eye.' Carter giggled. 'Like a ripe plum.'

'I don't like him,' said the boy softly. Surprised, Carter turned to look at him. His eyes, very bright, were dilated. 'I don't like him,' he repeated almost apologetically. 'I mean – I know he's your friend—' He stopped and drew in his breath. He sounded frightened.

Carter said,

'I wouldn't let it bother you. No one exactly loves Randy. Anyway, you like Todd, don't you?'

The boy unclenched his hands. He smiled brightly at Carter, protruding his soft underlip so that he looked almost babyish.

'Oh yes!' he said enthusiastically. 'I like him very much!'

Carter yawned again and stretched himself. He rubbed his back against the wall, enjoying the sensation.

'I shall have to go. I've got some beastly homework to do, and I've had three blowings-up already today about not doing it.'

'You all go to the same school, don't you?'

'Yes – the Grammar School.'

'I suppose the other two are in the sixth form.'

'Yes. They're both supposed to be awfully clever. Todd's marvellous at games too.' Carter sighed. 'He's good at everything, and he's got pots of money, lucky bastard.'

'Have you been friends long?'

Carter pondered this for a bit.

'A couple of years. It's funny – I don't quite know how. I mean, I don't really fit in with them.'

'Oh, I think you do,' said the boy politely. 'Have you got any more friends?'

'You mean people we do things with?'

'Yes, that sort of friend.'

'No – it's always been just the three of us. Funny, isn't it?'

'I don't think it's funny,' said the boy sombrely. He hunched his shoulders. For a moment his face looked pinched and old. Then it cleared. 'Do you suppose Todd will come and see me some time?'

'You bet he will!' said Carter.

'Will you come again?'

'You bet – it's been super this evening.'

'We could do the battle all over again and make it longer, and even better,' said the boy eagerly. 'You can be the pirate captain next time, if you like.'

'Thanks!' Carter was delighted. 'I'm sure you'll do the captain of the galleon jolly well.'

Well satisfied with each other, they climbed down into the cave. Carter sighed and looked round regretfully at the neat bed, the table and chair, the row of tins.

'It's a blasted shame having to go home,' he said. 'I jolly well wish I could stay here instead. It must be super sleeping here at night. I bet it's cooler than being indoors.'

'You can hear owls sometimes,' said the boy softly. 'And it never gets really dark. The birds start singing again almost before I've gone to sleep, the nights are so short.' He smiled shyly at Carter. 'I wish you could stay, too.'

'Oh well, off we go again up that blasted path.' Carter swung the rucksack over his shoulder. 'We'll all come on Wednesday. Have you got enough stuff?'

'Plenty. Good-bye. Thank you for coming.'

He put out a thin, grubby hand. Carter shook it awkwardly, surprised, yet somehow touched by the formality of the gesture. As he lowered himself out of the cave and was about to step sideways out on to the rock, the boy spoke to him again, casually, and in a low voice, so that Carter did not catch the words.

'What did you say?'

'Nothing – just that there's been someone down there, yesterday, and again this afternoon. I don't know if it matters.'

'What do you mean – down there?'

The boy described one of his wide, vague gestures.

'Down at the bottom, among the bushes.'

Carter pulled himself back into the cave.

'Who was it?'

'I don't really know. I was sitting by the entrance, just where you're standing, and I saw someone moving about.' He hesitated. He looked almost calculating. 'It looked like a girl.'

'A girl?' said Carter, startled.

'Yes. She was wearing something pink. That's why I noticed her. I could see a patch of pink moving about, and after I'd watched it for a bit I saw it was a girl's dress.'

'What was she doing?'

'I don't know. Just walking about, I suppose.'

'Was she by herself?'

'Oh yes, I didn't see anyone else.'

'Did she see you?'

'I don't think so. I was sitting a bit back in the cave, and I didn't move. I don't think she could have done.' He hesitated again. He seemed to be watching Carter closely as if to gauge the effect of his words. 'She stood still quite a long time and stared up. But I don't think she could have seen the cave.'

Carter stood still. He felt alarmed by this information. He was almost sure that the cave could not be seen from below, but the situation disturbed him. Eventually, he said,

'I wouldn't worry about it. But don't hang about too near the front of the cave, will you?'

The boy hastened to reassure him. Strangely, it was as if the prospect of discovery alarmed him as much as it did Carter.

'I'll keep well away,' he said. As if to show his willingness to connive at his own concealment, he went over to his bed and sat down on it, drawing his knees up to his chest. He looked brightly across at Carter.

'Are you going to tell the others?' he asked.

'I shall have to,' said Carter worriedly. 'They must know if there's anyone hanging around.'

The boy nodded. He clasped his hands round his knees and began to rock gently to and fro on the blankets.

'Oh yes,' he said. 'I think you should tell them. I really do. I quite agree with you. They certainly ought to know.'

Carter left him sitting on the bed, still gently rocking himself to and fro.

Todd sat down on the neatly arranged blankets and looked up at the other two. His face looked bleached.

'He's done it,' he said. 'He's gone.'

They looked back at him. There was nothing else they could do, nowhere else to look. Carter had even forced himself through the small aperture at the back of the second cave, pulling the loose stones away with his hands and wriggling along the small tunnel until he was stopped by blank rock. The boy was not there. Everything was, as usual, exquisitely tidy; nothing had been taken, not even, so far as they could judge, any of the food. The cup and plate on the table had been washed, the bed made. There was a sprinkling of moderately fresh earth in the trench at the back of the cave, and the bucket was half full of clean water. Of the boy there was no sign.

Todd sat on the blankets. His face was white. Even his lips had lost their colour. He clasped his hands between his thighs and looked down. He hunched himself forward and sat silent. After his frenzied search for the boy, during which he had scrambled down into the gully below and had run through the bushes calling recklessly to him to come back, he had collapsed into a kind of stunned helplessness. It was Carter and Randy who had carried out the grim, methodical search of the cave, looking for a message, a note left somewhere not immediately accessible, so that they should not find it too soon. They had found nothing. The boy had gone, as quietly and as mysteriously as he had come.

Randy looked at Todd with his bunched fists tight in his trouser pockets. He swung a little on his heels, his head cocked on one side.

'Perishing little bastard,' he said. 'We might have known it. We should have made sure he couldn't escape – tied him up, or something. I knew he'd do this.'

Todd looked palely up at them.

'He said he'd stay.'

' "He said he'd stay"!' mimicked Randy contemptuously. He turned away. 'Fat lot of good that's turned out to be. I knew this would happen.'

Something was worrying Carter.

'I say,' he ventured, 'do you think he'll go to the police?'

'What if he does?' returned Randy.

'Yes, but what if he goes and tells them?'

'Tells them what?'

'Well, that we brought him here, and kept him in the cave, and all that. I mean, it must be illegal or something. People must be looking for him. He's bound to tell them where he's been and about us.'

'What about us?'

'He knows who we are, doesn't he?'

'He only knows us as Todd, Randy and Carter.'

'We wouldn't be difficult to trace. He'd be able to describe us exactly. He's seen us often enough. They'd be on to us like a shot for kidnapping, or something.'

'So what?' said Randy contemptuously. 'We haven't broken the law. We didn't force him to stay. He could have walked out any time he chose – which is proved by the fact that that's exactly what he's done. We didn't stop him going, and we didn't ill-treat him. We gave him food, and we let him stay here in the cave, that's all. No one can get us for that.'

Carter pondered this dubiously.

'All the same, they'll think it's bloody odd,' he persisted.

'They can think it's as odd as they like, but they can't do a thing about it.'

'That's one reason why I didn't want to tie him up or any-thing.' Todd had been listening, although he had looked as if he were absorbed in his own private and agonising specula-tions. 'So that he couldn't say he had been forced to stay.'

'We can't prove that he wasn't tied up,' said Carter with a sudden flash of perception.

'He can't prove he was,' retorted Randy. 'It's three to one.'

'Do you think they'd believe us rather than him? He looks innocent enough to convince anyone of anything.'

'Well,' said Randy, 'all I can say is that if we had tied him up he wouldn't have gone, and we wouldn't be in this mess now. What on earth are we expected to do? Go rushing off all over the countryside looking for the little perisher? We haven't got a hope of finding him. He could be at the other end of the country by now. It's a bloody silly situation and no mistake.' He turned on Todd. 'And a right mess you've made of it,' he added with sudden savagery. 'What price your marvellous plan now?'

'Oh leave him alone,' said Carter, defending Todd merely because he was irritated with Randy. 'It's not his fault. Or at any rate, it's as much yours. You were in it too.'

'Not to mention you.'

'I wasn't, you know. I didn't know what it was all about. You thought it all up and I just joined in. You can't say I really had anything to do with it.'

'Backing out, now that things have gone wrong?' said Randy unpleasantly. 'You don't have to explain anything to me, you know. I'm not the police.'

Carter went pale. 'But I thought you said—'

'I said the police couldn't get us on anything. I didn't say they wouldn't try. And that means they might ask an awful lot of questions. You'd better save your explanations for them – you may need them.'

'Christ!' Carter sat down abruptly on the boy's chair. 'But what are we going to tell them? Hadn't we better get a story ready?' In his anxiety his hostility had completely vanished. He looked up at Randy in pure apprehension. 'What are we going to tell them?'

Randy raised his thin eyebrows.

'The truth, of course. Except for two small details. One is that the boy followed us to the cave; we didn't make him come. The other is that he stayed here of his own accord; we didn't tell him to, we only let him stay. Apart from that, tell them the truth. We didn't know who he was, or where he came from. Why should we want to keep a twelve-year-old boy here against his will?'

'You know why,' said Carter, puzzled – 'You said—'

'Oh for God's sake!' exclaimed Randy in an extreme of impatience. 'Must you be so bloody and unutterably stupid? Of course we know why. But he didn't, and we're not going to tell the police. Even with their filthy minds they won't be able to think up a convincing reason unless we give them one. Our side of the story's a lot more convincing than anything he can make up. There's no earthly reason why we should have made him stay if he wanted to go, which is proved by the fact that he was able to walk out when he'd had enough.' Randy spelled out this last sentence with extreme slowness and clarity, as if speaking to a small child. 'Got it?'

Carter thought about it.

'Yes, I suppose so.' He brooded. 'Let's only hope it doesn't happen.'

'It won't,' said Todd.

Randy turned on him.

'What won't?' he inquired silkily.

'He won't go to the police. I know he won't.'

'Oh, you do, do you? Well, if you remember, you were equally sure that he wouldn't clear out when he'd had enough. That didn't quite work out, did it?'

'I'm sure he won't go to the police,' insisted Todd.

'Indeed? I seem to remember you making him promise to stay. Did you make him promise not to go to the police too?'

'Of course I didn't. But I'm positive he hasn't told anyone, least of all the police.'

'Why do you suppose he's hopped, then? Just gone off home for a bit to tell them he's all right and not to worry about him, because he's being well looked after?'

'I don't know where he's gone,' said Todd miserably. 'How the hell should I know?'

'And I suppose he'll come back again tomorrow and settle down again as if nothing had happened. I can just see that happening!' said Randy, turning away contemptuously. He lit a cigarette and tossed the dead match out of the cave into the sunshine. 'I'll believe that when I see it,' he said over his shoulder.

Carter began to whistle between his teeth. He drummed his fingers on the table, watched Randy as he leaned against the wall, smoking quietly.

'For Christ's sake stop that bloody row!' Todd burst out. 'Can't you think of something to do instead of sitting there whistling?'

'What can we do?' inquired Randy in a tone of sweet reason. 'We've turned the place inside out, and he's not here.

He's gone; hopped it. Cleared off. It's finished, right? It was a mistake, and a failure, and it didn't work. You'd better face it, Todd, your little plan just didn't work out. And if you can think of anything sensible to do, you'd better tell us about it now, because I can't think of a damned thing.'

Todd looked at the two of them. Randy's face was reckless and hard, Carter's full of helpless anxiety. He got heavily off the bed and smoothed the blankets with his hand.

'There's nothing we can do. You're right, Randy, I've been a fool. It was a daft idea. I ought to have known it wouldn't work. We'd better go home and forget about the whole thing. Right?'

'Couldn't we find someone else?' suggested Carter with a spark of hope. 'I mean, you never know. Someone might turn up.'

'Look,' said Todd bleakly, 'we've waited two years for this. We won't get another chance. Anyway, it's too late. Term ends in a couple of weeks and I'm going abroad with my mother.'

'And Savory?' Randy put in unnecessarily.

'Possibly,' said Todd. 'That hardly matters now, does it? The point is that it's all gone wrong, and it seems to have been my fault. No doubt I should have tied him to the wall, or broken one of his legs so that he couldn't get away. I didn't think it was necessary. It turns out that I was wrong. The thing's over and done with, and we'd better forget it.'

He looked bleakly round the cave at the things they had made and accumulated. The sun had moved round and was not shining directly on to the floor, but it made a fuzzy golden glow in the entrance. It was almost setting, and had acquired a fierce reddish tinge which silhouetted Randy's black figure as if against fire.

'What are we going to do with all this?' Todd gestured round at the food, the clothes and furniture.

'Leave it as a memorial to an endeavour which failed,' Randy suggested.

'We can't just leave it all!' Carter was shocked.

'Why the hell not? I'm not dead keen on lugging it all back up that cliff, even if you are.'

'I just think it's a waste. And anyway, even if the boy has gone, it still makes a jolly good place to meet,' persisted Carter, looking on the bright side.

'I'm not coming here any more,' said Todd with flat finality.

'Nor me. Anyway, I'm getting a bit old for gangs and hide-outs,' agreed Randy.

'Well, I'm not leaving it,' said Carter stoutly. 'It's a marvellous cave, and it's a shame not to use it. I'm coming, even if you two don't.' He glared defiantly at them.

'Do as you please,' said Todd indifferently. 'I'm going. Coming, Randy?'

Randy unhitched himself from the wall and dropped his cigarette end on the floor. He ground it under his heel and settled his shirt in at the waist of his narrow trousers. He put out his hand and brushed it lightly down Todd's arm from the shoulder to the wrist. It was an unequivocal caress, tender, proprietary in the turn of his strong fingers on Todd's brown wrist. Todd suffered it with no response.

'Are you coming, Carter? Or are you staying to play cops and robbers by yourself?' he inquired over his shoulder.

Carter got up sulkily and followed them to the mouth of the cave. They stood and looked back together. Really, there was nothing to see, only the tidy domestic arrangements and the bright blankets where even the slight depression made by Todd's body had been smoothed away.

'What a pity,' said Randy softly. He was watching Todd sideways out of his narrow eyes. 'I feel we should make some kind of farewell gesture.'

Todd could think of nothing. He felt defeated.

'Perhaps we should sing a hymn. "Onward Christian Soldiers" or "Lead Kindly Light",' suggested Randy.

'Don't be an ass!' In spite of himself, Carter giggled.

'I feel we ought to hold a funeral service and bury something. Perhaps we could come back tomorrow and burn everything in a grand funeral pyre.' Randy peered into Todd's face, smiling. 'Can't you suggest anything?'

Todd shook him off and plunged out of the cave. They followed him, first Randy, then Carter. In silence they climbed up the path. Todd laid his hands on each familiar rock and root as if he were saying good-bye to them one by one. He wanted to destroy them after him as he went. Baulked of his prey, he climbed swiftly, easily outstripping the other two. He did not wait for them at the top but walked swiftly across the barren ground with his head bent.

As they got into the outskirts of the town he slowed down a little and they caught up with him. Carter was breathing loudly and sweating, but Randy was unruffled. They walked together along the wide pavement past the neat gates and hedges. It was a little cooler, but as usual the air was thick and motionless. A couple passed them, the girl clicking along briskly in her high heels.

'It can't last much longer,' she was saying in a clear well-bred voice. 'It's bound to break sooner or later.' The man said something inaudible, and they walked on laughing.

They turned into the high street. The street lights were on, fuzzy in the fading light. The air smelt of plush, of cooking, of stale smoke. They all felt hot and grimy.

Todd stopped suddenly under one of the street lamps and said,

'You wait here. I'll go and fetch the car.'

They looked at him, foreshortened by the yellow patch of light. Their faces were tinged with lurid colour and their bodies and legs tapered away into the dimness so that they looked like large-headed fish balancing on their tails.

'The car? What for?'

'We'll drive to the sea,' said Todd, inspired.

'But it's thirty miles.'

'Have you got a licence?'

'What'll your mother say if you take her car?'

They questioned him in whispers.

'She's away for the night, in town with my daddy-to-be. She won't even know. It'll be marvellous. We can be there in an hour. We could swim.'

They hesitated, doubtful. Then Randy said,

'We'll wait here. Don't be long. What about your mother, Carter?'

'Too bad. Let's sort that out in the morning. What about swimming things?'

'Don't be daft – it's much better without. I'll get a towel.'

'What about the licence? Have you got one?'

'No, I haven't. But I can drive all right.'

'What happens if we get nabbed?'

'That's another thing we can sort out in the morning. All right?'

'All right!' they whispered back, and watched his white shirt as it dwindled away up the street as if it were moving under its own volition.

He was back in the small red car almost before they would have thought it possible. The top was down, and he sat at the wheel with his shirt sleeves rolled to above his elbows and his sleek hair white under the street lamp. Randy got in beside him and Carter tumbled in at the back.

Todd drove well, with assurance and skill. He also drove extremely fast; but because he concentrated on what he was doing and made no unneccesary flourishes he communicated a sense of confidence and security. They rushed along the quiet roads which led to the sea in a roaring swirl of warm air; it slid over their skins and through their hair, exhilarating them. The sheer motion of it seemed to cool them. Randy lay beside Todd and rested his head on the back of the seat, letting the wind pour over his face and past him in a long continuous flow. He closed his eyes and spread out his legs and gave himself up to the sensations of speed. Carter, sprawled in the back, unbuttoned his shirt to the waist and did likewise. His body felt warm and heavy, as if he were being pulled very fast through warm water. He opened his eyes and looked up at the long sky above them, sometimes crossed and recrossed by a dark lattice of leaves and branches. An enormous golden moon accompanied them. It was low in the sky, and sailed along with them in a swift effortless passage through the darkness. When Carter looked away from it he could see that the night was not really dark at all. It was a dim pallor which enveloped them and showed every tree, every star, and the long lines of the hills with delicate precision. But when he looked back at the moon itself, everything else became dense with darkness.

Todd sat watchful and upright. He held the wheel lightly with both hands, resting one bare elbow on the sharp edge of the window beside him, which was almost fully wound down into its socket. That line of blunt glass bit into his skin and seemed to hold him steady in his seat. Without it, he felt, he might fly up and out, lose contact with the frail obedient machine which he controlled. His heels rested firmly on the floor of the car; through them every turn and leap of the engine seemed to be communicated up through his body to his brain, and out to his hands.

They swept through small towns where the windows of upstairs rooms momentarily showed as gold patches in the fronts of houses. Other cars flew along the road towards them; a pair of gleaming discs, the dark bulk looming between them, an increase of sound and of wind, and they were gone. On the entire distance nothing passed them. Todd drove the car to the limit of its speed. But even when the accelerator was pressed flat to the floor under his shoe his control remained absolute. He felt the warm air buffeting his head and blowing his hair back. Sometimes, streaming round a corner, he gulped in a mouthful of air and it went into his lungs like water. He expelled it in short deep panting breaths and crouched down a little on the slippery leather to avoid being choked by its rushes at his face and mouth.

They fled out of the last small town and down the straight stretch to the sea. The moon was higher and dipped and swung above the trees as they skimmed along the white road. Todd was making for a small private beach on the edge of a prosperous little seaside resort where wealthy week-end sailors kept their boats and where their wives drove on hot summer afternoons to give their children a few hours by the sea. The beach belonged to a sailing club of which Todd's father had been a member. The membership had lapsed with his death, but Todd and his mother occasionally visited the place during the summer to bathe, coming and going unquestioned. There was a white gate leading to the beach. On it in large black letters it said, 'Private. Members Only.' Todd coursed down the wide silent high street where the striped awnings hung out motionless over the pavements and where buckets and balls and straw hats blossomed like strange fruits bleached in the moonlight. He turned left, drove to the end of the rough road, and stopped beside the white gate. The engine beat softly in the air like a bird. He switched it off, eased the brake in, and moved his feet off the controls. The car shook and subsided into silence.

For a moment their ears were unable to pick up any sound. Then they all heard it, the soft, almost inaudible sound of water tipping itself gently over again and again on to small stones. It was a tiny shirring sound, like that made by hands ceaselessly stroking a length of taut silk. Randy turned his head towards Todd, cocking it up to listen. His eyes gleamed out from his bleached face from which the moonlight seemed to have sucked all colour.

'The tide's high,' said Todd quietly, in supreme satisfaction. 'Come on.'

'What about the car? Are you going to leave it here?'

'Why not?' Todd was already half out of it. His shirt gleamed against the dark leather. 'Come on, no one's going to pinch it. Get a move on.'

He swung himself out and pocketed the keys. Randy unfolded himself neatly like a large cat and Carter tumbled noisily out of the back. He had fallen asleep and stood gasping in the road, tousled and only half awake. He yawned prodigiously and shook himself.

Todd led the way to the white gate and felt for the catch. It was locked. Silently he motioned to the others and hoisted himself up and over, dropping with a light crunch on the gravel path. The others followed. He led them a little way along the path until, on their left, the low bulk of a building appeared, spreading its length indeterminately on rough grass. Todd turned right and climbed a low bank on which the scanty grass grew from thin, sandy soil. They saw the pale flash of his arm as he beckoned them, and his long body poised above them on the bank. Then he dropped out of sight, and they heard the heavy sliding crunch of his progress through the shingle.

Randy got to the top of the low bank and stood still. The beach, dark and shingled, sloped away from them to the edge of the water, and was enclosed by two breakwaters which stood against the sky like the ribbed skeletons of dinosaurs. They were fairly high, and ramshackle in places, where planks had disappeared and made gaps through which the water sucked idly to and fro. Between them, and out, beyond and to the low horizon, the sea stretched like an endless silvery plain. It looked corrunculated, ribbed with small motionless ridges. Nothing on it seemed to move, until the eye fixed itself on one particular ridge, and perceived the relentless motion towards the beach, so slow and even that it seemed not to be motion at all. At the edge of the shingle the water gathered itself a little and heaped itself up into sharp little waves which stood up for a moment and then toppled over on to their faces. The water fanned out a little, edged itself with silver, then silently drew back to make way for more.

Below them at the water's edge they saw Todd. He had taken off his shirt and it lay beside him on the shingle in a pale blur. He stooped, and in a quick movement pulled off trousers and underpants together and stood up naked except for his sandals. He kicked these off with quick flicking movements of his feet. He turned to look up at them. His hair shone as white as his shirt in the moonlight. He raised a long pale arm to beckon them, and they plunged down the shingle towards him, pulling their clothes off as they went. They bent, struggled with zips and buttons, executed some convulsive movements as they shed their pants and shoes, and stood up naked with the warm air running over their skins.

Todd looked like a narrow white wraith as he went ahead of them into the water. His small tight buttocks and narrow hips seemed insignificant below the broad white swing of his shoulders. His back sprang upwards and out from its tapering waist into the strong arch of the shoulder blades and powerful upper arms. His long flat thighs seemed to drive him forward like pistons as he stepped strongly down into the water. His calves rounded out and then thinned down to the anklebone and the solid hub of heel. His head, round and blond on the straight stem of neck, was thrust forward as he stuck his foot out and let the water run over his skin. He turned back to them, all his teeth gleaming his delight.

'It's warm!' he cried softly. 'Really warm, like a bath.'

He took a couple of steps forward, drew his arms up in front of him, and launched himself into the water. It shattered and splintered away from the impact of his body, darkening and turning over into silver as it ran away from him. He thrust his head up through it and swung himself over. His hair plastered itself darkly to his skull so that his head looked small and neat, like that of a swimming seal or otter.

'Come on!' he gasped, spewing water out through his mouth and nostrils. 'It's marvellous! Come on in!'

Randy, slim and straight as an adolescent animal, picked his way neatly over the shingle and into the water. His body was unmuscled compared with Todd's splendid machine. But it was wiry and developed, with power of a different sort in the flat spread of back and chest. Only his legs were insignificant, spindly and thin, dwindling to bony knees and straight, shapeless calves. When he stood up to his thighs in the water, however, he gave an impression of power, completely controlled, methodically deployed. He did not plunge himself under the water. He slid down into it almost surreptitiously, and struck out towards Todd with long neat strokes. His dark hair clung even more sleekly to his narrow head as he moved silently through the water.

Carter came last, launching his square strong body into the sea with a tremendous and satisfying splash. His build from thick neck and immense shoulders to bulging thigh muscles and calves, was simply and uncomplicatedly indicative of crude strength. He exuded health and power like an animal, and flailed through the water in a splashing froth of silver. He turned on to his back and wallowed along, kicking his legs up and down until he was enveloped in a fountain of spray. They all met some twenty yards from the shore and trod water together, panting and spluttering and shaking the moisture from their faces.

'My God, it's marvellous!' Todd bobbed up and down in a sort of incoherent ecstasy of release and pure happiness. 'Absolutely bloody marvellous!'

'I've never swum in the middle of the night before.' Carter executed a sort of wallowing somersault and emerged streaming and spluttering. 'Why on earth didn't we think of this before!'

'Come on,' said Todd. 'Let's swim out to that buoy.'

'Oh no you don't!' Carter plunged down into the water, grabbed Todd's legs, and pulled him under.

They went down together in a thrashing swirl of water, turning over and over each other as they fought and struggled. Todd bobbed to the surface first, took a huge gulp of water and air and thrust himself down again, grabbing at Randy's legs as he went and pulled him under too. In a moment the three of them were thrashing and twisting, tumbling over one another half below and half out of the water. Arms and legs broke the surface, white expanses of back and shoulder heaved up and over, and dark heads streaming with water shot up, snatched at the air like fish, and sank again. Carter got hold of Randy's legs and towed him along under the water like a twisting, coiling length of seaweed. Randy tore himself free, shot to the surface, and thrust himself forward on to Todd's shoulders, twining his legs round Todd's chest and standing up clear of the water for a dizzy moment. Then they both toppled over and sank again in an octopus-like entanglement of arms and legs. When they broke the surface again they were grabbed and up-ended by Carter, so that, when they all bobbed up together, the two of them rounded on him and splashed and ducked him until they had all had enough and had to stop for sheer lack of breath.

The outburst of high spirits disappeared as suddenly as it had come. Todd swam away and turned on to his back to float on the still surface. The sea seemed to seal itself round the edges of his body, and he lay idle and unthinking, rocking slightly with the tiny ripples lapping at his chin. By half opening his eyes he could see the moon stooping above him. He gently flexed his fingers and felt the water move between them.

Randy swam far out and away from the others, trying to reach the black speck of the buoy riding on the surface. He lacked Todd's elegance as a swimmer and could not match his speed; but his endurance was extraordinary. His neat economical strokes seemed to carry him on and on as if he could go on for ever.

Carter swam round aimlessly for a while and then went over to one of the breakwaters and hauled himself up on to one of its slippery joists. The beach shelved steeply, and he wanted to dive from the highest point of the groyne. It took him some time to decide whether it was safe, but eventually he launched himself into the water and came up, breathless, and delighted with himself. He repeated the dive several times until Todd joined him, and they dived in turn, Carter hitting the water with a huge splash, Todd's narrow body entering it with almost soundless elegance.

Randy came back from his excursion to the buoy and sat on one of the cross-beams to watch them dive. Their voices sounded small and far away as they climbed out of the water and called to one another perched like white sea birds on the dark planks. At last, regretfully, they lowered themselves into the water and swam to the shore. They came out of the water and dried themselves in turn on Todd's towel. They dressed in silence, turned away from one another as they pulled clothes on over their damp bodies. For some reason their exhilaration had died, and it left them not relaxed or restored, but exhausted in a sullen, dangerous way. They saw it in one another as they stood, dressed, at the water's edge. Randy had lit a cigarette, and its red tip glowed like a small luminous insect. It rose to his mouth, expanded itself for a moment, briefly illuminating nose, mouth and chin, then sank again to a pinpoint of light. The smell of the smoke was acrid, and it got into Todd's lungs, making him cough.

'Must you smoke those beastly things all the time?'

He flapped his hand irritably in front of his face to brush away the smoke.

'You smoke too,' said Randy imperturbably.

'Yes, but not all the time.'

'He doesn't smoke all the time either.' Carter kicked aimlessly at the shingle and stubbed his toe on a pebble. 'Damn and blast it!' He hopped around, clutching his foot. 'Damn this beastly shingle! You didn't tell us it was all stones, Todd. There isn't an inch of sand anywhere.'

'What the hell does that matter?' Todd snapped. 'We didn't come to sunbathe, we came to swim. And it was a jolly good swim, too.'

Carter sat down on the pebbles to nurse his foot in comfort. He took off his sandal and peered at his toe in the moonlight.

'It hurts like hell,' he said aggrievedly. 'I believe I've broken it.'

'Don't be daft,' said Todd crossly. 'You only kicked a pebble.'

'It wasn't a pebble. It was a dirty great chunk of rock.'

'It wasn't. It was a pebble. There aren't any rocks. For God's sake don't make such a fuss.'

'You'd make a fuss if you'd broken your toe.'

'You jolly well haven't broken your toe.'

'I jolly well have.'

They glared at each other.

Randy said,

'Have a cigarette.'

He held out the packet. Todd struck it out of his hand. Carter sat still, holding his injured foot.

'Pick it up,' said Randy.

'Pick it up yourself,' said Todd instantly.

Randy took a step towards Todd.

'I said, pick it up.'

'I bloody well won't.'

'Oh yes you will.'

'Oh no I won't.'

Randy said between closed teeth,

'If you haven't picked it up by the time I've counted three I'll make you pick it up, and I'll shove it down your throat afterwards.'

Todd put his hands in his trouser pockets and stood absolutely still.

'One,' said Randy.

Todd did not move.

'Two.'

Randy's eyes were dilated. He began to shake. There was a pause. He opened his mouth.

Carter pushed himself across the shingle on his behind. He picked up the packet of cigarettes and threw it to Randy, who automatically caught it.

'Take your beastly fags,' said Carter disgustedly. 'Honestly! Talk about a couple of idiots! Squabbling over a packet of fags.' He went back to nursing his foot. 'I don't know what's the matter with you,' he said virtuously. 'You took it out of me when Randy and I had a bit of a scrap, Todd, and now you're just as bad yourself.'

Todd stared at Randy. Then he took his hands out of his pockets and sat down suddenly on the shingle beside Carter.

'I'm sorry,' he said. 'I didn't mean it. Sorry, Randy.' He put his head down on his knees for a moment, then lifted it again and shook himself. 'I will have a cigarette, if you don't mind.'

Randy took a cigarette out of the packet and tossed it over. He lit a match and squatted down. The tiny yellow flame stood absolutely still between them in the still air. Todd inhaled deeply on a trembling breath and linked his hands round his knees.

'Thanks.'

He sat still beside Carter, looking out at the long stretch of sea. Randy watched him for a moment, and then stood up and wandered away towards the breakwater on their left. His feet made an appallingly loud noise as he slipped and stumbled slowly across the shingle.

'How's your foot?' Todd did not turn towards Carter.

'It hurts like hell.'

'Is your toe really broken?'

Carter gingerly bent his toe up and down and then wriggled it experimentally.

'Well, I don't think it's actually broken. But it jolly well felt as if it was. I've bruised the nail, and it's jolly sore.'

He began to put on his sandal, grumbling to himself and making exaggerated grunts and exclamations of pain as he did so.

'Do you think you can walk?'

Carter stood up and took a few steps, limping heavily.

'Sort of,' he said unwillingly. 'I'll walk about a bit and see if it improves.' He limped off towards Randy, lurching over the shingle.

Todd sat still looking out to sea. A tiny breeze just lifted the heavy lock of hair drying on his forehead and dropped it again. The waves went on smoothly piling themselves up and toppling on to the shingle with their relentlessly labial sound. On each side of him the two black breakwaters thrust themselves out into the water like sleeping animals. Through their ribs he could see the water almost white in the path of the moon. The sky seemed darker than the sea. There was no sound and no movement over its immense surface. It passed above his head and arched down on to the edge of the sea, where the elements seemed to fuse along a line which he could only perceive when he did not look directly at it. It was perceptible to him only out of the corners of his eyes, or when he glanced quickly at it and then immediately looked away again. His body felt superficially cleansed and relaxed, but the salt crawled on his skin as it dried and his hands felt rough. He rubbed his fingers together, feeling the salty crust between the skin surfaces. It set his teeth on edge and filled his mouth with saliva which was unpleasantly tainted with nicotine. He took a last deep pull at his cigarette, and tossed it away from him on to the wet shingle at the water's edge. It described a fiery loop and was immediately extinguished with a tiny vicious hiss. He exhaled the smoke from his lungs. It left his mouth and throat feeling foul, as if they were coated with tarry fur. He swallowed, and pressed his tongue against the roof of his mouth, tasting the nicotine. It combined most unpleasantly with the salty crust on his lips.

Randy's call, coming to him across the beach like the call of some seabird, startled him indescribably. He scrambled up on to the shingle with a lurching heart before he realised what it was. Randy called again. He was visible only as a white patch of shirt against the dark bulk of the groyne. His hair and skin and the rest of his clothes were swallowed up in shadow.

'Todd! Come over here.' The white patch changed shape

as an arm was raised and waved at him. 'Come over here.'

Todd got up and went over to him. The shingle shifted and slid away under his weight so that he could not move quickly.

Randy and Carter were standing together, looking up at a section of the groyne. Randy was holding something long and dark in his hands. When Todd got near enough he saw that it was a plank, dark with green slime.

'What are you doing with that?' he asked, looking at the plank, puzzled.

'It came away in my hands,' said Randy. 'I was trying to climb up. I wanted to see if I could walk along the top. But when I took hold of it, it came completely away. It must have been absolutely rotten.'

'I've walked all the way along it,' said Carter excitedly. 'It's all been rebuilt, except this section here. It doesn't really look much different, but it is. It's ready to fall down. It must have been here for years.' He looked up at the leaning structure of upright beams and planks almost in awe.

'He's right.' Randy's voice had a curious breathless note in it, almost of exultation. 'It'll come down at a touch.' He gestured towards the breakwater. 'Just you try.'

Todd looked at Randy, then at the plank he held.

'What do you want me to do?' he asked curiously.

'Just pull out one of the beams and see,' said Randy.

'Go on, you try.' Carter was jumping up and down beside them on the shingle, his injured foot forgotten. 'Go on, Todd, have a try.'

Todd advanced upon the breakwater, and studied the criss-crossing of planking. At length, he selected a long beam which protruded from the crazy structure like a broken bone jutting from a wound. He grasped it firmly in both hands and pulled strongly at it. It gave somewhat, but remained relatively firmly attached. He relaxed his grip a little, and twisted his head round to look at the others.

'Go on – try again,' urged Carter.

Randy said nothing. He merely tightened his hold on his own piece of planking and stared at the breakwater.

Todd turned back to his beam. He gripped it tightly, braced his feet on the shingle as firmly as he could, and pulled with all his strength. For a moment he thought it was not going to budge. Then there was a sharp crack, a tearing sound, a sort of rising scream as wood parted from wood, and the resistance abruptly gave. He staggered back, almost thrown off his balance, clutching the heavy damp length of wood to his chest.

Carter let out a shrill cheer.

'Well done! I say, jolly well done, Todd. Come on, let's get some more out.'

He threw himself at the crazy structure and seized one of the upright beams, clasping it to him and pulling at it in frenzied jerks. Randy silently began tearing at the planks, scrabbling at them with his nails as he tried to get a grip. He dragged one out and instantly attacked another, breathing loudly between closed teeth. There were the sharp rending sounds of splitting wood as the planks tore away and were flung down on to the shingle. A hole appeared in the dark structure through which Todd could see the light sea stretching out from the beach beyond. He hesitated no longer. He flung himself on to the breakwater and attacked the planks round the edge of the hole. First one tore away in his hands and then another. The noise seemed outrageous and enormous. The wood was rotten with age and with prolonged immersion in water, but it was tenacious. The three of them fought with it, tearing at it, kicking it, worrying at it like dogs as they tried to tear it apart, but it resisted them with frightening subbornness. The nails were firmly driven in and could only be detached by being twisted in the wood, and the upright beams were sunk so deep in the sand that at first it seemed as though they would never give way.

They worked silently, with complete concentration on

what they were doing. Carter threw himself on to the beams and worried at them with no husbanding of his strength. He pulled and strained and grunted, running splinters into his fingers and darting from one place to another as he thought he saw a better opening. He ran backwards and forwards tugging at the planks like a puppy. There was no system or order about it, but he was immensely strong and tenacious and his uneconomical methods produced results by the sheer brute force behind them. He wasted an immense amount of effort, but he had power to spare and unbounding enthusiasm. He was intensely excited and exhilarated by his struggles with the obdurate wood; he heaved away at it and wrestled with its opposing strength because the physical exercise gave him an uncomplicated pleasure.

Randy went silently at the breakwater and systematically destroyed it as if he were dismembering an animal. He concentrated first on the pieces of wood which were fairly easy to detach, and laid them down beside him in a neat heap as he pulled them clear. He had not got Carter's strength, but he used his intelligence instead, and methodically took the structure to pieces bit by bit with the controlled efficiency of a machine. He sized up each plank before attempting to detach it, so that his grip was always the most effective one he could apply, enabling him to free the wood with the least expenditure of sheer muscular strength. He husbanded every ounce of power, and did not even waste it in exclamations of triumph or despair as Carter did. He dissected the structure in front of him, and dismembered it in complete silence. But there was a frightening concentration in his movements which concealed his complete abandonment to the joy of destruction. He worked as if he were killing something, and as if he were enjoying the operation.

Between them, Todd worked blindly and almost as if unconscious of what he was doing. No doubt his mind directed his hands, but he was not aware of either. He saw the widening hole in front of him and felt the unresisting wood against his skin. He selected the best grip, the easiest stance, and gave all his intelligence and all his considerable physical strength to the destruction of the breakwater. Nevertheless, he worked blindly. The dismemberment of the animal brought to him no conscious pleasure as it did to Carter, no fierce, vicious satisfaction, as it did to Randy. He did it instinctively, as if he needed to do it. He seemed to be satisfying this obscure need with no sensual relief or enjoyment. He pulled and tore at the resisting wood with his eyes vaguely fixed on the still sea or on the placid sky above them. His body writhed and fought on the dark beach as if independent of his desires. He said nothing, hardly seemed to breathe any faster. Some remote but vital part of him remained untouched by what he was doing. But he took his full part in the operation, as if by virtue of his common humanity with the other two. They worked together in total co-operation.

Suddenly, the structure began to totter, to crack about them. Carter shouted something. Randy sprang back on the shingle dragging a length of planking with him. Todd, alone, stood stupidly beneath the swaying complex of half broken and detached beams, looking up at the low silhouette of the cliff as if he were thinking of something totally different. Carter grabbed him by the arm and dragged him roughly backwards, whirling him against Randy, who gripped him fiercely and held him crushed in the circle of his arm. There was a curiously human groaning sound on a rising note, as if some kind of question were being asked. Then what was left of the section of breakwater collapsed on to the shingle in a mass of rotten and shattered wood.

They stood in a row and looked at it. Todd could feel Randy's heart bumping against his side. The moonlight bleached the wood as it lay on the stones so that it looked like the scattered bones of some large dead animal. Here and there a great splinter stuck up, white and jagged. Planks lay split along their length or snapped across, some up-ended, some prone on the shingle. It looked like some chance discovery on a long abandoned battlefield. Behind it, through the gap where it had stood, stretched the revealed length of peaceful beach, identical with the one upon which they stood. It is indistinguishable, thought Todd, looking bleakly at it. They had broken through to it by means of this superb act of destruction, and it was simply the same; no better, and no worse. Somehow this distressed him greatly. His disappointment was irrational and acute. For the moment, standing sweating and exhausted in the iron support of Randy's arm, he felt he would never recover from it.

The other two stood beside him, silent. Presently, Randy stiffly relaxed his hold upon Todd and dusted his hands together with a dry, final sound.

'Well, that's that,' he said. He sounded exhausted and replete. His voice held a fat, thick note of satisfaction.

Carter giggled.

'What a mess!' he said softly. 'What a bloody marvellous mess.'

Todd alone said nothing. He contemplated the ruin, and turned away.

'Come on, I'll get the car. Let's go home.'

He plodded wearily off across the shingle. He climbed up on to the bank and heard the others following him. They trailed along the path in single file and one by one hauled themselves over the gate and into the road. The car stood where they had left it, compact and gleaming in the moonlight. They got in and slammed the doors. Todd started the engine and drove off along the empty high street. The thrust of the engine as he drove was vaguely comforting. The other two were asleep before they left the town, Carter sprawled in the back, Randy controlled and neat even in unconsciousness. Todd alone sat upright, staring unblinkingly through the windscreen at the white road leaping up to meet him in the headlights.

*   *   *

138

The following day after school they made their way separately to the quarry, drifting there without any knowledge of the others' intentions. All three had found themselves possessed by an intolerable restlessness, and each in turn had drifted towards the quarry without any intention of doing so. Thus, they met at the edge of the descent to the cave, surprised, and yet not surprised by the presence of the others.

Carter was sitting on the grass throwing pebbles down into the gully, and looked up when he heard Randy's approach. 'Hallo,' he said, and went back to his pebbles.

Randy grunted and squatted down beside him. He lit a cigarette and dangled his hands between his knees, looking across at the opposite slope. A cloud of small flies swarmed round them, filling the hot air with a languorous murmur. Randy scooped up some pebbles and began throwing them over the edge. Almost every stone fell with a distant clang on to the sheet of metal below. Neither of them turned when Todd came up and flopped down beside them. He took off his sun-glasses and rubbed the back of his hand across his face. It came away wet with sweat. He put the sun-glasses on again and rolled over on to his back. The light was so intense that the dark glasses were not sufficient protection as he looked up at the brilliant sky, and he had to cup his hands over his eyes.

'Any trouble about the car?' asked Carter after a pause.

'No. She's not back yet. She doesn't mind me borrowing it, but she gets a bit upset about me driving without a licence. I shall have to take the test this summer. She's afraid I'm going to be nabbed.'

Randy grunted.

'I'm not surprised. So she doesn't know where we were?'

'Of course not, you idiot. Did you see the evening paper?'

' "Unknown vandals destroy breakwater",' giggled Carter.

139

'And it was on the local news this evening. They seem to think it was a gang of local toughs. They can't get on to us, can they, Todd?'

'Of course not. However could they? Nobody was on the beach, and we couldn't have been recognised from the path. Frightened of the police again, Carter?'

'He's had a complex about them ever since he pinched that wood,' said Randy, but amiably, so that Carter grinned sheepishly.

'There was a picture in the paper, Todd. Did you see it? We made a damned good job of it, didn't we? Talk about a heap of old rubbish – they'll jolly well have to get down to it and build a new one now.'

'I call it very public-spirited of us, though I can't say it occurred to me in that light at the time,' said Randy reminiscently. He smoothed his hand over his immaculate hair and sighed. 'I could do with a swim now. It's blazing up here.'

It was – it burnt through their thin clothes and seemed to pin them to the hot earth. Todd rolled on to his stomach and chewed on a piece of dry brown grass. He looked sideways at the other two.

'Are you going down?'

'I don't know – I suppose so,' said Randy.

'We ought to get some of the things up,' said Todd as if trying to justify himself. 'The butter and bread and stuff. We ought to destroy it, burn it or something. It'll go rotten in no time in this heat.'

'I don't think I'll bother,' said Carter with elaborate casualness. 'I've had just about enough of scrambling up and down that beastly track carrying stuff. I'll wait here until you get back.'

'Oh no you won't,' said Todd firmly. 'You can jolly well come down with us and do your bit.'

They stood up reluctantly. All were unwilling to reaffirm the emptiness of the place, and all three sidled away so that they should not have to lead the descent into the cave. They watched each other nervously, ready to defect at the slightest sign of weakness from one of the others. In the end it was Todd, of course, who shrugged his shoulders and stepped forward to the edge. He swung himself over and dropped down to the stretch of his arms. They saw his face, neutralised by the heavy dark glasses, dip below the thin grass growing on the lip of the quarry. Randy hesitated, then followed him with the air of one who humours an eccentric friend. Carter came last with much *sotto voce* protestation.

Todd, stepping blindly into the cave muffled in its temporary darkness, edged forward with the uncertainty of the newly blind. He always loathed, and anticipated with much nervous shrinking, those few steps which had to be taken in trust. He always found himself picturing a newly opened chasm in front of his feet into which he would fall headlong and be for ever lost to the light. Today, he hesitated and fumbled forward, feeling out in front of him with the palms of his hands turned up and out as if he were about to press them to the upright face of an invisible wall. He felt forward with his foot, sweeping it hesitantly in a half circle to see if it encountered an obstacle. When it did not, he shifted his weight on to it and brought the other foot up to describe another trembling sweep across the floor. He put his hands out again into the absurd temporary darkness, and laid them upon a face.

He knew it was a face because he felt hair upon his skin and a mouth with teeth in it. He propelled himself violently backwards and let out a high scream of primitive, uncontrolled terror. It seemed to be dragged out of his chest without any conscious intention on his part. He heard an answering cry from Randy and feet coming swiftly up behind him. He swung his head round towards the mouth of the cave, seeing the aperture full of its irregular gold, then jerked back again to face whatever it was he had touched. His skin and flesh crawled under his clothes. But in that moment his eyes had accustomed themselves to the light. He saw the boy, standing quite still in front of him, close, and absolutely silent. He was so motionless, in fact, that he almost looked dead. His face appeared submissive, reflective, as if it would adapt itself to any mood with which it found itself in contact.

'Jesus Christ!' whispered Todd devoutly. It sounded as if he were praying. He put a shaking hand to his mouth and wiped away a trickle of saliva. 'Jesus Christ!' he repeated weakly.

The boy smiled timidly at him.

'Hallo,' he said. A look of anxiety, almost of solicitude, came over his face. 'I say, is anything the matter?'

'Who's that?' Randy peered over Todd's shoulder, saw the boy, and stopped abruptly.

'Well, well!' he said slowly. He looked the boy up and down. He put his hands into his trouser pockets and began to rock gently backwards and forwards on his heels. 'Well, well! This is a surprise.'

Carter came bustling forward, saw the boy, and stopped. Then he raised his voice in a joyful cry of welcome.

'He's back! He's back!' he shouted joyously. 'He's come back, Todd. I say, Randy, he's come back. I knew he would. He's come back! Isn't it marvellous, Todd? I knew he hadn't really gone. He's come back!'

'So,' said Randy, his cold voice cutting in on these noisy rejoicings, 'so we see. We, too, have eyes in our heads. Cut down on the noise, will you, Carter?'

'But he's come back! It's all right. Everything's all right. I say, you know, you didn't half give us a fright. We thought you'd gone for good. Where on earth have you been, rushing off like that? We haven't half been scared – we thought we'd never see you again.'

Todd had recovered himself.

'Shut up for a bit, Carter. There's no need to make all that din.' But he, too, turned to the boy. 'What on earth do you think you've been up to, going off like that?' he asked, anger asserting itself as relief made him tremble as though with cold.

The boy stood still in front of them. He maintained his timid, placatory smile, but he was watching them with alert eyes.

'I'm sorry,' he said. 'I didn't mean to cause any trouble.'

'Cause any trouble?' Randy repeated with cold astonishment. 'You sodding little perisher, you deliberately go off like that, without leaving us any message or telling us where you've gone, and then you have the face to say you didn't mean to cause us any trouble.' He turned his head aside and spat viciously on to the floor. The boy watched him with interest.

'Let's go and sit down,' said Todd. 'I want a drink.' He had regained his self-control, but he still felt shaken and unsteady. The sudden adjustment he had been called upon to make had destroyed his hard-won composure.

The boy went over to his bed. He sat down on the blankets, curling his legs under him with his usual neatness of movement. His thick hair was tousled and his eyes were bright in his brown face. He had rolled his sleeves almost up to his shoulders and he clasped his thin hands round his upper arms, spreading the brown fingers out over the paler skin. His immature muscles bulged slightly under the pressure. He looked clean, and alert, as if he were preparing to bring all his intelligence to bear on a thorny problem.

Todd and Carter drank some warm beer and Randy lit a cigarette. The boy, enthroned among his blankets, watched them expectantly. When Todd had drunk enough he wiped his mouth on the inside of his forearm and turned slowly to the boy. Now that the first shock of the return had subsided he felt intense curiosity take its place. But before he could speak, the boy said,

'I would have left a message, you know, but I didn't have a pencil or paper or anything, so I couldn't.'

This was not convincing, and Todd said so.

'You could have done something – scratched a mark on the wall, or on the floor. Anything would have done.'

The boy's face was illuminated with his wide, brilliant smile.

'I suppose I could have, but I didn't think of it at the time. I'm awfully sorry.'

Randy said, leaning against the wall,

'Messages are hardly the point, are they? What interests me is where you've been, and what you've been doing.'

The boy cocked his head on one side like a small intelligent bird.

'Well, I suppose I went because I got a bit bored. I mean, this is an awfully nice cave, and you've been marvellous about fixing it up for me and getting me food, and all that sort of thing, but there's not an awful lot to do. After I'd explored it and found out all about it, I suppose I just got a bit fed up. There's not much space really, when you're in it all the time, and sitting on the edge and looking out gets rather boring because no one comes, do they, and there isn't much to look at. You must have noticed that. After all, I suppose that's why you chose it. Please don't think that I don't think it's a marvellous cave, because I do, but when you come there are three of you, and you can talk and play games and things; it's not the same when you're on your own.'

'We should have tied you up from the very beginning,' said Randy grimly.

'But I did come back, didn't I?' said the boy eagerly. 'After all, I suppose I needn't have done, really.'

'You suppose you needn't have done?' said Todd, puzzled. 'There wasn't a damn thing to stop you getting out and staying out. Why did you come back?'

The boy looked at Todd with clear bright eyes which seemed innocent of deceit.

'You told me to stay,' he said. 'I didn't think it would matter if I went off for a bit – just for a change. I don't suppose I should have done, really, but I thought it wouldn't matter, if I came back.'

'But where did you go?'

The boy waved his bare arm towards the mouth of the cave in a gesture which seemed to indicate huge freedoms, vast spaces.

'Oh – just out, you know,' he said vaguely.

'We know that,' said Todd. 'But where? Where did you go?'

'Just out.'

'What you really mean is that you don't intend to tell us.'

He merely looked humbly back at them with his large childish eyes.

'Who did you see? You must have seen someone. You've been away for at least twenty-four hours. What did you eat? Where did you sleep?'

'Oh, I slept all right. It's so hot, isn't it? One could sleep anywhere.'

Todd persisted grimly.

'Who did you go to see? Why did you go?'

The boy did not answer for a while. Then he said vaguely,

'There was nothing to stop me coming back.'

He smiled placatingly at them.

Todd said,

'So you did meet someone. Did they try to stop you coming back?'

Carter asked suddenly,

'Was it the police?'

The boy withdrew his attention from Todd and gravely turned it upon Carter.

'What about the police?' he inquired, as if confused.

'Was it the police you went to? Have they followed you here?'

'Followed me here? How do you mean?'

'I'm asking you if you told them about us keeping you here,' said Carter desperately.

'But you're not really keeping me here, are you? I mean,

I can go whenever I want to. After all, that's what I did, wasn't it?'

He laughed in pure childish amusement, as if he thought he had said something exquisitely amusing.

Randy was leaning out of the cave. He put his hand out to them in a stiff gesture of warning. The boy stopped laughing. They all turned to watch Randy with sudden strained intensity. He knelt motionless as if he were watching something in the gully below. His neck was craned forward in rigid attention.

'There's someone down there,' he said softly.

'Who is it?' Todd whispered.

'I don't know. I can't really see. I just caught something move.' They waited tensely while he peered down, his body braced forward on to his hands. 'There it is again. It's someone down in the bushes, looking up at the cave.'

With a soft rustle of blankets the boy climbed off his bed and went across to Randy. He slipped in beside him as silently as a shadow and crouched down. He, too, craned his neck forward and out to look down into the gully. His figure was tiny and compact against the brightness. They both knelt quite still, looking down.

Randy drew himself back on his heels and swivelled round to look at the other two. His eyebrows were raised in a comical expression of surprise and disbelief.

'I believe it's a girl! I'm not sure, but I think I saw her dress. It's certainly something pink. It's almost impossible to see until it moves, but I'm sure it's a girl.'

'A girl?' Todd was relieved, but incredulous. 'What on earth is she doing down there?'

'God knows. She looks quite small, not much more than a kid.'

'Can you see what she's doing?'

'She's looking up.'

'Do you think she can see the cave from there?'

'I don't know. But if she's been there for any length of

146

time she must have seen us coming down the cliff and going in, so she'll know there's a cave here.' He paused, eyeing Todd. 'She probably saw the boy too.'

'You mean when he came back?'

'Yes.'

Carter and Todd stole across the cave and squatted down in the entrance. The boy was motionless beside Todd, his head bent as he looked down. His thick lock of hair fell away from his forehead. Todd's bare arm pressed against his shoulder. The contact left the boy seemingly unaware, while it dried Todd's mouth and made him shake. He forced himself to look down. He soon found the patch of colour, motionless in the low bushes. At first it was impossible to see it as anything more than a scrap of pink, surprisingly vivid between the greenish brown branches with their thin foliage. Then it moved and he saw her quite clearly, a sturdy, compact child of about thirteen with brown scratched arms and legs and a blob of black hair. She moved again, and disappeared. He almost felt as if she had never been there at all.

'Did you see?' whispered Randy. His words thickened with his excitement. 'It was a girl – I told you so.'

'Whatever is she doing down there?' Carter whispered. 'No one's ever been here before. I say, Todd, what do you think she's up to?'

'Snooping,' said Randy violently. 'She's just hanging round snooping, the silly little bitch.'

'What are we going to do about it?'

They paused to eye one another. At length Randy said, 'Go down and put a stop to it.'

The other two shied away from him like nervous animals. 'She'd see us,' said Carter, dry-mouthed.

'What about it? She's probably seen us already.'

'She'll tell someone we're here.'

'Will she?' said Randy, breathing fast. His eyes went to Todd. 'Do you think she'll tell anyone?'

Todd swallowed.

'We're not even sure she has seen us. She may not even know we're here.'

'Then why is she hanging about down there?'

'She's probably just playing some silly kid's game,' said Carter, encouraged to find himself on the same side as Todd.

'By herself?'

'Why not?'

'She doesn't look as if she's playing a game. She's just hanging about down there, watching.'

'What does it matter if she hasn't seen us?'

'Don't be a bloody idiot,' said Randy calmly. 'She's only got to say she's seen us here, and the boy, and the game's up. Finished. Done with. All over.' He made a graphic chopping gesture with his right hand. 'Don't you see?'

'What do you want us to do?' whispered Todd.

'Go down and settle it.'

'You mean – tell her to clear off?' said Carter with little hope.

Randy showed his teeth.

'Well, not exactly,' he said. 'That wasn't exactly what I had in mind.'

The others looked quickly at each other and then down into the gully. The scrap of pink was motionless in the bushes. Watching it, Todd said,

'I think we should leave her alone. After all, we don't know that she's seen us. I don't think we ought to go down, Randy.'

The boy moved back and sat up on his haunches.

'She's been here before, you know,' he said. 'She was here on Monday. I saw her clearly. She was looking up at the cave. I'm sure she knows I'm here, Todd, and she must have seen you coming down.' He watched them as they drew away from him into a little huddle of alarm. 'I really do think you ought to go down – now, while she's still there.'

They crouched together, looking down. The patch of

148

colour flashed between the bushes, and the girl stood up. She was curiously foreshortened, and her face was disfigured by the brilliant light pouring on to it into a patchwork of white planes and dark pockets of shade. But they saw her put a hand up to her eyes and look intently beneath it at the cliff face. Instinctively, they drew back.

'All right, that settles it,' said Todd. The boy let out a small whisper of breath. He looked down at his hands, clenched on his thighs, and Todd turned away from him in a kind of wondering disgust. 'Randy, get the knife off the table. You and I can find stones when we get outside, Carter. Get a flat one that'll fit into the palm of your hand.'

'Knife?' The boy looked up.

Randy was already padding back with it. He held it delicately by the bone handle with the blade turned back along the underside of his wrist. He smiled at the boy.

'Only to frighten her with,' he said sweetly.

One by one they swung themselves out of the cave on to the ledge of rock, and then down the cliff face into the bushes. They could no longer see the girl, but they were sure she could not have gone far.

The boy sat back in the shadows, his hands loose and open, palms upwards on his knees. His eyes were bright.

The three of them lay down among the dry bushes as soon as they got into the gully. They lay close together, with the brittle grasses scratching their legs. They could all see the girl. She had moved a little distance away from the spot where they had seen her looking up at the cave and was squatting down on the ground. She seemed to be doing something to her shoe. She was not a prepossessing child. Her black hair was cut close to her head in a square clump and her body in the pink dress was square and dumpy. But she looked strong and determined – not, thought Todd with a tremor, the sort who would frighten easily. She was obviously unaware of their presence. She finished what she was doing and stood up. She gave her shoe an experimental shake, seemed satisfied with

it, and began making her way slowly through the bushes
away from them. Todd knew that the defile narrowed, and
ended in a steep slope that led up to the waste ground in
which the quarry stood. Once up there, she would be clearly
visible from the road, and out of their reach. He turned his
head in the grass and motioned to Randy to move forward,
keeping to the girl's right, then to Carter to do the same to
her left. They began to edge themselves along the ground,
keeping well down among the bushes. Todd himself moved
forward with infinite caution, following more or less exactly
along the route which the girl had taken.

She was moving slowly, wandering along looking vaguely
around her, but even so Todd found that keeping up with
her speed required an agonising effort. He was soon drenched
in sweat which ran down his face and broke out on his hands,
mingling horribly with the dust caking his skin. He had to
move his arms forward in front of his body, dig his elbows
and fingers into the ground, and drag himself forward a few
inches at a time. He scraped his arms and legs on roots and
brambles, and crushed prickly branches under his body as
he moved. He was soon almost blinded by sweat and had to
keep stopping to brush it out of his eyes. It stung on his lips
and in the scratches on the undersides of his arms. The sun
poured down on to the whole length of his body. The bushes
gave him no protection from it, and all the time he felt it
running over him as if he were being sprayed with scorching
jets of air. He tried to control his breathing, but the urge
to pant with open mouth like a dog was almost irresistible.
The effort required to prevent himself from doing so gave
him an extra area of concentration which was intolerable.
As he dragged himself along with his face almost at ground
level, his ears were filled with an immense buzzing sound
which at first puzzled him. He thought it was the cloud of
flies which sluggishly accompanied him, attracted by the smell
of his sweat. Then he imagined it was actually coming up
from the earth, as if great dynamos were churning deep in

the rock. It was only as it increased with every foot of ground that he covered that he realised it was coming from the waste ground ahead of him, and that it was made by one, or possibly two, motor cycles. He cursed them and struggled on.

On his left, Carter was absorbed in his efforts to wriggle as quickly and as quietly as possible through the bushes. He could see the girl moving slowly along slightly below and ahead of him. He knew that he must not lose sight of her, that he must not let her see him, and that he must, if possible, catch up with her and head her off. What he would do if he were actually to confront her face to face he did not know. He had not, indeed, given the matter any thought. He had seen the knife in Randy's hand and he had selected a large flat stone for himself which he was carrying in his trouser pocket. He was carrying out the orders which he had been given, and should a new situation arise which they did not cover, he would ask for new directions. The actual enterprise in which he was taking part was completely unreal to him; only the pursuit existed. He wriggled along on his elbows and knees with the sun beating upon his head and shoulders. The scrap of pink moved ahead of him through the bushes, and he followed it, the stone in his pocket digging its sharp edges uncomfortably into his flesh with every move, so that he was strongly tempted to discard it. In the end, in disgust, he did so, and found his progress considerably less painful.

Randy, on the right of the girl, found the going comparatively easy. He was on a slope where the bushes grew sparsely, and between their roots there ran a kind of track, possibly used in the past by the men who had worked the quarry. It could hardly be called a path, but it was a well-defined track, and he moved along it fairly easily. He was also in the shade of the high ridge climbing above him to his right, and thus he had not the intensity of the sun's full heat to contend with. He found that he was able to move along in a crouching position, progressing in a series of short bursts. The bushes, though thinly spaced, grew to a reasonable height, and he was able to move from one to the next along the track, taking advantage of their scanty cover. He was not sure if they would afford him complete concealment, should the girl turn full round and look straight in his direction. But for the sake of added speed he was willing to take the risk. His intention was to skirt the edge of the gully and to station himself high up on the slope which the girl must at some point climb in order to get out on to the waste ground and thus to the road. Here, they would be bound to meet.

He kept looking down at her as she moved slowly, almost aimlessly along below him. Her brilliantly pink dress made her impossible to miss. There was no chance of losing sight of her in the bushes or of her giving him the slip. He felt positively grateful to her for wearing such a dress. Her clump of dark hair gleamed metallic and almost blue in the fierce light. She moved gracelessly, but she put her feet down firmly with an admirable disregard for the undergrowth, brambles and roots which straggled across her path. She looked a sturdy, compact little figure. Randy held the knife in his right hand; its handle frequently became sticky with sweat so that he had to keep stopping to wipe it. His immaculate trousers were wrinkled and marked with yellow earth stains at the knees. His shirt kept working loose at the waist, and in the end he pulled it out completely and let it hang loose. It made him feel considerably cooler, and it no longer impeded his movements by pulling under the arms.

He looked down, and saw behind the girl the movement of the bushes where Todd and Carter crawled painfully along. The noise of the motor cycle engines was now quite loud enough to drown any noise they might possibly make, but they did not seem to have realised this, for both of them were still moving slowly, and with extreme caution. He caught a glimpse of Todd's head raised for an instant among the bushes. It showed white in the bright sunshine, then sank again out of sight. Randy measured his position in respect to that of the girl, and then looked along the track ahead of him. He calculated the ground he had to cover in order to arrive on the slope ahead of her as she started to climb. He had to describe a considerable curve of rough ground on the hillside, whereas she had only to travel in a straight line along a moderately well-defined track. He wiped the sweat out of his eyes and looked down at her again.

To his dismay, he saw that she had stopped wandering aimlessly along, and had begun to walk extremely fast. She was covering the ground with long firm strides of her stout legs. He could see the brown sandals picking an unerring path along the bottom of the gully. With a start he realised that she had almost reached the bottom of the slope. Her speed was remarkable. Randy turned to look for Todd and Carter. Todd was just standing up. He rose from the bushes and stood motionless for a moment, looking after her. Randy was too far away to see his expression. Then he began to walk rapidly along the track behind the girl. He gained on her with every step. but Randy could see immediately that she would be over the cliff top and safe before he could catch up with her. Of Carter there was no sign. Presumably he was still happily crawling along through the bushes, quite unaware of the fact that his prey was rapidly disappearing out of sight.

Randy let out a groan, and began to run along the track. The noise of the engines was rising and falling in the hot air above him. He thought fleetingly that whoever was riding the motor cycles must be running them very near the edge of the cliff. Indeed, as he stumbled along with the blood drumming in his head, he thought for a moment that he caught a glimpsed silhouette out of the tail of his eye, like that of a man perched on a great black bird, swooping across the stretch of sky above him. He ran on. His feet slipped sideways at every step as the light earth on the slope threatened to pitch away under his feet and throw him down into the gully.

Thus he ran with a kind of lurching motion, constantly bracing his body against the downward pull, and this slowed him considerably. Also, the track began to get more thickly overgrown and more difficult to negotiate at speed. He fought his way through the thin tenacious branches, shielding his face, and tearing his clothes from their grasp. He could no longer see the girl but he knew that she must be at least halfway up the hillside, and he began to waste his scanty breath in swearing. Then he caught his foot under an arched branch and sprawled headlong and slithering on the ground. The knife flew from his grasp and skittered away into the undergrowth with a flicker of sunlight on the steel. He did not bother to search for it. He scrambled up and lurched off again with smarting hands and a pain in his side which caught like a knife at the deepest point of every breath.

When he burst out of the bushes, sobbing in his throat, he was momentarily blind. Bushes, hillside, sky, swam about in front of him in a meaningless jumble. When they had steadied, he saw her. She was two-thirds of the way up the slope and was climbing fast. Todd was behind her, coming strongly up, and below him Carter was scrambling furiously over the loose stones at the bottom of the ascent. Randy immediately saw that the girl had realised not only that they were after her, but that she was in some kind of danger. She looked back over her shoulder once, and then set herself to the climb again, legs and arms going like pistons as she pushed her strong little body over the rough ground. Out of the tail of his eye Randy again caught that high black swoop and roar as man and machine careered along the edge of the cliff and swerved off in a screech of engine noise. He began running again.

The girl sensed his approach – she could not have heard it above the engine roar – and waved her brown arm at him in a fierce gesture of repudiation. She did not stop climbing as she did it; indeed, she was only a yard or two from the top. Randy, his lungs bursting, hurled himself across the intervening space and forced himself over the few remaining yards on to the slope just below her climbing figure. He was almost able to touch her. With a desperate heave he threw himself up and grabbed at her foot. She kicked back savagely with the full strength of her bare brown leg and caught him on the cheek bone with her heel. Water spurted into his eyes and blinded him. When he was able to see again she was just going over the top in a jumble of brown flesh, pink skirts, and white cotton panties stretched tight over hard little buttocks. Randy hung on to the edge of the cliff for a long moment with his fingers hooked and scrabbling at roots and stones. Then his grip broke, and he slipped back a little so that he was lying pressed to the face of the cliff. His head protruded over the top, but he was shielded by a thin line of straggling bushes through which he could see the flat waste ground and the girl, trying to scramble to her feet.

There was a roar of engine noise on his right and he turned his head round among the branches. One of the motor cycles was careering across the uneven ground, jolting and leaping over lumps of earth and loose stones. It was coming straight down on to the girl. She crouched on the ground with one arm bent up across her face. Randy could see the rider's horrified face, mouth and eyes wide in the white flesh under the gleaming helmet. The girl threw herself forward, jerking her legs up under her and burying her face in the dust. The motor cycle roared past her in an insane curve, throwing a shower of loose pebbles and earth down on to Randy's face as he crouched in the bushes. It swerved away, and began to come round again in a narrow flattened circle.

The girl staggered to her feet and looked around. She saw the motor cycle bearing down on her again, this time from her left, bucking over the ground. Its driver was thrown from side to side on the seat as he clung to the handles in a desperate effort to control its course. He seemed to be shouting. The girl let out a terrified scream which was faintly audible even above the infernal din of the two engines. She began to run, staggering in a crazy zigzag. The rider of the other machine had seen her and was waving frantically to her, trying to signal her to come on, to go back – anything to get out of the path of the rearing, bucking thing which was pursuing her. It seemed to chase her as she staggered helplessly in front of it. The wheels slipped and swerved on the stones, throwing them out sideways in little spurts of dust. For a moment Randy thought she had escaped as the motor cycle skidded and almost tipped on to its side. Then suddenly, as if bewildered by the roar of the engine and the shouts of the two riders, she hesitated, half turned, and ran straight into its path. The machine, the black figure still clinging to its back, struck a stone, skidded on its back wheels, and reared up. They came down together with a scream, a roar, and a great explosion of yellow dust. Randy saw the rider fly off and hurtle sideways, hit the ground with a thud and skid into a huddle of legs and arms. The motor cycle fell over on to its side and lay there, its wheels spinning and its metalwork gleaming in the brilliant sun. The girl lay half underneath it. She was pinned to the ground at the hips, and lay twisted on to her side with her head turned away from Randy. One arm lay flung back behind her, and the fingers of the outspread hand twitched a little in the grass, then relaxed and lay still. Her black hair stuck stiffly out round her head as if it were glued into spikes.

The other motor cycle stopped some yards away. The rider switched off the engine, swung himself off, and began running jerkily across the grass towards the girl. The rider of the fallen machine groaned, rolled over, and sat up. He put his head between his knees and began rocking himself to and fro.

Randy decided he had seen enough. He loosened his grip and slithered a few feet down the slope to find Carter and Todd crouched beside him in the grass. They looked at him with wide eyes. Todd was trembling.

Randy shook himself, tucked his shirt in at the waist, and felt for his comb.

'Did you see?' said Todd.

'Of course I saw.'

'Do you think she's dead?'

'She's dead all right. She hasn't a chance under that thing.'

They watched him comb his hair.

'Do you suppose they saw us?'

'The chaps on the bikes? No – they couldn't possibly have seen a thing. We weren't in sight. Anyway, they had other things to think about.'

Carter pulled up a blade of grass and put it between his teeth.

'Well, she won't be able to tell on us now,' he remarked, with the air of one who looks upon the bright side of things.

'No, she won't, will she?' agreed Randy.

Todd, who felt like a murderer, said nothing.

That night, Randy, who was troubled by a feeling of business unfinished, went to the cave alone. He walked fast through the town and out on to the empty ground where the motor cycles had roared and circled. Now it was silent. The ambulance, the police, the reporters, had come and gone. The two youths had gone for questioning, one to be charged with manslaughter, their machines had been ridden sedately away. Now the open stretch of ground looked like a moon-scape in a children's paper, with silvery craters, dark hollows, and the distant line of trees like a range of mountains against the sky. The moon was full and painted everything with her sober deceptive silver. Randy walked carefully, occasionally flashing his pocket torch on anything in his path which looked dubious. A dog barked, far away and persistent. To his left a train hooted as it ran round the low hill sheltering the town. The air smelt warm and full and felt fuzzy on his face. He let himself over the edge and climbed carefully down. He knew the way so well that it was not necessary to see the path. He could have anticipated every stone of it under his feet, every root under his hands if it had been pitch dark.

The cave, as he stepped into it, was indeed pitch dark. But it was cooler than the outside air, and it smelt of human habitation – disinfectant, food, even, in an indefinable way, of human activity. Had he not known the boy to be there, Randy would immediately have smelled out a human presence. He hesitated, then switched on his torch with a gentle pressure of his thumb. There was no startled rustle of movement, no exclamation, to greet the sudden light. Encouraged, he directed the yellow circle of illumination on to the floor in front of his feet and padded softly over to the bed. He stood beside it for some time, quite still, trying to detect some sound from the occupant; but there was nothing, no breath, no movement, nothing to betray a presence except the indefinable awareness of another human body close to his own. The mouth of the cave gradually formed itself into an irregular grey circle.

At last, he lifted the torch and shone it directly on to the bed. All he could see was the surface of a small area of blanket, scarlet wool, ribbed with blue and thin lines of black. Out of relation to its surrounding area it meant nothing. It was impossible to tell whether or not there was a body beneath it. Cautiously, he moved the light up over the blanket, and thought he perceived the humped line of a thigh, a hip. The face sprang out at him with such terrifying abruptness that he almost dropped the torch. As it was, his hand shook so much that the half-perceived features executed a leaping dissolve, melting, then re-forming themselves as he looked at them. He clamped his free hand over the wrist of the hand that held the torch and steadied it.

The face was lit from below and the yellow light seemed to stream up from the chin and over the features into the darkness behind the head. Each projection threw its violent shadow upwards on to the area of flesh above it, the chin shadowing the lips, the nose shadowing the space between the eyes and so on. The cheek bones, particularly, set the eyes

158

deep in impenetrable pockets of shadow. The total effect was bizarre, grotesque even to Randy's steady imagination, and unsettling to his nerves. Then, realising how the trick was played, he raised the torch higher and shone it straight down on to the face. It resolved itself into that of the boy. He lay absolutely motionless under his one blanket, an arm crooked comfortably behind his head. His eyes were wide open and looked straight up into the light. He did not seem in the least dazzled by it or, indeed, surprised by Randy's presence. He stretched his mouth in a smile which showed an even, gleaming row of teeth.

'Hallo, Randy. Have you come to play with me, too?'

'Play with you?'

'Yes. Carter came the other evening. We had a lovely game of pirates. I wondered if you'd come to play a game too, though I don't suppose pirates would be much in your line.'

'No, I don't think they would.'

The eyes slid past the light as if searching behind it for Randy's face.

'I thought not.' He lay still for a moment as if trying to remember something. Then he said,

'You didn't come back this afternoon. I wondered what happened.'

'She was killed.'

'Killed?'

'She ran under a motor bike on the waste ground above the cave and was killed.'

The eyes widened and then drooped half closed again.

'I see. How awful!'

'Yes, wasn't it?'

'Did you see it?'

'Yes.'

'Did the others? Did Todd?'

'Yes, we were all there.'

'Oh. So that's that, isn't it?'

Randy turned away and laid the torch down on the table at the end of the bed.

'Get up,' he said.

The boy obeyed immediately, sliding out from beneath his blanket to stand, thin and childish in his shorts, beside Randy.

'Have you got any candles?'

The boy padded over to the boxes arrayed against the wall. He stooped, rustled among some paper, and came back with the two candles.

'They'll stand in cups,' he said helpfully. 'Cups make quite good candlesticks if you melt some wax in the bottom first to stick the candles in. The only trouble is that it's a bit of a job getting the wax out afterwards. You have to scrape it all out carefully or you get bits of wax floating about when you next use the cup.'

Randy lit one of the candles, stuck it upright in a cup and lit the other from it. The flames rose and fell, flickered a little, and then stood yellow and motionless in the still air. It was surprising how much illumination they gave. Randy sat down on the chair beside the table. He held the second candle upright in his hand, its little tree of light bright and still. He motioned to the boy with a deliberate movement of his left hand.

'Come here,' he said.

The boy looked steadily at him, and then moved two small paces nearer to him on the stone floor.

Randy beckoned again.

'Nearer,' he said.

The boy took two more paces.

Randy raised his left hand and snapped his fingers in front of the boy's face.

'Nearer. Come close to me and stand still.'

The boy came and stood close to his knees. His thin thighs almost touched the material of Randy's trousers.

'Put out your right arm.'

The boy did so.

Deliberately, and very slowly, Randy tilted the candle. The flame guttered, then flared as it caught the edge of the wax. A drop formed, elongated itself, and fell on to the tender white flesh of the boy's inside arm. He stood absolutely motionless, the fingers of his outstretched hand curved open and relaxed. Randy moved the candle a little and tilted it again. A second drop fell, then a third. Soon, a neat row of congealed droplets stood on the boy's arm from the inside of his elbow to the wrist. Randy held the candle upright again, and they looked at the arm together. The boy had not flinched or even drawn in his breath.

Randy put out his left hand, palm outwards.

'Stand still,' he said.

Very slowly, he began to move the candle flame towards the naked skin of the boy's chest. He did it so gently that the flame hardly flickered with the movement. Nearer and nearer it came, Randy's hand grasping the wax cylinder with absolute steadiness. The little yellow light illuminated the pale, taut skin of the boy's chest with a waxy glow, and still he did not move. Just as the flame was about to touch his skin the boy leapt sideways and, as if in the same movement, flung up his arm underneath Randy's wrist. The lighted candle was dashed up and back, and into Randy's face. With a smothered yelp Randy jerked his body backwards and away from the flame, lost his balance, and he and his chair tipped over backwards on to the stone floor. The candle rolled out of his hand and went out.

The boy, dancing up and down like an excited puppy, burst out into high, uncontrollable laughter.

'Oh, you do look funny!' he cried joyfully. 'You do look funny! Was that part of the game too? It's a jolly good game. Do get up, so that we can do it again.'

Randy heaved himself up with the chair clinging to his back like a giant shell. He flung it off, crouched, and threw himself forward. The boy ducked his body beneath the outstretched arm and writhed clear. He darted round the table and crouched over it, his hands flat on the cloth. The remaining candle, illuminating his face from below, turned his face into something resembling a Halloween mask – eye-sockets, nostrils and mouth full of yellow light. Randy swung round to face him. The boy moved his hands closer to the candle so that it stood between his fingers. Randy looked at the candle, then at the boy, and inched forward. He reached the table and shot out his fist in a lightning grab. But he was not quick enough. The boy snatched his hands together round the candle, swept it from the table, and darted towards the back of the cave.

Miraculously, the flame did not go out, although it streamed out flat beside the prancing figure like a banner. Randy grabbed his torch, snapped it on, and its broad beam shot out to illuminate the boy, dancing like an animal against the far wall of the cave. It caught his eyes, then his white teeth, then the gleam of flesh. The pale candle flame was almost swamped in its brighter light. Randy went slowly forward. He held the torch out in front of him as if it were a gun aimed at the boy's eyes. He stumbled over the uneven ground but he held the torch steady, and the boy waited for him with the candle held high above his head. When Randy was within a couple of feet of the now motionless figure he halted, shining the torch straight into the wide unblinking eyes. Then he kicked savagely out and up, carrying his weight well forward with the blow. The arm carrying the candle swooped down, and the flame seared Randy's neck, sizzled across the hair above his ear, and darted away.

Momentarily blinded and off balance, Randy lurched forward against the wall, trying to fend himself off with his free hand. The rough surface scarified the soft skin of his inside wrist and he caught his forehead a stinging blow. He swung himself round, breathing fast and clinging to the torch. The boy seemed to have disappeared. The candle must have gone out this time, he thought – it had made a considerably more effective weapon than he would have imagined possible. Without it, the boy would be helpless. Sooner or later he must be cornered.

Randy stood against the wall and began to swing the arc of light slowly to and fro across the cave like a searchlight. There was no sign of the boy, no glimmer of candlelight.

'You'd better come out,' he said loudly. 'I'll get you sooner or later. You can't get away.'

There was no reply. He repeated his manoeuvre with the torch, searching into every corner as far as the beam of light would carry. There was nothing. He switched it off and listened. The silence was warm and complete. He only heard his own uneven breathing and the blood beating in his head. He tightened his finger on the switch as if it were a trigger.

'You'd better come out. I know exactly where you are. I shall count three, and then I'm coming to get you.'

He paused to listen. There was no sound. He began to count.

'One.'

He waited several seconds, straining his ears with every nerve taut.

'Two.'

Nothing. He waited rather longer this time, then said, 'Three.'

The soft laughter came from his left. He sprang instantly towards it, snapped the torch on, and looked round wildly. The laughter came again, and this time, incredibly, it seemed to come from above his head. He looked up and saw the candle flame, and the yellow face grinning behind it, apparently floating in mid-air in front of and above him. He stared up, incredulous, frightened. The mouth opened and filled with light.

'Come on up – if you want to get me.'

'Where in Heaven's name are you?'

'I thought you knew where I was. Aren't you coming up?

It's quite easy – Carter managed it first go. We played a game up here too, only that was pirates, and this seems to be cops and robbers.' The face inclined a little forward over the flame, the eyebrows raised in two arcs of interrogation. 'Coming?'

Randy shone the torch on to the wall in front of him and the small upper cave, scooped out of the rock, sprang out at him. He swept the light up and down over the surface of the rock and saw the shallow footholds unevenly scarring its surface. He looked at them, then up at the cave and the boy, crouching on the ledge with the bare wall behind and no way out. He began to smile.

'Don't worry,' he said, 'I'm coming.'

At first he could not decide what to do with the torch, since he would need its light when he got up to the boy, and also because it made an excellent weapon. He saw that he would need both hands for the climb, and that he would not be able to manage the torch as well. Eventually he put it in the right-hand pocket of his trousers where it would be within easy reach of his hand and could not fall out on the way up. His trousers hung low on his narrow hips and the torch stuck out rather in the same way that a gun protrudes from its holster. He satisfied himself that it could not drop out and approached the bottom of the wall. The boy crouched motionless on the ledge above, peering down at him. Randy hooked his strong fingers into the first of the holds and began to haul himself up.

It was a surprisingly easy climb. The holds were much easier to grip than had at first appeared, and they were extremely well spaced so that each one fell exactly where it was needed. In a few strong heaves he was almost at the top. He steadied his feet, wishing he were wearing something more suitable than sandals, and prepared for the last pull on to the ledge. He braced himself and put a hand over the edge. Instantly, intense pain shot through the hand and up to the shoulder. He snatched his hand away with a yelp of agony.

'You little bastard! What the bloody hell are you doing?'

He could not see the boy's face because his own was pressed to the surface of the rock. His hand stung abominably.

'If you remember,' said the child's voice with a very unchildlike intonation, 'I've got the candle. It hasn't gone out yet, and there's plenty of it left.'

Randy crooked his arm across his chest and nursed his burned hand. The pain was horrible; nauseating, insulting. For the moment he found himself unable to concentrate on anything else. When, after an unidentifiable lapse of time, it seemed to have become a little more bearable, he was able, with much cursing and wincing, to use the hand to anchor his body fairly securely to the highest of the holds. Then he pulled himself up, resting his feet a foot or so further up the wall. This brought his face abruptly on a level with that of the boy. Randy let himself hang out at the length of his arm. His fingers were hooked strongly round a protruding piece of rock, and his arm muscles were powerful out of all proportion to his build. He swung there, looking at the boy. With his right hand he silently began to edge the torch up and out of his trouser pocket so that it slid forward, cool and heavy, into the palm of his hand. The boy looked at him with gleaming eyes.

'You know, you really can't come up,' he remarked conversationally. 'If you put your hand over the edge again I shall only burn it with the candle like I did last time, so I really wouldn't try it.'

Randy made no answer. Instead, he suddenly swung the torch up high above his head and brought it smashing down. He missed the boy, but he succeeded in hitting the candle with such violence that he not only smashed and extinguished it – he smashed his torch as well. The glass broke with a tinkle and a shower of splinters, and they were in darkness. The impetus of the blow carried Randy forward and then back on his perch. He knew he must fall, but he determined to take the boy with him. He lurched forward and clutched first at the air, and then again at something – an arm, a leg, he could not tell. They fell together, sliding and bumping against the wall. Fortunately the boy's weight, as he fell in Randy's grasp, held them close in to the wall so that they were not flung straight out and back at bodies' length on to the stone floor. They landed, neither uppermost, in a confused embrace.

Immediately they hit the ground the boy slithered away and almost succeeded in freeing himself. But Randy, in agony with his burnt hand, grimly hung on to a fistful of flesh, that of the boy's upper arm, and held tight. They twisted and rolled over each other on the floor, grunting and whistling for breath. Slowly Randy tightened his grip until his fingers seemed to penetrate the flesh and to grind on the fragile bone. The boy writhed his head back, twisting it round, and sank his teeth deep into Randy's shoulder. He bit like a dog, clenching his jaw and hanging on in silence. Randy began to groan. They remained locked together. Randy's nails had torn the flesh of the boy's arm and he could feel a sticky trickle of blood over his hand. The boy made a sound in his throat as if he were being strangled. Suddenly, they let go together, and rolled apart.

Randy lay flat on his back, his knees jerking. His chest felt as if it would burst. He could hear the boy close beside him breathing in quick animal pants. His teeth seemed to be chattering. It was too dark for them to be able to see each other. Randy's hand burned and ached and his shoulder was piercingly painful. He also felt sick when he thought of the sharp little teeth closed on his shoulder. Sodding little bastard, he said weakly to himself, the fucking little savage. The boy crouched, panting and shivering, close behind him in the darkness.

Presently, he heard the boy getting to his feet. The stumbling footsteps crossed the cave, and he heard the slight sound of the blankets on the bed being moved about as the boy lay

166

down and wrapped them round himself. Then there was complete silence. After a while he got up and groped his way towards the entrance of the cave. His body felt stiff and encrusted with dried sweat. As he passed the boy's bed he stopped, and stood still to listen. He could hear the deep even breathing of childhood sleep. He felt that he could lie down beside the boy and instantly fall asleep himself. He stood beside the bed, his own breathing steadying into the rhythm of that of the boy. They seemed to sleep together, one lying among the blankets, the other on his feet.

Todd woke late on Saturday morning to hear their voices below his window. He lay still, covered only by a single sheet. Savory seemed to be explaining something to his mother, for his voice went on and on in a soothing monotony, punctuated by Clare's quick little interjections of assent. Mark had driven back with Mrs Gascoigne late the previous evening. Todd, working in his room, had heard them arrive, but had not gone down to greet them, and by the time they came up he had switched his light off and was pretending to be asleep. For some reason he had not wanted to tackle his mother – or, for that matter, either of them – at that particular moment.

Now he lay flat under his smooth white sheet and watched his light yellow curtains filled with sunshine as he listened to the voices on the gravel below. He turned his head on the pillow to look at the time. A quarter past nine. He kicked over on to his side and humped one knee up towards his chest, luxuriating in the comfort of his bed. He was almost asleep again when his mother came in.

She wore a brief straight dress of pink cotton bound with white, and her dark hair hung down her back in a silky pigtail. She had bound the end with a pink ribbon and her lipstick matched her dress. She came over and stooped to kiss him. Her eyes were bright. He saw the smooth white division of her breasts and wondered if Savory had seen it too.

'Todd darling, how late you are. I saw you were working last night so I didn't come in. Hurry up and come down – we're going to have breakfast in the garden.' She smiled down at him. 'You look marvellous, darling. Brown as a berry, and that gorgeous bleached hair! How I envy you being fair.'

Todd rolled over and stretched his arms high above his head.

'Nice time in London?'

'Marvellous. Tell you about it later. Come on, get up, lazy. We want you at breakfast. Mark's dying to see you. He says he really wants to get to know you this week-end.'

'Does he now. Am I supposed to be flattered?'

'Be whatever you like, darling, only for goodness sake get a move on.'

Todd stretched, and grinned up at her.

'I was awake when you got in last night, but I didn't want to see you.'

She ran a finger down his chest.

'I know, darling. Funny boy.'

'It wasn't only Mark. I didn't want to see you either.'

Her bright enveloping affection seemed to grow even more tender.

'I know. I understand how you felt. Come on down and have some breakfast. I'll do you bacon and egg. Get up, lazy!'

She twitched the bedclothes away and revealed his naked length in the bed.

'Gracious, Todd, I didn't know you slept in the raw! Though I must say I do too in this heat. What a gorgeous boy it is.' Todd pulled at the sheet and she put her hand up to her mouth and giggled like a small girl. 'Don't be an ass, Todd – I've seen it all before, you know.' She went to the door and peeped back at him as she held it half open, still giggling. 'Though you've grown a bit since I last bathed you and put you to bed, I must admit!'

168

He heard her heels tapping away down the passage and her voice, high with happiness, as she called out of the window to Mark in the garden below.

'He's coming at last. I've just managed to drag him out of bed!'

When Todd came down he saw them together on the lawn in wicker chairs, the table between them covered with breakfast things. Mark wore a bleached linen jacket and twill trousers. He looked younger and browner, somehow less formidable than Todd remembered him.

He stood up with his usual precise courtesy to shake hands.

'Good morning, Todd. I was sorry not to see you last night when we arrived, but your mother tells me you were already asleep. We got back later than we had intended.'

'Good morning, sir.'

Todd held the strong fingers briefly in his and felt the alert grey glance on him. He sat down and helped himself to fruit juice.

'Your bacon's on the hot plate, dear. Hurry up or it'll spoil.'

His mother lay back with her coffee. Pale blue smoke curled aromatically from her cigarette. Mark ate a small piece of toast liberally spread with butter and marmalade and watched Todd as he finished his juice and uncovered a substantial plate of bacon, egg, tomatoes and mushrooms.

'A hearty English breakfast, I see,' he commented, wiping his fingers carefully on his napkin. He took a small sip of his coffee and savoured it richly. 'Delicious, Clare, quite delicious. Your touch with coffee verges upon the miraculous, as usual. Try some, Todd.'

'I intend to,' said Todd gravely.

The spectacles beamed jovially upon him as he drank.

'Delicious, isn't it?'

'It is indeed.'

Todd finished his bacon, feeling as he did so that he was doing something rather vulgar. Clare smiled affectionately at them both.

'He's always had a hearty appetite and he's working hard at the moment, so he needs feeding up.'

Todd felt as if she were apologising for his appetite and felt correspondingly embarrassed. Defiantly he helped himself to a large slice of toast and buttered it thickly, and then spooned marmalade on to it. Savory selected an apple from the fruit dish and rubbed it meticulously on his napkin. Then he took a small knife in a leather sheath from his pocket and peeled it with skilful little movements. The peel grew between his fingers into a long curl and Todd watched it, fascinated. When he had finished peeling the apple Savory quartered and cored it, cut it into neat pieces and began to convey them one by one into his mouth. During this operation he gazed about him with a remote and abstracted air, as if he were not eating at all; rather as if he were outwardly occupied with some trivial matter while his mind moved freely among higher preoccupations.

Todd lit a cigarette and lay back in his chair. The sunlight was full on the grass already and the shadow fell around them in a translucent fragility of greens and greys. It was already withdrawing before the sun's increasing strength. Soon, they too would have to retreat, but for the moment they lingered, fed and comfortable, under the trees. Savory lit a small gold-tipped cigarette and looked at Todd in friendly fashion.

'What about our game of golf this morning, Todd? We might get in a few holes before it gets too hot. Your Mama professes to have some shopping to do, and admits that she prefers to go alone. She maintains that the male animal is an encumbrance on such occasions, in spite of its willingness to carry parcels.'

'You go off and have your game,' said Clare lazily from the depths of her chair. She had perched a large flat straw hat on top of her head and with her black rope of hair drawn forward over her shoulder and her bare brown legs she looked like a beautiful Chinese girl. 'Todd needs some exercise. He's been spending too much time at his books.'

'I'd like a game if you would, sir.' Todd turned politely to Savory. He felt his manner was in danger of becoming infected with some of Mark's courtly elaborations. 'There's usually at least a breath of wind on the course, and we should get in a few holes before it gets too hot.'

'As for me,' remarked Savory, laying his finger-tips together in a donnish gesture, 'I do not feel the heat. The hotter it becomes the more I relish it. I think of myself as a desiccated sponge, soaking up sun as a sponge soaks up water.' He paused to consider this image and did not appear altogether satisfied with it. Todd cut in hastily before he could attempt to improve upon it.

'Are you sure you don't mind, Mama?'

'Quite sure, darling. Just try to get back for lunch, about one. I thought we might drive out somewhere for a swim when it gets cooler. Do you swim, Mark?'

'I did when I was young. Now I feel my appearance in a bathing suit would be an affront to the aesthetic sensibilities of my friends and a sad insult to my conception of my own human dignity. But I shall be delighted to accompany you and to watch you disport yourselves.'

He really is unbelievable, thought Todd – until he looked up and saw the formidably intelligent eyes looking at him. They were lit by a wicked, convulsive mirth, and Todd felt sobered, and wary.

Savory drove to the golf club under Todd's directions. He drove magnificently, with a loving understanding of his machine, and Todd's respect grew. They purred out of the small town along the wide winding road and climbed steadily up to the course. As they nosed upwards the countryside fell away below them in a green and golden panorama of fields, hedges and woods, set here and there with little white houses and with toy cattle and sheep on the jig-saw fields. The sky above them was blinding and blue, and crossed only by the long white ribbon left by a silver fish of an aeroplane circling in the sun in vast idle loops.

171

The club house, trim with white boarding and brilliant little flowerbeds arranged in the gravel, was comparatively empty. It was both too early and too hot for the usual Saturday throng of liberated week-end golfers. They were soon out on the immaculate turf carrying their own clubs. Savory's were housed in a well-used bag – there was nothing of the newly-purchased-for-the-occasion look about them. He saw Todd looking at them and, disconcertingly, seemed to catch with uncanny accuracy at his thoughts.

'Yes, I play quite a lot. I have a cottage outside London where I spend most summer week-ends, and I usually get in a Saturday morning's play.'

He strode out well over the grass, his chest open and his arms swinging. He seemed to have shed some of his affectations with his smart city clothes and his horn-rimmed spectacles. He had produced an ancient pair of sun-glasses and a disreputable linen hat which perched oddly on top of his magnificent head. His sleek hair protruded beneath it at the back as if it were painted on to his skull. The effect, combined with the round childish sun-glasses, was endearing, if peculiar. He looked like an eccentric ornithologist, armed with golf clubs instead of field-glasses.

His game proved to be excellent, far superior to Todd's. What he lacked in strength he made up in sheer skill. His putting was unerringly accurate. It soon became obvious that once on the green he was unbeatable. Todd panted along behind, increasingly depressed and dishevelled. The heat bothered him far more than it did Savory, and he was showing dark patches under his arms and a face running with sweat when Mark was still completely cool and unruffled. The man's as dry as a dead stick – he simply doesn't sweat, thought poor Todd, irritably scuffling around in a bunker while Mark stood patiently on the green waiting for him like a meditative stork. He was more than grateful when Savory said,

'Let's sit down for a bit in the rough over there. It's getting

172

too warm for striding around in the sun. You play a decent game, Todd.'

'I've been playing a ghastly one today,' burst out Todd. He kicked crossly at his ball, and it bumped gently into the hole. 'I don't know what's the matter with me. I'm not usually as bad as this.'

'You're not bad at all,' said Mark serenely, leading the way into the rough grass. 'With practice you could be really good. I play extremely well, that's all, and you have allowed yourself to become ruffled. Foolish, dear boy. Very foolish.'

That completely took the wind out of Todd, and he plumped down into the grass beside Savory's long figure feeling at a considerable disadvantage. Savory selected a blade of grass and put it between his teeth. He chewed delicately at it, his ridiculous hat tilted well forward over his face so that Todd could only see the dark shadow of his sun-glasses and the rhythmic movement of his jaw as he chewed. Presently he said,

'Your Mama seemed quite pleased that we should come out here for a game this morning. Why was that?'

Todd shrugged. Savory supplied the answer himself.

'Could it be that she wanted us to get to know each other better?'

Todd found this so exquisitely embarrassing that he rolled over on to his face in the grass.

Savory calmly went on,

'That, of course, is absurd. One cannot manufacture a relationship. If you and I are to achieve any kind of understanding it will not be due to anyone else's manipulation of the situation.'

This was plain speaking. Todd cocked his head on to his arm and listened.

'You must know that I wish to marry your mother?'

'I had guessed something of the sort,' Todd agreed guardedly.

173

'Very well. That being so, it seems to me important that I should have some idea of your feelings upon the matter.'

Todd said, perhaps with some idea of gaining time,

'Do my feelings really matter?'

'Of course they do,' said Savory energetically. 'Be sensible, dear boy, and try to use your considerable intelligence. Your mother is a very sensitive and affectionate person. She is a widow and you are her only son. For a good many years you have supplied her with an object for her affections. She has lavished her devotion upon you. Now you are mature, and you are about to leave school, doubtless for a university career of some distinction. And then? You will leave this rather suburban little town and settle elsewhere, probably in London. In time you will no doubt gather unto yourself a wife, a family, a home of your own. Your Mama is an intelligent woman; she must have foreseen all this. She is considering re-marriage; now that her duties towards you have been discharged she feels herself free to do so. Indeed, she must see it as the only sensible course she can adopt. Nevertheless, she will consider you in her choice of a new mate. Your approval will be vital. She is devoted to you – I have occasionally thought too devoted, although I have no doubt that I can modify her devotion by channelling a certain portion of it in my own direction. But if she thinks you do not approve of her choice she will unhesitatingly reject me. This is what I wish to avoid. It is essential to my interests, and to hers, that we gain your approval: more – I might even say your warm commendation.'

He paused. Todd rolled over and sat up. He felt that a recumbent posture was not sufficiently formal for the reception of such confidences. He hooked his arms round his knees and pondered. Savory gazed serenely ahead, chewing his piece of grass.

Todd said,

'You have been very frank. May I be the same?'

A grave inclination of the head was his answer.

'You have told me that you wish to marry my mother, and I have reason to think that she is willing to marry you.'

'You have?'

'Yes. I think you are right. She is too close to me – she makes demands—'

He stopped. Again the stately inclination of the head.

'I assume she must be fond of you – that she likes you, in fact. Her experience with my father must surely have cured her of wanting to marry someone completely unsuitable.'

'It was not, I gather, a happy marriage?'

'It certainly was not.' Todd spoke with bitter emphasis, remembering the quarrels, stifled in his presence, the long absences, the sustained outbursts of hysterical weeping.

'So I had thought.' Savory's voice held a certain note of gratification. 'He was not, of course, at all the right type of person for your mother. She needs attention, protection, a certain quality of – what shall I call it? Insensitivity? Let us just say that she can do and say things which should not be taken completely at their face value.'

'Anyway,' Todd persisted, 'I think she's willing to marry you. What I want to know is, do you love her?'

It sounded hideous, and in the vilest of taste, but he felt better for having said it. Savory stopped chewing his grass and turned his face towards Todd. The sun-glasses, by concealing his eyes, made his face peculiarly expressionless.

'Do I love her?' Savory suddenly rumbled and shook all over with a vast subterranean chuckle which he cut off as abruptly as it had begun. He waved a deprecating hand. 'Forgive me. I should not be amused. Your amazing maturity of approach to many subjects leads me to forget that you are, after all, only eighteen.' He composed himself. 'Do I love her? Love does not, I emphatically repeat, not, enter into the matter at all. That emotion, with all its irrationality, its ability to confuse the issue, to cloud the judgement, is totally foreign to me. I would not do your mother the disservice of loving her. I like her, I admire her. What is most important, I covet her.'

'Covet her?' Todd was startled.

'Covet her.'

'Why? To go to bed with?'

'That too, if she insists.'

'She probably will,' said Todd, driven to crudity.

'In that respect, as in all others, I shall comply with her wishes. Physically, she is a most desirable woman.'

Todd was too dumbfounded to attempt an answer.

Savory continued, his serenity unimpaired,

'When, however, I say that I covet her, I mean something completely different. I have wanted her for my wife since I first met her, twenty years ago. She has all the things I want, and all the qualities I wish to possess in a woman: intelligence, wit, gaiety, courage, acerbity; she stimulates me, we sharpen our minds one upon the other. She has abundant warmth and life, and I need to be in constant contact with these things. I need to warm my hands before her fire, to prolong my life through hers.' He blinked, and clenched his hands upon his knees.

They sat together in silence for a while.

'And her?' ventured Todd at last.

Savory unclenched his fingers and made a stiff, but expansive and expressive gesture.

'She shall have everything she wants. I have waited a long time for my opportunity, and I shall make the most of it. She shall have money, clothes, a fine house, all the gaiety and luxury she could ask for. More; total freedom. My demands shall be minimal – merely, a small proportion of her charm, her wit, her good humour to be expended upon me. She will find it easy, delightful, to do that. I can give her all she wants, and that will make her agreeable, faithful, compliant, within reason. She will have too much to lose were she not so. She will be happy, Todd, I promise you that. I understand her, and I know how to make her happy. You need have no doubts on that score.'

In spite of his prejudices, Todd began to find this magnificent. He said thoughtfully,

'It sounds to me as if you are buying her.'

'That, dear boy, is exactly what I am doing,' Savory agreed, with the nearest approach to eagerness Todd had yet seen in him. 'She is an object which I dearly long to possess, and I am willing to give everything I have in order to do so. My only fear is that it will not be enough.'

'I wouldn't worry too much. I imagine it will.'

'You really think so?'

'Well, you must admit, it's a steepish price to pay.'

'I am convinced it is worth it.'

'And how much of all this,' continued Todd, 'do you intend to tell the lady?'

'Not a word – not a word!' Savory was genuinely shocked. 'Women are romantics, and your mother more than most. I shall offer her,' he said with dignity, 'my love, my devotion, my protection. My worldly goods—' he coughed delicately. 'Well, she knows they are considerable, and that they are a necessary adjunct to my affections. You think she will accept?'

'She will,' said Todd with conviction.

Savory drew a deep breath of satisfaction.

'I am glad to have your assurance. I confess that I had hoped so. I could not fail to notice some indications of partiality – even of affection. But she is mercurial, hard to interpret in some moods. I am much relieved.'

'So that just leaves me.'

Savory gave the impression that he was marshalling his forces for the second phase of the battle.

'I have been completely frank,' he said. 'I have placed myself at your mercy, within your power even. I rely upon your discretion.'

'You may do so,' said Todd with dignity.

177

'And your approval?'

'That is another matter.'

'It is indeed. You require time?'

'I do.'

'May one inquire how much time?'

Todd thought it over.

'A week – ten days. Until my exams are over.'

'They are next week?'

'Yes.'

'It gives me time to consolidate my position. I will not ask her to marry me until I have your approval – or otherwise. A fair bargain?'

'Very fair.'

'You understand that I shall ask her in any case?'

'I do.'

'I must take my chance.'

'Of course.'

'And meanwhile you will not attempt to prejudice my case?'

'I will say and do nothing to further or to prejudice it.'

On this stately note they paused. Todd felt they should sing a few bars of the National Anthem – at least shake hands. Savory, however, made no move. He sat still in the grass beside Todd. After a moment he shook with a brief resumption of his curious chuckling.

'What's amusing you?' asked Todd.

'Nothing, nothing. Just a thought. Shall we resume our game?'

They finished the game in silence. Savory finished at the eighteenth by sinking his putt in a brilliant four, and Todd's game improved to become positively respectable. They drove home, still in silence.

Mrs Gascoigne met them on the lawn. She had pinned her hair up and looked coolly beautiful.

'Did you have a good game, darling?'

She spoke to Todd, but her glance slid past him to Savory,

standing behind him in the shade of the house. Todd leaned
forward to kiss her cheek.

'Very good, thank you, Mama.'

She smiled contentedly, but he knew that the smile, like
the inquiring look in her brilliant eyes, was not for him, but
for Mark, chequered and almost invisible in the green patterns
of the shade.

'Bless me, Father, for I have sinned,' said Randy, smelling
the mothballs on the dark serge and feeling the hard edge of
the stool biting into his knees. He tried again.

'Bless me, Father, for I have sinned. Since my last
confession—'

'Yes?'

The thin face behind the chequered grill turned placid inquiring eyes to him.

'Which was two weeks ago—'

The face dipped a little in approval, inclining itself into
the brown shadow as if into water.

'I have neglected my prayers, I have sinned against charity,
I have lied.'

His mouth was dry. He was humiliated and hurt that he
should have to tell these things to the half-seen face behind
the grill.

'And I have sinned against chastity.'

The face waited for his elucidation. It did not come.

'With a woman?'

Randy thought of Daphne, of the girl in the cinema opening her sticky thighs to his hand. Could you call them women?
Technically they were.

'Yes.'

'A married woman? Your fiancée?'

'Just a girl.'

The low voice, disinterested, bent only on assessing the
extent of the misdemeanour, persisted.

'Was the act completed?'

'No.'

Shame made his mouth drier still, so that he had to suck in his cheeks in an attempt to collect saliva in order to speak.

'I see. Did this occur often? Once? Twice? Many times?'

'Twice,' he said quickly. He had long decided not to count anything that involved the areas above the waist. Breasts, he had decided, were permissible.

'I see. You must try to avoid the occasions of temptation. These habits can easily lead to serious sin. Is that all?'

'I have also sinned against chastity with myself. By touch.'

He could not bring himself to pronounce the word 'masturbation'. In any case it could not do justice to the terrible need which had driven him to this insufficient easing of himself.

'That, too, is a dangerous habit,' said the serene voice. 'One which you must try to overcome.' There was a pause. The face dipped again and Randy glimpsed the hands linked loosely and white on the dark serge. 'You are obviously unhappy and in need of an outlet for your physical urges. But these are not the means of finding satisfaction.'

Randy listened, hoping for something which might supply him with an answer, knowing it would not come. There was a gentle sigh, a movement of the head.

'You must avoid the occasions of sin, and try to occupy your mind with other matters before you sleep at night. Keep up your prayers and frequent the Sacraments. For your penance—'

Randy recited his act of contrition. He looked at the figure on the cross. That head, too, seemed to be dipped forward into the brown shadow of the wooden box in which he knelt.

'Go in peace and pray for me.'

He went out. A woman passed him and knelt where he had knelt. The murmuring began again.

He crossed the aisle to kneel before the statue of Mary and the Holy Child. Their faces were full of placid serenity. He recited his penance, shaping the words with his lips. The absolution would not work if he merely went over the words in his mind. When he had finished, he knelt on, looking up at the figures. They beamed at him, remote, and sinless. 'Help me,' he prayed.

When he got home his aunt and uncle had begun their meal. He saw to his disgust that it consisted of corned beef and salad. They looked up at him as he came in, and he thought they seemed to draw together as if seeking mutual protection. He sat down and helped himself to meat and salad. They sat together, not eating, trying to look as if they were not watching him. He began to fork the food rapidly into his mouth, sprawling forward a little over the table. When he reached out with his fork to spear a tomato and convey it to his plate they shrank back as if in fear of physical violence.

He peeled a banana, pulling the skin off and dropping it on to his plate of half-eaten meat and salad. He ate it slowly, looking round him at the tall room with its great windows where long red velvet curtains were half drawn across the glass to keep out the sun. It was a fine room with a magnificent ceiling, moulded into swathes and loops of white plaster. But the paint was dark, the furniture massive and cumbrously uncomfortable. It was a place designed for stately family repasts which now housed only the three of them, eating their meals in glum hostility. Beyond the windows lay the garden, uncared for, rank in the hot sun. A half-ruined greenhouse glittered among dark laurels and a sundial struggled to keep its head above the surging grass on the lawn. Apple trees, so long unpruned that they had grown into fantastic shapes, had their trunks swathed in ivy and other vegetation up to a height of several feet. Mr and Mrs Johns had long ago retreated in the face of such unbridled fertility, and all this fecundity had over-burgeoned and had destroyed itself. The house stood among its trees and bushes like a stranded ship driven upon rocks. It survived, but only just. It was enormous, empty. Only a small corner here and there was inhabited. Most of its rooms housed nothing but old furniture, and unidentifiable

181

and long-forgotten faces peered forlornly out from behind dusty glass. Randy hated it.

He finished his banana and pushed back his chair. Mrs Johns looked quickly at her husband and then spoke, almost nervously, to him.

'I wanted to ask you – your exams are this coming week, aren't they?'

'Yes. Why?'

'I really feel, dear, that we should have a little talk.'

'What about?'

'Well, about your future. What happens next.'

'Go on.'

'The point is that I don't think we can afford to go on keeping you any longer. I don't want you to think it's just because you've been taking money, or because of what happened the other night. It's just that – well, things have become very difficult for us, and if you get this scholarship and want to go to the university—'

Confronted by Randy's cold eyes, her voice tailed away. She swallowed, and looked down at her hands. Randy tilted his chair on to its back legs and rocked himself backwards and forwards.

'You don't have to give me any reasons,' he said. 'You don't want me here any longer, and I don't want to stay. So far as I'm concerned, the thing is settled. I'll stay until I've taken the exam.' He got up. 'After that, you won't see me for dust.'

He went out and shut the heavy door on them, together at the long, empty table. He went upstairs and along the passage to his room. It was full of sunshine, but even in the full yellow glare it felt chilly. The ceiling was enormously high, so that the heat seemed to rise and become trapped in the dusty air just below its cornice. He lay down on the bed and shut his eyes. The house was completely silent. Through the blur of his lashes he could see the green-laden branches of a tree stretched across the window. He felt comfortable and relaxed. After a while he took a book from the pile on the table beside his bed, propped himself on his elbow, and began to read.

The football results came to an end and Daphne reached up to switch over to music. Mrs Carter picked up the paper. Randy had seen it, the blurred pictures of the two youths on the front, the enormously enlarged face of the girl, enigmatic between two slabs of straight hair.

'Isn't it awful about that poor child?' Mrs Carter shook her head over the pictures, lingering on the headlines with ready sympathy. 'Poor little kid – I don't know what her mother was thinking of, letting her play about near that quarry all by herself. A little kid like that! Those awful motor bikes ought to be banned. It sometimes gets me really worried about Gordon having one, seeing things like that.'

'Oh, Gordon's safe enough,' said Carter carelessly.

'Is that the girl killed on the waste ground near the quarry?' asked Randy.

'Yes – isn't it dreadful? Right near where you go and play your games, whatever they are. I wonder you didn't see it happen. Poor little thing, one of them ran her down and killed her. The boy broke his leg. It says here she ran straight under his wheel. A likely story! Why on earth should she be running about without seeing where she was going in a great open space like that. He was going too fast, more like, and got out of control, and ran her down. It really makes me angry, that sort of thing. I hope he gets sent to prison for a good long spell, that's all. It says here he's been charged with manslaughter. Murder, more like.'

'What were they doing out there on motor bikes, anyway?' asked Daphne. She had been painting her nails and was peering over her mother's shoulder as she waited for them to dry.

'It says they were having a race,' said Mrs Carter, looking down the column. 'A race! I ask you!'

'She looks a funny sort of kid,' Daphne studied the picture. 'Sort of sensible and grown up. Not the type to go running under motor bikes.' She turned to Randy. 'Don't you think so?'

Randy had started on a banana.

'I don't know,' he said. 'I haven't really looked at the paper.' He bit off the end of the banana. 'Perhaps something frightened her and she lost her head. After all, she was only a kid.'

'Frightened her? But what could have?'

He shrugged.

'I don't know. I wasn't there, was I? Perhaps she saw something.'

'Perhaps she saw you, hiding in the grass.'

'You never know – perhaps she did!'

They laughed together.

Carter said, avoiding Randy's eye,

'Did the two boys see anything?'

'It says they were too busy trying to avoid hitting the girl once they'd seen her to notice anything else,' said Mrs Carter. She turned to the back page to finish the story. 'It's a shame! She was an only one, too, and her mother says she was ever so sensible and good. I don't know what we're coming to, I really don't.'

Carter pushed his cup forward and she poured him more tea.

'Where're you going tonight?' she asked him.

'We thought we'd go to the cinema with Daphne and Anne,' said Randy. He tried to avoid Daphne's eye.

'I can't think what you want to go to the cinema for on an evening like this. It's far too hot.' Mrs Carter blew out her cheeks in a parody of exhaustion. 'Why don't you go swimming instead.'

'Because we went this afternoon,' said Carter.

The noise of Gordon's motor bike roared through the open window again.

'Oh, that boy!' Mrs Carter put her hands to her head. 'Every evening it's the same. I can't think what he keeps doing to it.'

'Taking it to bits and putting it together again just for the hell of it,' grinned Carter. 'Come on, Randy, let's go and have a word with the old boy.'

In the yard Gordon raised a filthy and smiling face from the machine and shouted something above the din. The heat in the small garden seemed to dance with the noise. Tools and mysterious pieces of machinery lay on the grass. Gordon switched off the engine and wiped his hands on an oily rag.

'Hallo – come to have a look?' He stood back and surveyed the gleaming machine with pride. 'Lovely, isn't she? Going like a bird at the moment. I was just thinking of taking her out for a spin. Want to come, Randy?'

'No thanks, I can't. We're going to the pictures.' But Randy walked up to the machine and looked at it with interest. 'Bloody great things, aren't they?'

'Not half.' Gordon aimed a loving kick at the front tyre.

'Pretty dangerous, I should imagine.'

'Not if they're handled right. Safe as houses if you know how. It's only the half-baked idiots or the speed merchants who come to grief. You're a lot safer than you would be in a car if you know how to handle them.'

Randy went on looking at the machine.

'Read about those two who ran that girl down near the old quarry?'

Gordon clicked his tongue against the roof of his mouth.

'Bloody idiots. That's the sort I mean. Riding machines far too heavy for them on that sort of ground. They were asking for it. I've seen it up there. You couldn't keep proper control of a kid's tricycle over ground like that at any sort of speed, let alone one of those. Poor kid – she looked a decent sort. Bloody murderers, I'd say.'

'What do you suppose actually killed her?' Randy ran his

hand over the massive front tyre. Carter watched him intently. Gordon shrugged.

'Going by the paper, I'd say the front wheel hit her and the impact threw the thing off balance. She fell, and it came down on top of her. It was bad luck, though. She had a fair chance of only getting a couple of broken legs, but she fell crooked and the machine crushed her pelvis and did some sort of internal damage. She was dead when the ambulance got to her. Bloody shame. They shouldn't sell these big machines to anyone under twenty-one or who hasn't had at least a year's experience riding the things. They're lethal in the wrong hands. It was odd, though – she had plenty of time to get away. Must have caught her foot or something. Though I've seen some odd things.'

Randy swung his leg over the machine and sat on the saddle. He put his hands on the handlebars and gripped them tight as if about to drive away.

'Odd things?' he inquired.

'Pretty odd. I once saw a chap being chased by one of these. That was in a field too, plenty of space. He just couldn't get away. It seemed to go on for ages. Whichever way he ran the thing went after him. The bloke riding it said afterwards he just couldn't control it. It had a will of its own, he said, and it went after the chap as if it was going to do murder.'

'Was he killed?' asked Carter.

'Oh no, he was O.K. He got behind a tree, and the machine crashed into the trunk and just folded up. The driver was pretty smashed up, though. Concussion and a broken nose and his face was not a very nice sight. He swore he'd never ride one again.'

'Sounds as if something like that happened to that girl,' remarked Randy. He turned his hands on the handlebars. 'Massive brutes. I certainly wouldn't like to have one after me.'

Gordon laughed.

'Well, I don't suppose you ever will. Pity you can't come

186

for a spin. I'd like to show you how sweetly she can go. Perhaps some other time.'

Reluctantly Randy swung himself off the machine and followed Carter round the side of the house and into the road.

The film was a Western, slow-moving and beautifully set against golden prairie lands and huge skies. Daphne sat modestly upright and gazed at the screen with prim attention. Her profile, serene in the half light, looked remote, even beautiful. Randy looked surreptitiously at her cheek, her throat, and the soft curve of her breast. He knew by the tightening of her mouth and jaw that she was aware of him. He lit a cigarette, replaced his lighter in his pocket, and pressed his upper arm against hers. She did not respond, but neither did she draw away. He put his hand on her thigh and tightened his fingers. She drew her breath in a little gasp. He could feel her muscles tighten under her skirt. Randy drew his hand back as if he had been stung, remembering the flesh and fragile bone of the boy's arm grinding under his fingers. He felt sick.

Above him, on the brilliant rectangle on the darkness, guns flashed, horses reared, men rolled on the ground and died in every conceivable attitude of agony. Randy sat still and sweated under his clothes. Daphne had drawn herself away to the very edge of her seat and sat stiff with mortification, but she no longer concerned him. He wondered, in fear, whether every physical contact, every touch of flesh on flesh, would, for him, be for ever tainted by the violence of that futile struggle with the iron fragility of the boy's body. The notion terrified him. He locked his fingers round his knees and sat still, trying not to contemplate the appalling extent of the damage the boy had done to him.

In spite of Savory's visit, Todd shut himself up and worked all day on Sunday. Occasionally he heard Mark and his mother in the garden, and he stopped for twenty minutes to eat the cold meal she brought him on a tray. Apart from this short break he kept himself steadily at it all day.

When his mother came up and crept in to see him soon after nine he had more or less given up because he was unable to absorb another word.

He blinked at her as she came in. His eyes seemed to be out of focus so that her figure, outside the circle of his lamplight, had furry edges, and her face, in reality so vivid, had lost all its definition. She came and stood beside him as he looked blearily out of the light at her.

'Still at it? Darling, you really must stop now. Twelve hours is enough for anyone. You'll overdo it, you know, and that's as bad as not doing anything at all.'

He pushed his books and papers away and yawned prodigiously. His scalp prickled. He put his hands up and scratched his head vigorously, feeling the bleached hair brittle against his skin.

'I'm stopping now. I can't read another word. Has he gone?'

'Mark? Yes, a few minutes ago. He wanted to say good-bye, but I persuaded him not to. I knew you wouldn't want to see him. Don't scratch your head like that, Todd – anyone would think you'd got fleas.'

'It helps me to relax.'

'Oh, come on, big boy, I'll stroke it for you. Lie back.'

He tilted his head back in the chair and she went round behind him. She began to stroke his hair back from his forehead to the nape of his neck with long firm strokes. He could feel the tension running out of him.

'Lovely,' he said, with his eyes shut.

Her fingers went on, strong and rhythmical.

'You've done it often enough for me when I've been nervy and tense. It works, doesn't it?'

'It's marvellous.'

'It's nice to be just us again,' she said after a pause. 'I love having Mark here, of course, but it's nice when he's gone, too.'

'Darling Clare!' he said, laughing at her. 'I had the impression you doted on the man.'

'Oh, I do. But all the same—'

She left the sentence unfinished. He wriggled round to squint up at her.

'Don't jump around like that. You're meant to be relaxing.' She went on with her stroking. 'Did you really enjoy your game yesterday?'

'I told you I did. He plays damn good golf.'

'Oh,' she said, a little disconcerted. 'Does he?'

'Yes. Much better than mine. He beat me hollow.'

She gave the impression of trying another tack.

'What did you talk about?'

'Darling Mama, one doesn't really talk when one's playing with a chap as good as Savory. One concentrates on one's own miserable game and tries to pick up a few tips for improving it.'

She gave his hair an exasperated tug.

'Oh Todd, you wretched creature. You know what I mean.'

'Yes, I do. You want to know if we talked about you.'

'Well, why not?'

'Why not indeed?'

'Did you?'

'Of course.'

'What did he say?'

'Curious, aren't you?'

'Oh come on, Todd – tell me, or I really will pull your hair!'

'He said all sorts of charming things, from which I gather that he intends to offer you his hand and heart.'

She stopped stroking his hair and came round to stand beside him. She looked earnestly at him.

'Did he say that?'

'Yes. Of course, I can't say when he'll actually make you the offer – he doesn't strike one as a creature given to mad impulses, does he? But he made it quite clear that sooner or later he will offer you his all.'

She clasped her hands loosely in front of her body and went on looking at him.

'I thought so,' she said, brooding on it, 'but he hasn't actually said anything, and I couldn't be sure.'

'Well, you are sure now, darling, so you'd better start thinking about your answer, hadn't you?'

She looked closely at him.

'I say, Todd, are you supposed to be telling me this?'

'Telling you what?'

'That he's going to ask me to marry him.'

He shrugged.

'He didn't actually make me promise not to. He's probably relying on me being a little gentleman. He's a model of discretion himself, so he probably thinks I am too.'

'Thank goodness you're not. What else did he say?'

'Oh, all sorts of nice things about your character. He thinks you're a splendid person. Wit, courage, gaiety – I really can't remember all the nice things he mentioned.'

'Did he now!'

'He also made it clear that you'll be leading a life of some luxury. He must be pretty well off, the wily old bird.'

'Oh, he is. But I've got a bit of my own, you know, Todd. Guy was doing pretty well by the time he died, and I got the lot. I don't do too badly.'

'I know you don't, darling. After all, quite a bit of it rubs off on to me, doesn't it. But this would be in a different class altogether. House down here, flat in town, servants, expensive holidays, all the clothes and fripperies you want – it's worth thinking about.'

'I suppose it is. He was pretty frank, wasn't he?'

'He was. I was surprised.'

'I'm not.'

'What do you mean?'

'Oh, it's easy to see what he's up to,' she said impatiently.

'He's trying to get you on to his side. He couldn't tell me all this directly, so he told you.'

'Knowing I'd pass it on?'

'Exactly.'

'Like I said – he is a wily old bird.'

'He is. He must want me pretty badly.'

'Oh, he does.'

She frowned at him.

'Did he happen to mention anything about love?'

'No, but I did.'

' "Sir, do you love my mother as a man should love the woman he hopes to make his wife?" '

'Yes.'

'Don't tell me he professed passionate and undying love.'

'He did not. He said, so far as I can remember, that he wishes to warm his hands at your flame.'

'Good heavens. How extraordinary.'

'Well, are you going to let him?'

'Let him what?'

'Warm his hands and so forth.'

'That, dear boy, is what I am trying to decide.'

They laughed together.

'How I loathe being called "dear boy",' remarked Todd.

'Oh, it's just one of his mannerisms. He's pure Victoriana in some ways. I don't think he listens to himself any more.'

'If he did, he wouldn't do it.'

'However. To return to our muttons,' said Clare after a pause. 'What am I going to do?'

'Act according to the dictates of your heart, dear Mama.'

'Oh, shut up,' she said absently. 'The dictates of my heart don't come into it, as you very well know. Did he try to get you to do any pleading for him?'

'Oh no. He was the soul of honour. He spoke of your deep affection for me, the only son of his mother, and she a widow, and all that. He seemed to think you would do whatever suited me, so he made me promise not to prejudice your decision either way.'

'Good Lord! What a man. Did you promise?'

'I did.'

'Well, you haven't done any prejudicing so far, I'll give you that.'

'He also said that he wouldn't pop the question until I'd told him which way I was voting – for, or against.'

'I see. Poor old Todd. So it all depends on you.'

'So he seems to think. I forbore to remark that you would probably make up your own mind irrespective of my feelings in the matter. That would have shattered his illusions about our beautiful relationship somewhat too rudely.'

Suddenly serious, she said,

'You know, that's not altogether true. If you're dead against me marrying him I shan't do it. However much I want all these things he's offering me I'm not going to risk losing you, Todd.'

'How touching, darling. By the way, can we clear up one small point? I presume you're not in love with him?'

'No, I'm not. I was in love with Guy, God help me, so I know what I'm talking about. But I like him; he amuses me. Our minds work the same way. That's enough for me. And I'm tired of being on my own, Todd, I really am. I'm only forty-three, and I know I'm still attractive. I'm wasting time.'

'Savory thinks you're attractive, too,' he said calculatingly.

'Does he?'

'I think he wants you for other purposes besides – well, warming his hands at your flame and so on. Perhaps just warming his hands, let's say.'

She flushed an ugly pink which made her look old and raddled.

'Need you be so crude?'

'I thought perhaps it might be as well if you were to realise fully what you're letting yourself in for. I don't suppose

192

there'll be any separate bedrooms stuff for him. He's been a bachelor long enough.'

'All right, Todd – you've made yourself quite clear.'

'Good.'

She looked down at her hands. Her thin fingers moved restlessly, turning a fine gold bracelet round and round on her wrist.

'Damn this tan. It makes me look like a gipsy. What am I going to do, Todd?'

'How should I know? I promised not to prejudice you either way, remember?'

'Don't be an idiot. Tell me what you really think about it.'

'But I can't. I don't know what you're feeling, how badly you want a husband, any husband, how much you want to get away from here, what your real feelings are about Savory. How can I?'

'You can try. You must understand a bit of what I feel.'

'Well, I don't.'

'What about Mark, then? You must know how you feel about him.'

'Oh, I do. I think he's amusing, and clever, and witty. But then I'm not thinking about marrying him.'

She moved away from him and went to the window. She leaned on the sill to look out at the stifling darkness. She said over her shoulder,

'If I marry him, will you come with us on our honeymoon?'

'Come with you?'

'Yes. He'll want to get married at once, I can feel it. He'll want us to go away this summer. I can easily say that I won't go unless you come too.'

Todd was profoundly shaken.

'But darling! Do you think—'

'I don't think anything,' she said impatiently. 'I just want you to come with us.'

'I can't,' he said flatly. 'I won't. I simply don't want to.'

'You must, Todd. I shan't ask you to do anything else. We were going to have a holiday together, weren't we? Well, this will be it. Mark will be there, but he won't make that much difference. I shan't let him.'

'Not even on your honeymoon?'

'For heaven's sake, Todd, I'm not a blushing bride.'

'And Savory's no spring chicken either?'

'Exactly.'

'What if he refuses?'

'Then I shall turn him down.'

'Just for the sake of having me with you on this damn bridal spree? I just don't understand. Why does it matter so much?'

He was exasperated, but there was more to it than that. He felt menaced, as if his mother and, through her, Savory, were trying to draw him into their orbit. Once in, he felt, with a sudden sense of panic, he would not be able to free himself. He looked at his mother in fear and hostility.

'If you won't come,' she said, 'I shall tell him about the quarry.'

For a moment he did not understand what she was talking about.

'The quarry?'

'Yes.'

'But what can you tell him? There's nothing to tell.'

'Oh yes there is,' she said contemptuously. 'You're up to something which means a lot to you and your nasty little friends. I don't know what it is because I've never bothered to find out. But it wouldn't be difficult. I'd only have to drop a hint or two to Mark, and he'd be on to you like a shot. He's a curious sort of bloke – he just loves a mystery. He was interested that evening when he first came and you came back with the other two. I haven't encouraged him since, but it wouldn't be difficult. And you wouldn't like him to go poking his nose into whatever it is, would you?'

194

I damn well wouldn't, thought Todd. And she's quite capable of it.

'Go ahead and tell him, then,' he said idly. 'I've told you before it's not important. You're too bloody dramatic, darling – building up big mysteries for yourself. What on earth could I be "up to" as you so elegantly put it, that I wouldn't want Savory, or anyone else for that matter, to know about?'

'I don't know,' she said cunningly. 'But I could find out.'

'I'd love to know what you think's going on down there,' he remarked, testing her.

'I can think of a dozen things. I know you, darling, you're capable of almost anything.'

'We both are,' he said without thinking.

'Aren't we?'

'Blackmail included.'

She made him a little bow. It reminded him of Savory and, at a remove, of the boy.

'I admit it. Pure blackmail. But it's quite simple – you come with us, and I'll keep your boyish secret, whatever it is, and fend Mark off if he starts showing signs of interest. After all, darling, you get your holiday, and I won't let him get in the way and spoil it. It'll be just us, really, like we planned it. We could go to France, Italy, Spain – anywhere. Mark can afford it. We'll have a marvellous time. I'll make it worth your while.'

As he considered it she went on watching him, pleating a fold of his yellow curtain round and round her wrist.

'All right,' he said at last. 'I don't mind.'

She was not deceived.

'Promise?' she said. 'It's a real promise? Hope to die?'

'Promise. Hope to die.'

Instantly she came to him. She put her arms round him and rubbed her cheek against his shoulder.

'Darling Todd,' she said.

'Darling Clare,' he said wearily.

'Good boy now?'

'Good now.'

She linked her wrists behind his head and smiled up at him. He felt the length of her body against his.

'I'll make it lovely for you,' she said. 'Promise I will. It'll be just like we said.'

He held her, betrayed, and very tired.

Much later he got out of bed, dressed, and went to the cave alone. He thought at first of taking his mother's car, but eventually, afraid that the noise would wake her, he got his bicycle out of the garage and wheeled it quietly over the grass verge of the drive and out into the road. The moon was high over the trees and everything showed up with almost daylight clarity. He got on to his bicycle and rode quickly away, running easily down the long hill into the town and along the silent high street, past the houses and shops leaning together, masked by one another's shadows, and out on to the road to the quarry. He hardly seemed to use any effort in pushing the bicycle along. He seemed to float over the smooth surface of the road as if he were being towed over water.

As usual, there was no wind – not the slightest breath of it. The only movement was his own, and that of the air he displaced as he skimmed along. He saw his own hands and forearms, the skin silvered by the moonlight. The landscape through which he rode, ordinary enough in daylight, was much dramatised by the moon. Trees and houses became humped shapes menacing him like illustrations from a child's book of fairy tales. The open ground, when he came out upon it, looked like a strange sea ridged or pitted with motionless waves. It was all unreal, theatrical, slightly absurd. Todd felt that he must keep a firm hold upon his imagination in order not to be seduced by it; but nevertheless, it affected him. He caught his breath in unwilling surprise when he stood on the edge of the quarry and looked down into the gully below. Everything stood motionless and drained of colour. Silver bushes sprouted, glistening, from silver earth, and from their feet black shadows spilled on the ground like ink. The path below him crawled down over the cliff face like a runnel of fire. It was a fairy landscape, designed to appeal to a child's fantasy of fairyland. Todd was almost afraid to put his foot on the path in case it should peel away from the rock like a strip of silver paper and float away into the valley perhaps taking him with it and casting him into that intimidating landscape of silver bushes and black shadows.

When he actually made the descent he was surprised to find that it was extremely difficult for him to climb down that altered path. Distances were telescoped or fantastically extended, obstacles, enlarged by their shadows, looked enormous, even insurmountable. It was a dream country where things moved which were ordinarily not capable of movement and where his arms and legs seemed weighted with lead. As he clambered painfully down his sense of unreality increased until it became oppressive. The silver light became extremely trying to his eyes, and it made him climb so clumsily that he repeatedly tore his skin on objects which he did not even see until the damage was done. By the time he reached the ledge of rock and stopped to rest with his body pressed close to the reassuring hardness of the stone, he was tense and exhausted. He almost determined to go back without going into the cave at all. But something, probably sheer habit directing the movements of his body, made him step sideways and then forwards into the complete blackness in front of him.

As he did so he regretted, too late, that he had not brought a torch with him. The darkness was so thick that he could hardly bring himself to move through it at all. He felt as if he should raise his hands and push it away from his face as if it were a curtain, hanging too close to him and hampering his breathing. He stopped and felt in his pockets. In one of them he found a small book of matches. Immediately, with the means of producing light at his disposal, his composure returned. He moved confidently forward, his fingers clenched tightly on the matches held in his trouser pocket. The place smelt familiar – of warmth, of disinfectant, very slightly of stale urine, a smell which was more or less inevitable in a closed atmosphere in excessive heat. There was also another smell which he could not quite define – not of food, or of the proximity of a human body. Thinking it over, he could only presume it to be the natural smell of the place itself. It seemed to be compounded of earth, of stone, and of age; there was even a slight freshness in it, as if of vegetation, of moving water or of air. It was definitely odd – some might even have found it distasteful. In Todd it inspired comfort and confidence.

He stood beside the boy's bed for some moments listening to his light breathing. The place was so absolutely quiet that the regular intake of breath sounded quite loud. He wondered whether to wake him – if, indeed, he wanted to do so at all. Having come to the cave, and having heard the even breathing of the boy's sleep, he felt almost satisfied. The need actually to see him and to talk to him was much eased. He felt the jumping of his own breath steady and his tensed muscles relax. He stood uncertainly in the darkness, holding the matches. An owl, crying outside in the darkness, hardly startled him at all. It was a brooding, indolent sound which was more a part of the silence than a disturbance of it. Curiously, however, it roused the boy. There was a pause and a catch on an indrawn breath and then absolute silence, so intense that Todd felt the listening consciousness beside him as clearly as if it had been part of himself. The blankets rustled and there was the small sound of abrupt movement.

'Who is it?'

The voice did not sound startled or particularly frightened.

'There's someone there. Who is it?'

Todd stood still. He sensed, rather than felt, the arm put out towards him. The contact of the small strong fingers touching the back of his hand made him start violently. The fingers touched him again, then grasped him firmly. Their grasp was steady, and surprisingly powerful.

'Is that you, Todd?'

'Yes. I'm sorry. I woke you.'

'You didn't. It was the owl. I often hear it.'

'How did you know I was there?'

'I didn't. I knew someone was there.'

'But you knew it was me.'

'Not until I touched you.'

The fingers gave an impatient little tug at his hand. Helpless to detach himself, Todd moved nearer the bed.

'Is there anyone with you? Any of the others?'

'No.'

The boy gave a little laugh. It was almost a chuckle. To Todd, it sounded triumphant.

'I knew you'd come,' he said.

Todd did not reply. He felt in his pocket and brought out the matches.

'Have you got a candle?'

'On the table.'

The fingers loosened their grip and slid away. Shaking, Todd struck a match. The boy's face, raised smilingly to him, leapt up at him out of the darkness. The lips curved upwards at the corners showing the two rows of white teeth slightly parted. The feathery lashes threw two little furry arcs of shadow on the cheeks. The skin looked as if it were frosted with a slight bloom, like that on ripening fruit. Todd saw that the boy's chest and arms were bare and that his two long straight legs were bent sideways under his buttocks. The arch of his thin shoulders looked too frail to support the rounded head with its thick crop of hair which hung heavily almost to the eyes. The eyes themselves were very bright. In each pupil Todd saw a tiny flame reflected.

'You'd better light the candle,' the boy laughed up at him. 'You're going to burn yourself.'

199

Todd did so. The light was small, but quite steady in the motionless air. It was sufficient to show him the heap of disordered blankets, the clothes thrown over the chair, the boy's white shape almost naked, coiled in the dimness like a snake, or a flower.

The imperious hand came out again, to pat the blankets beside him.

'Sit down. I can't talk to you when you're standing over there.'

Todd obeyed. He, too, curled his legs under his body, so that they sat on the bed facing each other, their knees almost touching. They looked as if they might be going to play a game of cards as they bent forward to each other.

'I still don't see how you knew it was me,' said Todd in a low voice. Instinctively, they both spoke almost in whispers.

The boy shrugged.

'The other two have both been to see me by themselves. It was your turn.'

'What did they come for?'

'Carter came to play pirates.'

'Pirates?'

'Yes. We played a game where he was a pirate captain, capturing a Spanish galleon. In the end I walked the plank. He played it very well. He enjoyed himself very much.'

'And Randy?'

'Oh – he came to play a game too.'

'I can't imagine Randy playing pirates.'

'It wasn't pirates. It was gangsters.'

Todd was looking at the boy's right arm. In the candlelight the huge bruise looked black. It was staring on the white skin. The boy caught his glance and looked down. Todd gestured at the mark.

'How did you do that?'

The boy looked unwinkingly at him.

'I fell. It doesn't hurt any more.'

'It looks horrible.'

'Does it? I'm sorry.'

Todd clenched his hands between his knees.

'And what game have I come to play?' he inquired.

'I don't know.'

Todd looked sharply at him and found the answer accompanied by a smile of such absolute candour that he was silenced by it.

Presently he said,

'I shan't be coming for the next few days.'

'Oh yes – the exams.'

'I must do some work. It's important.'

'Of course.'

'Carter will come and bring you food and all that.'

'Good. We can play some more pirates.'

'You won't go, then?'

'Go?'

'You did before.'

'But I came back, didn't I?'

The boy was patient, and most unchildlike. Todd felt he was talking to someone considerably older, not younger than himself. He also felt dominated, and enjoyed his submission. The boy waited, sitting at his ease. Behind him the candle burned steadily. It darkened his face and edged his crop of hair with a furry golden halo.

Todd said,

'Why won't you tell us anything about yourself?'

The boy looked back at him, puzzled. Todd tried to explain.

'You always answer our questions with another question, not a proper answer.'

The boy still looked as if he did not understand. Frowning, he said,

'I don't mean to.'

Todd said,

'You must be able to tell us something. You behave as if

you didn't exist before we found you that day and brought you here.'

'But you haven't told me anything either, you know.'

'I'm willing to tell you anything you want to know – where I live, about my mother, my school, what I do when I'm not here. I can tell you about the others too.'

The boy put out his hand, palm outwards, as if he were directing a stream of traffic.

'I don't want to know.'

'Why not? You must be curious about us, why we brought you here at least, if nothing else.'

'I'm not.'

'But why?'

'I don't want to know anything about you. It would bore me.' He brought it out flatly, with insolence. 'That's why I don't ask you any questions.'

Todd, conscious of the light full in his face, compressed his lips with irritation. The boy said, in a softer voice,

'Don't you see – all that sort of thing is a waste of time. It doesn't make any difference to us as we are now.'

'Don't you even want to know what's going to happen to you? I can tell you if you want to know,' said Todd. It was a kind of desperate threat, but the boy still did not respond, either with fear or with curiosity.

'I don't expect you to tell me anything, so I don't see what you can expect from me,' he said, smiling up at Todd. 'It's a sort of bargain, isn't it?'

'A very lop-sided one,' Todd began irritably, but the boy just went on smiling. He leaned forward a little and put his hand on Todd's clenched fist.

'Don't be angry,' he said. 'You ask quite a lot of me too, you know.'

Nothing about him was childlike now, except the easy pose of his body and the high, light voice.

'I suppose so,' said Todd wearily, abandoning it.

'Are you tired?'

'I shouldn't have come. I've been working all day.'

'Can't you sleep here?'

Todd propped his weight on a hand and pushed his hair away from his face.

'I don't know – perhaps.'

The boy uncurled himself and knelt up. He was wearing his brief shorts, and his flat chest and thighs showed pale in the candlelight.

'Try,' he said. 'Lie down.' He patted the blankets with the flat of his hand. 'It's quite comfortable. Come on, try it.'

The hollows made by his body were flattened by Todd's weight, but the depression in the folded blanket which formed the pillow received his head exactly. He stretched his limbs out tentatively; trembling with a desire to draw into himself, he forced himself to extend his body and to lie unprotected in front of the boy. It was delicious to lie on the soft blankets. Looking round him he could see the darkness gradually thicken until it became impenetrable. He felt as if he were enclosed in a shell of darkness. The boy crouched beside him on the bed.

'It is comfortable, isn't it?' he said exultantly. 'I told you it was.'

Todd closed his eyes. After a while he felt the fingers on his forehead, pushing the hair away, smoothing the side of his cheek and then his neck. He lay absolutely still. The hand, cool and knowing, moved on the skin of his shoulder, under the open neck of his shirt and across his chest. It travelled down his forearm, across his wrist, and touched the inside of his hand between thumb and forefinger. He felt the small even breaths on his face. Half opening his eyes, he saw the body crouched beside him and the intent face with its delicate feathering of hairs beside the mouth. He closed his eyes again. The touch of the fingers on him was very light, but it was purposeful, and it seemed to demand something of him – complicity, decision. When he put his own hand up, trembling, to meet it, it leaped to respond to him with complete understanding.

The next day Todd and Randy began their exams. After the first paper Todd went over to Randy who was standing by his desk at the other side of the room methodically tearing up sheets of used scribbling paper and piling the pieces neatly beside his row of pens and pencils. His face, stooping expressionlessly over his moving hands, looked calm and remote.

'Ready?'

Randy tore the last sheet across and added it to the heap. He stood contemplating the torn paper.

'Nothing is to be taken away from the room in which the Examination is held,' he remarked conversationally.

'Oh, come on,' said Todd impatiently. 'We'll be in here again in a couple of hours, you know.'

Randy patted the pile of torn paper.

'So much for my great thoughts.' He turned away from the desk and slipped an arm through Todd's. 'Come. We need nourishment.'

They went out together. The glare of sunshine on the stretch of grass under the high windows was intolerable. Todd literally stumbled under it as if he had been struck. Only Randy's arm, held rigidly under his own like a rib of steel, prevented him from falling. Dazed, he allowed himself to be led across the grass into the shade of the row of trees which bounded the field. Here he sank down, to lie on his back, arms spread, eyes closed. He seemed to undergo some limitless period of sleep, at least of arrested consciousness, before Randy, kneeling beside him with a large plastic cup in his hand, woke him, and made him sit up.

'Drink it,' he said. His arm, hard through its cotton sleeve, pressed into Todd's back as he gulped the fruit juice down. It was delicious, very cold. After the first few mouthfuls he was able to hold the cup himself and to drink more slowly. Randy squatted beside him in the grass.

'You've overdone it, you ass. I suppose you worked all last night?'

Todd put down the empty cup and wiped his mouth with the back of his hand, then licked the moisture from his skin.

'Not all of it. I went to the cave.'

'Oh, you did, did you?'

'I didn't mean to. I'd done as much work as I could and I wasn't taking it in. So I went.' He squinted up against the sun. 'Well, you went too, didn't you?'

'Did he tell you that?'

'The boy?'

'Yes.'

'He said you'd been, and Carter.'

'Carter too?'

'Yes.'

Randy pondered this, holding his cup in his clasped hands as if it were some kind of offering. He had the sun behind him and his face looked dark.

'Did he say anything about it?'

'You mean when you were there?'

'Yes. What we did, or anything?'

Todd laughed suddenly.

'Only that you played some sort of game.'

'Game?'

'Yes.' Todd tried to remember. 'Wait a minute – I've got it. He said he played pirates with Carter, and cops and robbers with you. Which, I must say, sounds quite incredible.'

'Quite a sense of humour the lad's got,' remarked Randy after a pause. 'Now I come to think of it, he said much the same thing to me.'

Todd, who was feeling better, reached out to help himself to a sandwich from the pile on the grass between them.

'And did you?' he inquired with his mouth full.

'Did we what?'

'Play cops and robbers.'

Randy laughed.

'I suppose we did in a way.'

'Did you enjoy it?'

'Not much. For one thing, he cheats.'

'He does, doesn't he?' agreed Todd.

'And what did you play?'

'We didn't play anything.'

'Oh yes you did – we all did, you included.'

'All right, if you're so sure – what do you think?'

Randy laughed again. He put out his hand and ran his fingers over the skin of Todd's arm from above the elbow to the wrist.

'Never mind what I think – it doesn't really matter what we call it, does it? I hope it was fun.'

Todd rolled over on to the grass. His half-eaten sandwich was flattened under his thigh as he moved.

'Messy!' said Randy reprovingly. He rescued the sandwich and replaced it carefully in his tin. 'Look what you've done to your nice clean trousers!'

He leaned over Todd and rubbed at the mess of melted butter with his folded and immaculate handkerchief. Todd lay still, his face pressed down into the grass, as the deft hands busied themselves about him.

He took Randy home with him for the evening meal. Mrs Gascoigne met them in the drive. She looked as if she had been watching for their arrival, and she took them straight round to the lawn where she had put out long wicker chairs and a table with drinks and a jug of iced fruit juice. Todd, as he rounded the corner of the house, half expected to see Mark Savory's long figure unfold itself from one of the chairs to greet them, but there was no one there. They sat in the shade and drank cold fruit juice. Mrs Gascoigne went into the house and emerged after a time with a tray of cold food. It was light and appetising. Todd, finding he was very hungry, ate with relish. His mother watched him with bright proprietary eyes. Occasionally she exchanged a glance with Randy. Todd could sense their conspiracy of concern directed towards him, but had no energy to protest.

When they had finished eating, Clare asked him how the papers had gone. It was done with tactful hesitancy, and he was grateful for her reticence.

'Not bad,' he said, lighting a cigarette. He felt drugged with food and reaction. 'Better than I expected.'

Randy enlarged, and his mother listened. Todd sat still. He heard their voices as far away exchanges of question and answer, unrelated to himself. After a while he closed his eyes and thought about the boy. He wondered if Carter would remember to take him regular supplies of food and drink during the next ten days. He had decided not to go again until the exams were over. He had explained this to the boy and the strange eyes, dark in the candlelight, had seemed to look up at him with perfect, even tender understanding. He had tried to make it clear that his motive was one of selfish self-consideration, but the boy, with one of his wide, airy gestures, had brushed the explanation away and had turned it into something absolutely reasonable, even commendable. Todd winced as he remembered this incident. He had found it touching, but it also frightened him.

They sat on in the garden while the shadow of the house crept towards them over the grass and drew itself over them, so that the harsh colours of daylight were softened down into a gentle, uniform grey. The birds began to make small liquid sounds as they rustled among the leaves. Randy stubbed out his last cigarette and rose to go. He lingered for a moment beside Todd's chair. His shirt, as crisp and clean as it had been in the morning when he put it on, glimmered in the dusk.

'Good night,' he said. 'Don't do any more work, will you, Todd?'

His concern seemed genuine, and again Todd was touched, and grateful. Yet, mingled with this surprised gratitude, was the sense that yet another demand was being made upon him. He felt that no sooner had he extricated himself from one position of responsibility than another was thrust upon him.

During the next ten days, Todd felt as if he had embarked upon some easy course where everything arranged itself for him with the minimum of effort. Randy came home with him almost every night, stayed for a meal and a chat with Mrs Gascoigne, then quietly took himself off. Everything which was vicious or unstable about him seemed to be in abeyance at this time and Todd found his continued presence and support acceptable. It was a curious interval in Todd's life – a loop in the line, so to speak, a period of dreamlike relaxation which unexpectedly intervened when he had most anticipated tension and difficulty. Randy, too, seemed quiet and softened. His eyes, turned on Todd, held concern, complicity. It was as if they were protecting each other, deliberately being extraordinarily kind to each other – a curious relationship which soothed Todd, and which at the same time stimulated him to the necessary point of application during the actual hours of the examination.

When they had no papers they lay in the grass in the school grounds or dozed together in Todd's garden, wearing bathing trunks and browning like red Indians. They smoked a good deal and hardly talked at all. Their bodies, so dissimilar in detail of build and structure, grew alike as they lounged and slept in the sunshine. Occasionally, one of them moving unexpectedly in the grass, or sprawling out in a chair, their limbs touched and drew unhurriedly apart again without self-consciousness. Mrs Gascoigne came and went, feeding them, talking occasionally when they wished to talk, mostly silent.

Only at the week-end, on the Saturday evening, did the pattern briefly change with the arrival of Mark Savory, come to stay over the Sunday. Todd, lying on his stomach under an apple tree, heard the car draw up on the gravel and cursed briefly and comprehensively as he got to his feet for the encounter.

'Ah! Our student.' Savory looked Todd up and down, his eyebrows raised in gentle surprise. 'I had expected to find you at your books, young man, not disporting yourself in the sun.'

'He did far too much work before the exams started.' Mrs Gascoigne smiled protectively at Todd. 'I'm glad he's got the sense to give his books a rest. I'm sure it's doing him much more good.'

'Oh, quite so.' Savory turned his gentle beam upon her. 'I was merely joking.' He let his smile broaden upon Todd. 'You look remarkable, dear boy. The picture of health and relaxation. And how are the papers going?'

Todd shrugged his naked shoulders. Confronted with Savory's immaculate summer guise he felt at a disadvantage – the bathing costume, he felt, was no match for light flannel trousers, gleaming shirt, and loose linen jacket.

'Quite well, thank you, sir.'

'Good, good. And your friend? Let me see – Randolph, was it?'

'Randy.'

'Ah yes. Randy,' repeated Savory with mild distaste. 'And how is he getting on?'

'I don't know. He hasn't said.'

Savory shrugged delicately, dismissing Randy.

'I'll get you a drink,' said Todd hastily, escaping into the house to cover his nakedness. In a state of high ill-humour he put on a shirt and slacks and carried a tray of drinks out on to the lawn.

'I suppose your little affairs at the quarry, or whatever it was, are being somewhat neglected at the moment,' remarked Savory, accepting a glass of orange juice. 'You must have more important matters on your mind at the moment.'

'Oh, that's all being attended to,' said Todd airily.

'Really? Surely your friend Randy is also rather occupied?'

'There's still Carter, you know.'

Savory frowned, as if in an effort at recollection.

'Ah yes. I recollect Carter. And you entrust your business to him?'

'Why not?'

'Indeed – why not? Save that he appeared a little young, a trifle unthinking, perhaps, for an affair of such moment?'

'He's all right,' said Todd shortly.

'Mark darling, for goodness sake don't go on about that dreadful old quarry!' Mrs Gascoigne laughed brightly from one to the other as if to draw them both into her confidence. 'Todd's only teasing – there's nothing going on, you know. He's just playing you up, aren't you Todd, you wicked boy?'

She reached out to pull a lock of Todd's hair as if in fun. It was a playful movement, and it seemed to deceive Savory; but it hurt, and brought tears of startled pain into Todd's eyes. He interpreted it as a warning.

'Have you decided anything about High Clere yet? I mean whether to buy it or not?' he asked.

Savory responded immediately.

'I have not decided,' he said with a meaningful glance at Mrs Gascoigne. She looked properly conscious and he beamed at Todd. 'It depends, you know, on various things. I hope to be able to reach a decision within the next week or so.'

That gave them all something different to think about, and the danger was past.

Savory cooked a meal for them that evening, a Spanish omelette with a green salad, and after they had eaten it he produced, with a modest flourish, a huge box of crystallized fruits filled with liqueurs. Mrs Gascoigne, who loved sweet things, fell on them with delight. Todd, distrusting the motives which had prompted the gift, did not. Savory, basking in Clare's approval, consumed several of the sweets, licking his fingers neatly after he had conveyed each luscious morsel to his mouth. He eats like a great cat, thought Todd, and looked past him to the garden, grey in its shadows outside the long windows.

Savory washed up too. He put on a frilly apron, and wore it gravely, seemingly unconscious of its incongruity with his lean angular form. He rolled his shirt sleeves high on his arms and secured them with arm bands. He handled the glass and china with fastidious care, and when he had finished he scrubbed out the sink with scouring powder and rinsed the washing up cloth in several changes of hot water.

'They can so easily become offensive in this weather,' he remarked as he draped it carefully over the edge of the sink. 'One has to be most careful. I boil mine frequently – much safer, I think.'

Mrs Gascoigne, going to and fro with the clean china, agreed with gravity. Todd wondered at her, and kept his own counsel.

'I know!' Todd's mother, coming back from putting away the last of the cutlery, suddenly put her hands together under her chin and looked at Savory with brilliant eyes. 'Let's go for a swim!'

'A swim? Now?'

'Why not? It wouldn't take us more than an hour to get to the coast. Oh Mark – do let's – it would be marvellous! And I'm sure it would do Todd all the good in the world after all his hard work.'

So they went, throwing swimming costumes and towels into the back of Savory's car and setting off in the twilight which was still luminous with heat. Mark opened the roof of the car and the air rushed in and past them and gave at least an illusion of coolness. Todd closed his eyes and thought about nothing. The sensation of speed helped him to empty his mind and he gave himself up to it, grateful for the lessening of tension. Only once was he roused, when his mother, sitting in front with Mark, suddenly turned her head to him, exclaiming,

'Oh Todd! Look! There's Randy on a motor bike!'

Todd sat up quickly and looked out of the rear window. All he could see was a red tail light whisking rapidly away behind them.

'How do you know it was Randy?' he said crossly, settling himself again. 'He hasn't even got a motor bike.'

'Well, he was riding this one, a great big black thing.'

'Surely you can find out from Randy himself?'

Mark mildly put this in as he drove at considerable speed through the darkness, and for the moment it put an end to the matter. But later, as Todd lay indolent and unthinking in the warm water and Clare splashed and circled around him like a shining seal, her black hair streaming on the water, he thought about it again. The idea of Randy on a motor bike was, for some reason, disturbing to him. It was as if the conjunction of two such potentially dangerous animals constituted a menace which he did not wish to contemplate. He lifted his head and saw Savory, a dim outline, sitting primly on the shore watching them. The sight suddenly made him feel joyous. He flipped over on to his stomach and streaked off after his mother, who was visible as a faint froth of white water and the occasional gleam of an arm upraised.

However, it had indeed been Randy. Roaring illegally and exultantly through the night on Gordon's motor bike he had recognised Savory's car, he himself was not quite sure how, and he had flashed out a hand to it in salute as they passed.

Arriving at Carter's house to give him supplies to take to the boy, he had dispatched Carter, and had then gone round into the back garden where Gordon, as usual, was tinkering happily with his machine.

'Still at it?' he inquired. 'It can't be that much of a machine if it needs all that repairing.'

'Oh, it doesn't. I like to keep it in good order, that's all.'

Randy gestured over his shoulder towards the house.

'Out,' said Gordon. 'Mum's taken Anne with her to see one of the neighbours, and at the last minute she dragged Daphne along too. Probably wouldn't leave her in the house in case you turned up.'

'Probably.' Randy fished out a packet of cigarettes and tossed one to Gordon. 'Is that thing going?'

'Like a bomb.'

They smoked, looking at the machine. Randy rocked to and fro on his heels. Voices came quietly from one of the gardens to their left. There was the steady beat of music pulsing from some open window. A mower purred rhythmically over the grass a few gardens along. It moved steadily backwards and forwards, surprisingly quiet in the still air. Gordon trod out his cigarette and dusted his hands down the sides of his trousers. He gestured towards the motor bike, standing black and stocky between them.

'Like to have a go?'

Randy went up to the machine and put his hands on the handlebars, grasping the rubber handgrips closely and enjoying the firmly ridged rubber against his skin.

'On the road, you mean?'

'I'll take you out for a bit. We can find a quiet stretch where you can have a go. It's a bit dark, really, but it's easy once you get the hang of it.'

Randy looked curiously up at him.

'Aren't you afraid I'll smash it up or something?'

'You won't. I can tell. Come on.'

Gordon wheeled the bike round the side of the house and swung himself on to the seat. Randy climbed on behind and put his feet firmly on to the rests. Gordon looked over his shoulder.

'Hold on round my waist. It's safer if you're not used to it.'

The machine lurched under his feet, sprang up, and roared into shattering noise.

'Ready?'

Randy linked his arms round the sturdy compact body. 'Ready!' he shouted back, and they were off in a great smooth swerve as if they were flying. Randy, his face full of air, gulped, and ducked, clung rigidly for a moment, then instinctively adjusted his body to the swing of the machine. Immediately, he began to enjoy the sensations of speed, of movement, and of his own physical co-operation with the machine. When they drew up on a quiet stretch of road, well out of the town, he slipped forward on to the front seat and gripped the handlebars with eagerness and complete confidence. He felt he hardly needed the patient explanation and demonstration which Gordon insisted upon giving him.

'I know, I know all that,' he said impatiently, hardly listening. 'I know what to do.'

'All the same, you can jolly well listen for a bit,' Gordon persisted equably. 'It's not a toy, you know, it's a lethal weapon if you don't handle it properly, and while I don't give a damn if you smash your own head in, I do care what happens to the bike. So you can jolly well listen, or you're not having a go at all.'

Thus admonished, Randy listened, followed his instructions, and presently set off alone on a wide and erratic course down the road. At first he was immensely conscious of weight, of power trying all the time to pull away from him, and of his own body's inclination to swerve, not with the machine, but in opposition to its movement. Once, however, he had grasped the fact of this tendency, he was able to correct it, and at the same time to loosen his convulsive grasp upon the handle-bars. He managed to turn, scraping the side of one shoe in the road as he did so, and came back to his starting point on a tolerably straight course.

'Not bad.' Gordon looked critically at him. 'Lean forward a bit more. Go with it. You won't control it any better by cocking your arse on the back of the seat. But you're not bad, not bad at all. You're doing nicely once you get going.'

On his second attempt Randy did very nicely indeed, and knew it. He felt, as he roared back towards Gordon, a small black blob at the roadside, that the machine was obeying him – that, in fact, they were working together rather than in opposition. On his third trip he went a considerable distance down the road, rounded a corner, and increased his speed until he was bucketing along with the engine shuddering between his legs and the air buffeting him round the face as if it were slapping him with great cupped hands. He swung round, exhilarated by his now complete control of the machine, and streaked back, rounding the corner and roaring up to Gordon in a scream of tires. In the resulting silence Gordon looked closely at the machine and then at Randy.

'Are you sure,' he inquired suspiciously, 'that you haven't been on one of these before?'

Randy lifted his hands from the handlebars in an exultant gesture, like that of a boxer who has floored his man.

'Never!' he declared. 'Never been on one in my life. Why not, I can't imagine. It's marvellous. Absolutely bloody marvellous. I'm off – just once more.'

'Well, don't go too far. It's getting pretty dark, you know.'

Randy roared the machine round and stood up in the road, his legs astraddle.

'Here goes!' he shouted, and was off.

Thus it was that Mrs Gascoigne, looking out in the half dark, saw him flying past them, crouched on the machine, and recognised him not by his face, which was, in any case, invisible, but by the exultation, the extraordinary atmosphere of achieved desire which his very position in the saddle expressed as he flew by.

Gordon drove them back to the house. Randy, a little sobered, but still exalted, clung on behind and tumbled off into the road outside Carter's house, executing a grotesque series of dancing leaps as he led the way through to the garden. His self-possession was momentarily abandoned. With no one but Gordon to see him, he gave way to a rare impulse to clown, to perform, to express his achievement in bodily movements which he would not normally have allowed himself.

'I did it!' he kept repeating. 'I did it! I did bloody well, didn't I? I rode her like a veteran, didn't I? Did you see me go round that corner? Like a bomb! You're a beauty, you old cow, you're a real beauty.' He slapped the seat of the machine as if it were a horse's rump or a girl's bottom.

'You did all right.' Gordon bent to adjust something on the machine and spoke casually. 'Ever thought of going in for it professionally?'

'Racing them, you mean?' Randy thought about this. After a pause, he said, 'I'd have to buy one, and get some experience.'

'Easy. Start by going in for some small local events. If you're any good, and if you survive, you'll make it into the big stuff.'

'Do you think I'd do?'

'You'd do all right – you take to the things like a duck to water.'

Randy squatted down beside Gordon.

'I'd like that,' he said. 'I think I could be really good at that.'

Already he was hugging the idea to him with love and excitement.

Carter, coming back from his trip to the cave, found them still out in the garden discussing the plan. Randy looked fleetingly up as Carter approached, but he asked no questions about the boy.

'Everything's all right.' Carter stood beside them, tired, a little awkward. 'What are you doing?'

'Just talking.'

Carter could not see their faces, but he smelt the warm fumes of the engine and the acrid smoke of Randy's cigarette.

'Don't you want to know how things are?' he said, lingering. Randy's face, lifted in the pallor of the thin summer night, was cleansed of expression.

'Not particularly.'

He bent his head again to Gordon.

Carter, who had spent an exhausting, but most enjoyable evening playing at the cave with the boy, said crossly,

'Oh, all right then—' and went indoors.

He had been the only visitor to the cave during the whole week. He had taken food to the boy, and had prolonged each visit in order to play ever more elaborate and complicated versions of the game which they had played together on his first visit to the cave alone. The boy, perhaps because Carter was the only person who remained in contact with him, seemed increasingly glad to see him, and became ever more inventive in his contribution to this game. He and Carter, together in the resounding spaces of the cave, worked out every possible permutation of the original situation, ranging from chases across the high seas to pitched battles between pirate ship and galleon; they rode out innumerable tempests, they delivered an infinite number of broadsides, they captured, sank or took in tow countless enemy vessels. They were scrupulous in their division of role, taking the coveted part of the pirate captain in turn. On one occasion Carter even tried to introduce a romantic element by prevailing upon the boy to play a captured damsel, love-sick for the pirate captain. Before long, however, the boy rebelled openly against the lines supplied for him by Carter, and the attempt was abandoned.

It was their only disagreement. On everything else they concurred, and performed the action as one. It was delightful to play, fully and freely, in the large privacy of the cave. Only occasionally did Carter, coming to the end of some impassioned tirade, turn, and meet the cold, curious eyes gleaming at him out of a face which seemed infected with the disconcerting pallor of the prison. The eyes, calculating and remote, would remind Carter. He would falter, and fall silent, standing apart and fearful. Almost at once, as if ashamed, the boy would start up the feverish play again, making up for his lapse by the range of his invention, the fantastic vigour of his imagination. These incidents, though rare – they occurred perhaps four times in all during this time – seemed, nevertheless, of profound importance to them both. They were not referred to; indeed, they seemed to pass almost unnoticed. But their play, immediately after they had occurred, became feverish, heightened by their mutual determination to behave as if nothing had happened. They performed at, rather than played with each other, as if each were trying to distract the other. Carter found these incidents exhilarating, and they stimulated him to higher flights of fantasy. The boy seemed merely to become more entirely absorbed in his efforts to please Carter, and to fall in more fully with his suggestions.

During this period Carter returned home remote, and still preoccupied with his experiences at the cave. Temporarily cut off from Todd and Randy, he was, nevertheless, very conscious of his own importance as the line of communication between the three of them and the quarry. The atmosphere at school was much relaxed, due to the examinations and the approaching end of term, and he found that little more than actual bodily presence was demanded of him there. His own future was not discussed, and he did not give it any thought; if he considered the matter at all, it was merely to presume that something would 'turn up', although he had no idea what. He supposed that things would settle themselves, and contented himself with that. He had looked ahead at nothing in his life so far, and he did not intend to start doing so now.

Todd and Randy sat their last papers on a Friday afternoon. It seemed to Todd, as he came out of the hall with Randy for the last time, that a lifetime had elapsed since his last encounter with the boy. He stood by the notice board in the passage, waiting for Randy, who had gone to the cloakrooms, and felt vaguely disappointed at his lack of elation. Randy

joined him and they walked out of the building and across
the field to their usual place under the trees on the other
side of the stretch of dry, brown grass. Randy flung his brief-
case down and dropped full length in the shade. After a
minute's hesitation, Todd stretched out beside him.

'Thank God that's over.' Randy accepted a cigarette and
lay smoking for a while in silence. 'What a bloody waste of
time. Not for you, of course. No doubt you'll go and join
the rest of Britain's gilded youth at Oxford or Cambridge
on the strength of your efforts this term and next.'

'Not particularly gilded nowadays.' Todd inhaled smoke
and blew enormous smoke rings which lingered, round and
perfect, in the air above his face. 'Lots of Grammar School
boys like us, and bags of democracy. A pity – frankly, I
could have done with a spell of gilded youth after seven years
in this dump. Anyway, what about you? Aren't you staying
on to try for a scholarship? You'll get one all right.'

'Not me. I'm not coming back for another term of this.'
Randy gestured with peculiar viciousness at the bulk of the
school buildings across the grass.

'What will you do, then?'

'Oh – I've got my plans. Get away from this place, for a
start.'

'Where to? London?'

'Not on your life. I like suburbia. I like the tarty little
housewives with their tight little arses pushing prams in the
high street. That's what Daphne Carter's aiming at – a couple
of kids, a pram like a yacht, and a husband who gives it to
her good and proper twice a week and no messing.'

Todd laughed.

'Do you see yourself as the husband?'

'No bloody fear. I'm not getting tied up with any of the
silly bitches yet awhile, and when I do it'll be one with a
lot more class than Daphne Carter. I just like looking at them,
that's all. Better than a whore any day.'

'So speaks the expert.' Todd could not resist it, and afterwards tried to soften it with a laugh. 'You're quite right, though. I can't see you settling down in a place like this, Randy.'

'I shan't. Don't worry about me – I've got my future all mapped out, after this little business is over.'

Carter came plodding across the grass towards them, a small figure square against the immensity of brick and glass behind him. He plumped himself down beside Randy and blew out his cheeks.

'Hotter than ever.' He squinted up at the sky, showing almost colourless through the trees above them. 'You wouldn't believe it could get worse, but it's been bloody awful today. Three chaps passed out in assembly. My head feels lousy. Probably tramping out to that cave every day. It's no joke in this sort of heat.'

'We haven't exactly been having a rest cure,' Todd pointed out mildly.

'I bet you're glad it's finished. No more work for you, you lucky bastards.'

'I'm certainly glad.' Todd rolled over on to his stomach and plucked up a blade of grass to chew. 'Everything all right?'

'Fine,' said Carter briefly.

'I suppose the pair of you have been living on chocolate cake and sausage rolls.'

Carter grinned.

'More or less.'

'We'll go tomorrow evening, then,' said Randy.

They both turned their heads to look at him. He lay on his back in the grass, one leg cocked over the other at the knee, a shoe dangling.

Todd said, chewing his blade of grass,

'As soon as that?'

'Why not? We said as soon as the exams were over. Well, they're over, aren't they? So what are we waiting for?'

'I didn't mean that. It's just that it seems so soon. Why can't we leave it for another week? It won't make any difference.'

'Exactly,' said Randy. 'It won't make any difference. So why don't we get it over and done with? I want to get shot of this place.'

Carter looked startled.

'Where are you going, Randy?'

'I'm going to pinch all the money I can lay my hands on from old Ma Johns, and then I'm going to get a job. Somewhere away from here.'

'What sort of job?'

'Anything – it doesn't matter, so long as I can scrape up enough money to buy a motor bike and learn to ride it.'

'Good God! You're going to try racing the things?'

'That's the idea.'

He lay looking at them, his thin cheek pressed down into the grass.

'You're incredible, Randy,' said Todd. 'Ever since you saw that girl killed you've wanted to ride one of those bloody machines. That's it, isn't it?'

'So what?'

Todd said, after a pause,

'You frighten me sometimes, you really do.'

'Think about yourself, and you'll be even more frightened.'

'I am.' Todd spoke sombrely. 'I'm dead scared.'

'Backing out?'

'Of course not.'

'Sure?'

'Sure. Not after all this time.'

Carter, who had been watching them, said,

'What do we do then?'

'Meet on the cliff above the cave tomorrow at midnight,' said Randy promptly.

As if with an effort, Todd bestirred himself to take command.

'Don't be dramatic, Randy. Not midnight. Much too late. Make it half past nine. It won't take more than an hour.'

'All right, half past nine.'

'You bring the things, Randy. Carter, you bring the paraffin. Plenty of it. It's got to be done properly.'

'All right, Todd.'

'Randy, you know what to do.'

'Yes, I do. Don't worry, I'll be there.'

'I'll bring torches, and I can use the car as Mama's away for the week-end. We ought to get back as quickly as we can afterwards in case anyone sees anything.'

'No one could.'

'No, I don't think they could, but all the same we'd better not hang around. The girl was there, remember – there just might be someone else.'

'I jolly well hope there won't,' said Carter fervently.

'Right. All settled?'

They looked at one another. Randy, lying in the grass, breathed quickly and smiled at the others. Todd was pinched round the mouth, but calm.

Carter suddenly threw himself into the grass and kicked his legs up. He gave his little high-pitched giggle.

'Little bastard,' said Randy. He drove his fingers deep into the grass. 'Stinking little perisher. About time he learnt his lesson.'

Carter stopped giggling. Todd put his chin down on to his folded arms and watched Randy with bright eyes. A patch of sunlight, moving surreptitiously between the leaves, fell on the grass between them. It bleached the colour from the grass, as if its very touch was enough to maim, to kill. They all lay and looked at it as if it were an animal crawling about on the ground, trying to find a way out of the circle they made with their bodies.

Randy would not kneel. He stood in the side chapel and looked up at the painted figures. The mother stood tall, impossibly slender, and held the fat beaming baby on her arm.

Its head was covered with symmetrical blond curls and its stout legs dangled against the blue robe. Their faces simpered down at him as he stood in the quiet dampness of stone and plaster and smelt the sanctity of stale incense. Beside him on the stand the candles, lit by the faithful, burned serenely. The church was empty. Although it was late, and dusk was already settling outside – indeed, the church itself was almost dark – the wide doors still stood open. It was absolutely quiet.

'All right,' said Randy aloud, looking up at them, 'if I'm worth saving I'm worth a miracle. Surely that's fair? Show me, just show me once, that I'm worth bothering about, and that it's all true and I'm not wasting my time, and I'll go on with it. I'll stick to it, confession, holy water, miracles, the lot. But prove it to me. Do something. Anything. Put out your tongue. Dance the can-can. I don't care what you do. But prove it.'

The painted figures remained motionless and serene in the candlelight. No shadows flickered across their faces to give a semblance of expression or movement. Nothing came in answer to his demand. Randy stood still, sweating slightly, and feeling ridiculous. It was a superstitious test of his will to believe, one which he knew was absurd and doomed to failure. Yet, he felt, if some ultimate demand were made, and some great expression of his need were still ignored, he would be free to feel that the bargain had not been kept by the other side and that he could in all honesty withdraw his allegiance. The links had worn very thin, the burden had for a long time been not only too heavy but increasingly meaningless. Now he had reached the stage where, with his instinct for the dramatic, he wanted to free himself by means of some action as ritualistic, as meaningless, as the hoops through which he had forced himself for so long.

He clenched his body and directed all his will on to the figures standing above him in the twilight.

'Work a miracle,' he said to them. He fixed his eyes on the painted faces and defied them. 'If I'm worth it make me believe in you and in all the rest of it. Move your head, blink your eyes. Say something. Say my name. Randy. You ought to know it by now. Say Randy Randolph. I dare you. Say it.'

Absolute silence, absolute immobility answered him.

'I shall give it all up.' He threatened them as if he were a rebellious child. 'I shall go away and I shan't come back. This will be the end of it all. I'm warning you – I mean it. It's your last chance. I shall count three.'

His neck had begun to ache, and the cold struck up through the soles of his shoes. Indifferently, he began to count.

'One.'

The candles stood straight beside him, rising like a triangle of jewels.

'Two.'

He hardly waited, hardly looked at them, before rushing on triumphantly to,

'Three.'

He stared up, trying to be fair, giving them an extra second or two in case. They smiled on, unresponsive.

Randy put out his hands in a wide gesture. He went out of the side chapel and into the aisle. Beside the altar the Sanctuary lamp glowed like a red eye in the darkness. He felt that he had been behaving absurdly, and was glad that no one had seen him making his farewells. The episode sank into unimportance as he hurried down the aisle and out into the porch. Automatically, he dipped his fingers into the Holy Water, and then remembered. Ostentatiously, as though making the gesture for someone who, though unseen, might still be watching him from the dark interior of the church, he wiped his hand on the seat of his trousers and hurried off to meet the others.

'There's a wind getting up,' Todd whispered incredulously. 'I can feel it on my face.'

'There can't be. There hasn't been any wind for months.'

'Well, there is now. There it is again. Can't you feel it?'

They all stood tense, braced against the descent, their heads strained up. Todd felt it again, a sluggish movement of the damp hair on his forehead. There was no coolness or refreshment in it, but the air was definitely in motion.

'Good God!' Randy whispered beside him. He sounded, if anything, awed. 'Do you think the weather's going to break?'

Carter was fidgeting.

'Let's get a move on!' he urged restlessly. 'What does it matter if it is going to break? Come on, Todd, let's get down there before someone sees us.'

Todd turned his head to look at the car. It stood under the ragged fringe of trees on the edge of the waste ground, just visible as a faint gleam of the metal here and there on its darker bulk. Then he looked up at the sky. It was still a taut, greenish stretch above them, but here and there a wisp of grey cloud crept across its expanse. The wisps were thin and nebulous, and seemed to float motionless; but as Todd watched one immediately above him, he saw that it was imperceptibly extending itself across the green background of the sky, and that others, even fainter, were also crawling forward, as if to meet it. It was a curious sight, the fingers of cloud edging out over their heads. As Todd watched, the wind came again, small, and cold.

'God damn it – I believe it's clouding over,' said Carter uneasily.

They all stood and looked up at the sky. Todd heard Carter breathing nervously and unsteadily beside him. Randy stood motionless with his hands in his pockets, cocking his head up. His shape was humped and thickened by the rucksack slung on his back. As Todd watched him, he brought his head down and grinned at them. They saw the white glimmer of teeth in his face.

'All the better,' he whispered. Todd could smell the reck-lessness in him. He exuded the rank odour of dangerousness. He swung himself gently to and fro on his heels as he grinned at them. 'Who goes first? Follow-my-leader, eh? Todd first, then Randy, and little Carter to bring up the rear.' He pushed out with his elbow to give Todd a vicious little shove. 'Come along, dear boy – after you.'

They climbed down swiftly and silently. Carter, encumbered by the heavy tins of paraffin slung on his back, slid down in the rear, bringing a shower of pebbles and earth bouncing down round the other two. Randy, clinging to the rock face, lifted his face to curse him in a vicious whisper.

'Stop that bloody row! You'll bring the whole lot down on us in a minute.'

Carter mumbled some inaudible reply and clambered down after them, sliding the last few feet on to the rock to cling there, shaking and sweating.

Todd went first into the cave. He moved a few paces forward, then snapped on his torch. A moment later a second beam of light joined his, then, after a pause, a third wavering beam played unsteadily on the floor in front of them. Todd moved forward again, shading the torch with his cupped hand. He found the table, and directed the cone of yellow light on to it. The checks of the cloth sprang up at him. On it, four cups, each with a new and unlighted candle set upright in it, were arranged, one at each corner. The white shafts of wax stood immaculate against the darkness. Behind him, Todd heard Randy's breath hiss in his throat.

'All ready for us!' The words were a mere breath in the stillness.

Carter whispered,

'Who did that?'

'Who do you think? He did, of course.'

Todd stared at the candles.

'Right.' He felt in his pocket. 'Let's light them, shall we?'

Randy stepped up to the table. He held his lighter in his hand; it shone between his fingers in the mingled light of their three torches. He snapped it on and the small yellow flame leapt out. He was about to apply it to the first of the four candles when Todd's hand slid forward into the light.

'Thank you,' he said.

He took the lighter and began to light the candles. The wicks were long and unused. Each one sputtered slightly as the flame rose, wavered, then rose again, crept up, and began to burn tall and steady. When they were all burning Todd handed the lighter back and stood a little away from the table. They slowly turned towards the bed and saw the boy, sitting cross-legged on his neatly folded blankets, watching them.

The light given by the four candles was considerable, certainly strong enough to illuminate his face with perfect clarity. It was grave, unsmiling and perfectly composed. The wide childish forehead, shadowed by the hair, was smooth. The hands lay loose, one cupped lightly over each bare knee. He seemed to be waiting for them to speak – to address him, or to require something of him.

Randy, with a small movement, swung the rucksack from his back. He turned himself slightly away for a moment and busied himself with it. When he had finished he moved next to Todd, his hands behind his back. The three of them were stationed close to one another – so close, in fact, that anything passed from hand to hand behind them would not be visible to the boy.

Todd said,

'Stand up.'

The boy obeyed. He was so much shorter than the other three that, in order to see their faces comfortably, he had to tilt his head back and look up at them. He stood loosely, his hands by his sides. At first his gaze passed across all their faces, scanning them earnestly as if trying to search out some meaning from them; then it settled gravely, almost pensively, upon Todd.

'Bring the chair and put it down here.'

Todd gestured precisely with his hand to the exact spot where he wanted it placed. The boy fetched the chair dragging rather than carrying it. Its sturdy weight as he struggled with it emphasised the fragility of his thin arms. He got it into position, and stood back, breathing fast from the effort.

Todd sat down. The other two stood one on each side of the chair, their hands hidden behind their backs. Todd leaned forward, laying a forearm along each thigh and letting his empty hands hang down between his knees. The boy stood before him. He now looked down at the ground, shifting his feet slightly in the shadows.

'Prisoner at the Bar,' said Todd, 'do you plead Guilty, or Not Guilty?'

The boy looked up swiftly. He looked almost relieved.

'What is the charge?' he inquired gravely.

Todd, motionless, waited.

Randy said,

'The charge is immaterial. What do you plead?'

'I can't plead until I know the charge. I can't play unless I know the rules.'

'It isn't a game,' said Carter. He giggled. 'We mean it this time.'

'Yes, I know you mean it, but after all, it's still a game, isn't it? Only this time we all play,' the boy added, as if explaining it to them.

Todd merely repeated,

'What do you plead?'

The boy looked at them again, hesitated, then shrugged his shoulders.

'Not guilty.'

A movement ran through them all. It started with Todd and communicated itself outwards to Randy and Carter, then seemed to leap forward to the boy so that he jerked his shoulders back and ducked his head as if to avoid a blow.

'Not guilty,' he repeated, more confidently.

Todd leaned back. He spread himself physically so that he seemed to grow bulkier, more formidable, while the boy, in contrast, crouched himself down a little and hedged his body with his thin arms.

'If you are not guilty,' said Todd, 'tell us why we have come.'

The boy straightened himself slightly. He looked surprised.

'Don't you know?'

'I want you to tell us.'

'There's no need to tell you something you know already.'

Todd disregarded this. Inexorably, he repeated,

'If you are not guilty, why have we come?'

The boy shrugged again, and smiled fully at them.

'After all,' he said, 'I set out the candles.'

They all turned to look at the four white columns tipped with gold, then back again to the boy.

'Admission of guilt,' said Randy, motionless beside the chair.

'Agreed?' asked Todd.

The boy made no reply, but his lip turned downwards in contempt. The candles, burning tranquilly beside him, threw a little dip of shadow under his chin, but otherwise swept his face clear.

'You can't really blame me for not answering your questions,' he remarked. 'After all, we have played quite a lot of games. How do I know this isn't just another one? Anyway, it's not fair. It's three against one. I haven't had time to—' he paused, searching for the phrase – 'to prepare my defence.' He looked triumphantly at them, as if pleased with himself.

'You have had time,' said Todd. 'Twelve years.'

'Oh,' said the boy. He hesitated, thinking it out, then said, 'You mean I'm on trial for being here with you, like this?' He gestured round them at the cave.

'You could call it that,' said Randy.

The boy ignored him. He concentrated his strong gaze upon Todd.

'Is that what you mean?'

Todd put his left hand slightly forward, palm downwards. He moved the hand up and down once or twice, as if he were patting something into place. The boy watched him. After a moment he nodded, as if he understood.

'Yes, I see. That's true,' he remarked. 'All the same, Carter's only fifteen.'

'Three years,' said Todd. 'Anyway, he's leaving school. An entirely different matter. Surely, if you think it over you must agree.'

The boy looked Carter up and down as if he were taking into account the breadth of shoulder, the powerful barrel of the rib cage, the legs straddled wide. Then he held out his own childish arms and looked at the delicate bones of the wrist knobbed under the skin, and at the tracery of blue veins on the backs of the thin hands. He sighed as he contemplated them.

'Admission of guilt,' said Randy, his hands behind him.

'All the same, I came with you.' This seemed to occur to the boy as a strong point and he produced it with pride.

'But you were there,' said Todd, inexorable. 'We had waited for two years, and we came down that slope on that particular day, and in that place, and you were there. You can't deny it. You were undoubtedly there.'

'I could have refused to go with you.'

'But you came.'

'I could have run away.'

'But you stayed.'

'Does that make it worse?'

'Much worse. More serious, you are still here, at this moment, with us. We did nothing to make you stay, but you didn't go.'

'You made me promise,' the boy pointed out.

'A promise?' Todd leaned forward and laughed at him. 'You should have broken it.'

'I did.'

'But you came back.'

The boy wrinkled up his face.

'Does that make it worse too?'

'Much worse. Irrevocable, in fact.'

The boy described one of his wide gestures. It looked as if he were saying, 'And tonight?'

'That was worst of all. That you are here now.'

'Admission of guilt,' said Randy. He made a thrusting gesture with his right shoulder as if pushing something out of the way.

'It mounts up,' said Todd.

The boy went on looking at him. His face was not hostile, acquiescent merely, as if he agreed.

'Again: you knew we were coming. The fact that you set out the candles proves it. And still you made no move.'

Todd paused. The boy, who seemed to feel that something was expected of him, mildly said,

'No.'

'Why not? Not because you had promised. You had broken your promise once – why not again? You are guilty of conspiracy.'

'Conspiracy?' repeated the boy, frowning.

'With us,' said Randy.

'You invented the games we played,' remarked Carter suddenly. 'You had all the best ideas. They wouldn't have been any good without you. You thought of all the best things we did. I wouldn't have wanted to come at all if you hadn't been so good at all the games we played.'

'That's true,' said the boy with some pride. 'I was much better at it than you.'

'Much better than all of us,' said Todd.

'Admission of guilt,' said Randy. He shifted lightly on his feet. 'How do you plead?'

'Oh, guilty,' said the boy immediately. 'Guilty, of course.'

Todd let out his breath in a slow sigh. He pressed himself against the back of the chair.

'Guilty,' he said. 'That is the verdict of us all.'

The boy dipped his head slowly before them. His hair hung forward over his face.

'The verdict of us all,' he repeated obediently.

Todd closed his eyes. His hair, his skin, and the material of his shirt were all reduced to the same featureless pallor by the candlelight. Randy's dark hair and clothes were absorbed into the background and only the light length of his face stood forth in illumination. Carter, overlaid by the shadow of Todd's bulk, was grey and indeterminate. He was the furthest from the source of light and was hardly touched by it.

The boy alone stood in complete illumination. Every detail of his skin and hair, his physical structure, was drowned in light, played upon by it, outlined, sharpened, edged by it. It defined and confined him, almost seemed to give him his existence. He did not shrink from it. Rather, he seemed to put himself forward to it as if it were a source of warmth and an establishment of identity. Because the light was full upon him he looked out at them from it as if across an abyss, or some vast empty area of twilight. He seemed to stand back from them as if to say, 'This is not my doing. I am not concerned in any of this. I cannot be held responsible for any of it.'

'You've accused me,' he said softly across this great space. 'Now it's my turn to accuse you.'

'Accuse us?' Randy laughed contemptuously. 'We are not on trial. You are the prisoner.'

But Todd suddenly half rose from his chair. He pushed himself up on one hand, putting out the other, edge to the boy. The line of his body, thrusting forward to the straining head, expressed urgent attention.

'Go on,' he said. Without turning to the others he threw back at them, 'Let him speak. It's only fair.'

The boy stood quite still looking back at Todd. A curious expression began to spread itself over his face. It was compounded of fear, of helplessness, of appeal – mostly of appeal. The life seemed to be draining out of him, as if he were pouring it into this, and all the time he focused himself at Todd; threw himself forward, so to speak, across the space which separated them. Carter shuffled his feet, turning his head aside and blinking under the intensity of this appeal to Todd. Randy drew in his breath. Silently, he slid in behind the chair. Without taking his eyes from the boy he put out his hands and gripped its back, so tightly that the knuckles started out white under his skin.

Todd suddenly levered himself away from the chair and stood completely upright.

'How can I help you?' he called out. He sounded anguished, terrified. 'What do you want?'

The boy said nothing, did not move. Slowly, Todd began to walk forward. He moved stiffly away from the other two with his arms rigid by his sides. He seemed to go on moving for an infinity of time, further and further away, dwindling and diminishing as he went, until he stopped at last face to face with the boy, his back squarely to the other two. But even as he dwindled the boy, standing still with upturned face, seemed to enlarge himself as he stood so that when they met he seemed somehow the larger figure, looming over Todd with infinite menace. They could see his face quite clearly. It was very pale, and a fine sheen was spread over the skin. A tight line appeared, drawn from the inner edge of the eye to the nostril and from there to the mouth. It quivered a little, making his face blur and jump as if it were in the process of dissolution. Todd stood absolutely still, his head hanging stiffly forward.

Randy opened his mouth to shout to Todd. But even as he made the movement the boy suddenly tensed his body as if gathering himself together for some kind of mental spring. He moved his mouth, his hands came up and a little away from his body. But it was Todd who spoke.

'We are accused,' he said in a high, loose voice utterly unlike his own, 'not of wanting to destroy you, because that is perfectly natural and understandable. We are accused because we intend actually to do it, because we are striking at shadows, and because we intend to destroy something which is no menace to us, which makes minimal demands, and with which we could co-exist, at least in part, almost indefinitely.'

He stopped. His body sagged a little. But the boy did not move or relax his intensity. They saw Todd's shoulders tense again under his shirt, the material running away in little creases as he bunched himself together for another terrible effort. He started again in his new, unrecognisable voice.

'We are also accused of being too literal. We are being asked to compromise, not to be too quick to take the final step. There is no need to cut ourselves off with such violence. It could be done slowly, so that in the end it would be done and none of us would know exactly when or how it had been achieved.'

Randy leaned forward over the back of the chair and spoke across, not to Todd, but to the boy.

'You are not practical. The thing couldn't be done. We are breaking up now – we have reached a point where we can't go on together any longer and you are included in that.'

The boy's face changed a little. But he did not deflect one ounce of his concentration from Todd.

Carter said suddenly,

'I am leaving school. Randy is going away. It wouldn't work.'

'You are included in that,' Randy repeated as if Carter had not spoken.

Todd jerked and shuddered. He said,

'We are your prisoners as much as you are ours.'

Randy said, still to the boy,

'Ever since you came with us it has worked both ways. You came, you stayed, and you are still here.'

The boy blinked rapidly once or twice. Then he sighed, a long, even intake of breath which he seemed to hold for a long time.

Todd said,

'You must pronounce sentence on us. Randy was right – it works both ways. We've given you your chance. You have had your way.'

Slowly, he began to back away from the boy. When he was about three feet away from him he put up a hand and did something to his face – they could not see what, for his back was still fully turned to them. They saw the boy hesitate, then drop his eyes. He let the breath trickle out of him in a long, slow sigh – an infinitesimal fall under the white shirt.

Todd turned fully round to face them. His face looked quite normal.

'We have already paid,' he said, and came back to them. He reached the chair and unhurriedly sat down. Randy slid back to his place. The boy shrugged his shoulders slightly and turned indifferently away.

A sudden sound, strange and far off, startled them all. The boy put his head up and opened his eyes wide. They listened; without looking at one another, they yet moved closer together, even the boy, who shrank up to them unnoticed. The sound was not unlike a human groan, very loud, yet very distant, as if it came from deep in the ground beneath their feet. Nothing moved, but the sound crept up around them, rose to a muttering mumble, maintained its note for some seconds, and then fell away again into silence. The candles burned straight and undisturbed and they had felt nothing, no movement of the ground or surrounding air. Yet they were all aware of a change of some kind, a re-settling of the atmosphere.

'I've heard it twice before,' the boy said.

'What is it?' whispered Carter. 'It sounded like an earthquake.'

'Just the earth settling. Something to do with the heat.' Randy sounded uneasy.

The boy put his hand on Todd's knee.

'What do you think it is?'

Todd looked down at the fingers hooked on to his knee.

'It's nothing important,' he said obstinately. 'It doesn't matter.'

The boy's grip tightened. A moment later the sound was repeated. It was a little louder, but still infinitely far away. The fingers on Todd's knee grasped him with surprising strength. The pain was considerable, but Todd sat still and endured it. The boy's face was close to his own. It was waxy with fear, and glossy, as if some greasy secretion had spread itself over the skin. The eyes looked past him. They looked as if they were filmed over with apprehension. Todd could see the infinitesimal fair hairs laid softly over the skin above the upper lip. They made the mouth look childishly vulnerable, and yet, at the same time, mature. When the sound had ceased the painful grip on his knee relaxed, but the fingers, widely separated over the dark cloth, remained. Todd's hair prickled.

'It's gone.' The boy turned his eyes upon Todd. The film had cleared, and Todd could see the colour diffusing itself over the face until, in a moment, it looked as usual.

'You've heard it before?'

'Yes. Never so loud.'

Randy looked round, up at the invisible roof, down at the rough ground on which he stood.

'It's time we were going.' He turned slowly to face the boy. 'There remains the sentence.'

Todd made a violent gesture with his hand, brushing the boy away from him. He seemed to be gathering himself up for something. The others waited without interrupting him, the boy as well.

Todd said,

'We are going to kill you. The sentence is death.'

The boy remained smiling and calm.

'Do you agree?'

After a short hesitation, the boy gravely nodded.

'Aren't you afraid?' Carter whispered.

The boy's eyelids flickered, as if in contempt, but he made no reply.

Todd stood up. He went to the boy and, shielding him from the others with his own body, he raised his hands and began to unbutton the boy's shirt. They stood so close together that at various points, at thigh and at knee, they were actually touching – in fact, the boy arched himself a little forward from the waist so that the contact should be made, and maintained. Todd bent his head over the boy and saw every detail of the fine fall of brown hair, the tender line of forehead and cheek. He did not attempt to remove the shirt, merely pulled it wide open and drew the ends round behind the boy's waist and knotted them there. The material strained back from the shoulders and upper arms, but did not fall away. Between its white edges the smooth skin, unmarked by hair or by blemish of any kind, stretched from throat to navel. It was a wide and easy target.

When he had finished, Todd stood perfectly still for a moment. He let his hands fall away to his sides, but he remained bent over the boy as if in profound meditation. The boy was motionless. He did not tremble, his body was relaxed.

Behind them Randy said,

'Do you wish to be blindfolded?'

The boy raised his head. He could not see Randy because his vision was obscured by Todd's shoulder, and in any case he made his reply, such as it was, to Todd.

'Why? Do you want to hide from me?'

Todd looked down at his face. They were poised, mouth

close to mouth, in the attitude of embrace. For Todd to have lowered his head a few inches would have brought mouth on to mouth. They gazed, dreamily and consideringly, at each other's faces. The boy put up his hand and gave Todd a light push in the chest. It seemed a friendly, almost reassuringly impatient gesture.

'Go on,' he said softly. 'Go back to them, Todd.'

Todd stood back.

Randy threw out a hand in which the blade leapt in the candlelight.

Todd cried out,

'Not his face – Randy, don't touch his face.'

Carter moved forward, bringing his hand stiffly away from his side with the fingers crooked round the handle.

Randy shouted back to Todd,

'Why not his face? Why not?'

Todd came forward last. He struck up and out, and felt the impact up his arm to his shoulder and to his brain. There was a burst of movement round him as bodies made contact and swung away again. There was a brief whirling of bare arms; feet scraped on the floor, the chair fell over on to its side. A candle tottered, swayed, its flame looped to the floor and went out. There was the sound of short panting breaths, a grunting sound from Randy as he struck again and again. They stooped over the boy, slashing at him, terrified because he would not fall.

When they felt it must be enough – and curiously, they all seemed to feel this at precisely the same moment – they simultaneously stood back. Standing in a line, a little apart from one another, they leaned fearfully forward to see what they had done.

The boy stood in front of them as though untouched. He made no sound. It seemed impossible to tell whether he had been struck or not. He looked much as usual, a little dishevelled, perhaps, but certainly not mauled, or marked with blood.

'But I got him,' Randy whispered. 'I got him, just there.' He gestured towards the boy's chest and stomach.

'So did I.'

'So did I.'

The boy seemed to be looking back at them. He stirred, and walked briskly forward. They shrank back, horrified, sweat breaking out on them like blood. The boy went up to Todd and hesitated, gazing thoughtfully into his face. Convulsively, Todd started away from him. The boy wavered, and then went slowly down on to his knees. He steadied himself for a moment with one hand pressed firmly, palm downwards, on to the ground beside him. He remained in this position for a short while, and then toppled soundlessly over on to his side. He drew his knees up to his chest, and then stretched his body out full length on to the floor, his arms laid at his sides and his head turned away from them so that they could not see his face.

They all stood motionless, looking down at him. Randy made as if to move forward, but Todd brushed him away with the flat of his hand and went to kneel beside the boy. He put his left hand delicately on the breast over the heart and waited for a few seconds. Then he placed his hands on the floor, one on each side of the body, and leaned close down to the face.

'He's dead.'

'Who—?' Randy's question tailed away.

Todd searched the body briefly, hardly touching it.

'There are a number of wounds, almost any one of which would have been enough,' he said gravely.

He took out his handkerchief and shook out its whiteness and laid it over the face. One foot, in its brown child's sandal, was bent under at the ankle and he straightened it beside the other. They watched him greedily. When he had finished he stood up and came back to them. They moved away from him as if he frightened them. His face was grave, almost stern. He gestured round him at the cave and its contents.

'Everything,' he said.

In silence, and with great speed, they began making a heap of furniture, blankets, clothes, and food on the floor near the back of the cave. Each article was handed to Todd as he stood beside the growing pile, and he sprinkled each with paraffin before adding it to the heap. The place began to stink. The candles burned steadily on until, last of all, the table was heaved to the top of the mass of stuff. Then Todd set them at the four corners of the cave, where they glowed thinly in the darkness.

When it was all done, Todd stood back, with the can of paraffin in his hand.

'I'll do the rest. Randy, you go outside with Carter and wait for me in the gully. I won't be long.'

They went quickly, hurrying away to the mouth of the cave. As they went, they looked back, and saw Todd going to the boy, the can of paraffin in his hand.

They waited in the gully for what seemed a long time. Both felt cold. They noticed, even in their preoccupation, that the wind had grown much stronger. It moved across their bare arms and faces in sluggish gusts, cooling their sweat and making them shiver. Carter's teeth began to chatter. Both fixed their gaze expectantly on the patch of darkness which concealed the mouth of the cave.

Suddenly the cliff face was slashed with a sheet of orange flame. It died instantly, was replaced by utter blackness, then silently burst out again. This time it remained visible for several seconds, and against it they both saw the black figure, thin and fantastic as a paper cut-out against the orange. Again there was blackness, and then another burst of colour which this time did not waver or die away, but leapt and expanded like a gigantic blossom on the rock face. The black silhouette hovered in its heart for a further moment, then flashed down and out of sight. A moment later Todd came scrambling and sliding down the slope towards them, and fell into the grass at their feet. Randy clutched at him. He was dripping with sweat and heaving with shuddering breaths. They crouched together, raising fearful faces, and watched the huge orange and yellow light spraying the cliff above them. By now they could hear it, a deep hissing roar which filled the humid air like the sea. The light leapt above them as if it were threatening to spill out and engulf them. As they watched it, it seemed to swell, a huge ragged ball of fire with frayed edges like petals. Sharp cracks, like gunfire, came from it, and an increasing roar and splutter rose triumphantly into the silence.

Randy suddenly leapt to his feet, dragging Todd with him. He began to shout something which they could not hear above the tumult, but when they looked at him, faintly illuminated by the huge light above them, they saw that he was starting to dance – a mad, exultant dance, in which he leapt, stamped, flung his arms out and whirled among the bushes. His dark hair swung about his face as he stooped forward and then arched his body back in this furious dancing.

In a moment Carter had joined him. They whirled together, spun round, leapt high in the air, then dashed themselves together again. Todd, sick and staggering, began to dance too. He flew unsteadily round them; he grabbed a hand here, an elbow there, touched a cheek, a back, brushed a thigh. He drew them against his body, flung himself away from them, fell on his knees with his face in the earth, then scrambled up and dashed at them again.

Suddenly the noise above them changed. At first the roar of the flames seemed to deepen and to fill out; then, motionless and crowing for breath, they realised that what they were hearing was, in fact, a totally different sound – that of earth and rock stirring, shifting, starting to slide forward in a huge crumbling mass. Fascinated, they clung unsteadily to one another, and stared upwards to see the silhouette of the cliff top, black against the sky, rear up a little, crumble, and break off. A few small pebbles and pieces of baked earth began to bound down towards them and to explode into the grass at their feet. Silently, they began to shrink back, moving away across the gully until they were crouched together against the opposite cliff face. The fire burned on, brilliant in the dark rock, but the whole face of the cliff was now in motion. A great slab of rock near its top, roughly illuminated by the reflected light of the flames, began to rear itself up preparatory to starting its descent. They watched it stir, tilt itself, hang for a moment as if undecided, and then begin to move with gathering speed down the face of the quarry. As if it had started a general movement with it came smaller rocks, pebbles, sheets of earth, which moved down with it and gathered speed in an increasing roar of sound.

The three of them crouched back against the rock face. The ball of fire burned on undiminished. Then, slowly, it seemed to shrink, to flatten itself at the top and become rapidly smaller. A spurt of flame and sparks shot from its bottom edge as if sucked out by a huge draught of air. It hovered above them, curled up and out, then retracted itself and disappeared. The flattened circle became a wedge, then a crescent. Suddenly, with a roar it was obliterated. Rocks, earth, and small stones poured over it like a torrent of raging water and cascaded down into the gully. Everything round them seemed to be in tumultuous motion. Small stones bounced on the hard earth and were flung towards them. A shower of loose earth rained against their arms and faces, stinging like hail. A huge sheet of rock landed on its edge, heaved itself up, then tilted over on to its back in a mass of shattered splinters. Todd felt something strike his cheek, and a furrow of burning pain like fire ran down his face and neck. He sprang up.

'Come on,' he shouted. 'We'd better get out of here!'

More stones, larger than before, were being hurled at them. They struck the ground and ricocheted in all directions. Shielding his face, Todd threw himself at the rock face behind them and began to climb. As he heaved himself upwards he felt Randy on one side, Carter on the other, scrambling upwards with him. The stinging hail of stones struck at their thighs, then at their ankles, and finally ceased. Choking, they flung themselves over the top of the cliff and wriggled forward into the grass.

'The car! The car!' shouted Carter. 'Get to the car!'

'We'll have to go round. Come on!'

Randy was already away, running across the uneven ground with arms and legs flying. They scrambled up and raced after him. Behind and below them the roar continued, a little muffled, but still terrifyingly loud.

'There can't be much more to come down,' panted Todd.

'The whole bloody lot's coming down. We'll have to get out of here. The whole place'll turn out to see it.' Carter lurched and sobbed beside him.

They doubled round the end of the quarry, skirting it as closely as they dared. Todd pulled up for a moment and looked across the open ground which lay between them and the car. Half-way across it, just visible in the greenish light, Randy was running swiftly, crouched low. As they stood still, they heard, above their own harsh breathing, the scream of first one siren, then another.

'My God! They're coming already.'

They broke away into the open ground and raced across it towards the car. Randy reached it when they were still only half-way across. He wrenched the door open and leaned inside. They heard the engine start and saw him spring out towards them, waving his arms as if the gesture could add to their speed. Todd got to the open door and fell into the driving seat. He grabbed the wheel, wrenched at the gears, put his foot down and shot away, bouncing over the rough track without waiting to see if they were all safely in. The car flew along the path, bucked round a corner, and shot off down the road away from the quarry towards open country. When they had gone a few hundred yards Todd braked and brought it slewing to a stop.

Randy jumped out into the road and peered back towards

the turning on to the waste ground. They all heard the bells clanging as the first of the fire-engines turned in and stopped. They could still hear the steady rumble of the rock fall.

Randy came back. He climbed in beside Carter and sat shaking in the dark.

'Someone must have seen the fire and telephoned the police.'

'I wonder what made it all come down like that.'

'The heat probably. It was a bloody furnace in there. Everything's as dry as tinder.'

Carter giggled.

Randy said,

'It'll make a marvellous tomb.'

'Yes. No one will ever get in there now. There must be tons of rock on top of it.'

Todd sat with his hands loose on the wheel.

'Come on,' said Randy. He yawned noisily in the dark. 'It's finished. Let's go home.'

Carter sat on the edge of his bed and looked at himself in the wardrobe mirror. It was like looking at a stranger, he thought, and put up a vague hand to touch his filthy face, his disordered hair. The skin of his palm and inside wrist showed clean and startlingly pink against his face. The front of his shirt was streaked with yellowish stains, the sand of the quarry coated his trousers and was caked thickly on his sandals. A long scratch which had bled a little showed lividly down his cheek. His body throbbed with fatigue – his very skin surfaces felt tender with it.

He stood up and, moving away from the mirror, quickly undressed. He wrenched his shirt over his head, kicked off his shoes, and pulled the rest of his clothes off in one convulsive movement. Instantly, as he flung them away from him and stood up naked, he felt restored, refreshed, as if the air moving freely over his skin both cleansed and healed him.

He picked up his shoes, and, holding them carefully at arms length, went over to the window. He shook them out into the darkness, feeling the fine thin stream of sand trickle on to his skin and rush between his fingers, down and away.

He went on standing at the window. He could see little; the night seemed to him unusually dark, and after a while he realised that a small cold wind was blowing on his face and trickling over his chest and shoulders. At first he thought, incredulously, that it was rain. Then, as he leaned there, he heard, far away, the first thunder. The curtain moved sluggishly against his cheek. A door in the house slammed suddenly. The quarry seemed a long way away.

He turned contentedly from the window to go to bed just as the rain began, and the first heavy drops splashed down unnoticed on the dry earth below.

Randy burst into the dark house, switched on the hall light, and flung up his head to listen. Except for his own heart the silence was absolute.

'Hey! You! I'm back,' he shouted, lifting his voice and letting it go out of him like a trumpet. Cocking his head for the reply which did not come, he seemed to hear his voice moving away from him, diminishing through the empty rooms, dying away to a whisper, then going out like a candle. He stood still for a moment longer, waiting.

Then he went quickly to the drawing-room door, flung it open, and switched on the light. There was no one there, nothing but the two chairs arranged by the dark window in a kind of stiff intimacy. He turned away and ran across the hall to the dining-room. When he put the light on here the long strip of table sprang out at him, gleaming between the high backs of the chairs. He began to run through the house, throwing open the doors, switching on all the lights so that he left a blaze behind him as he went. Up the stairs, into this room and that – the empty rooms were left in a bleak glare

245

of light, dusty and surprised, until last of all he came to their door and flung it open and burst in as if he thought he might find them there, crouched like two frightened animals.

The room was empty, and he pulled up, disconcerted, some of his assurance gone. He stood still, panting a little, looking round him. He wondered whether to wait for them. But there did not seem, at the moment, any impetus in him towards further violence.

He went to the chest of drawers and began methodically to turn its contents out on to the floor. Socks, handkerchiefs, shirts, underclothes, all were flung out in armfuls and made a growing pile around his feet. He trod on the things, kicked them away from him so that they spilled out of their folds and trailed over the carpet like the lifeless victims of some indiscriminate act of violence. In the bottom drawer under a heap of her underclothes he found what he was looking for and straightened up with the wallet in his hands. He counted out the notes. Six pounds. Not much, he thought, but enough to be going on with – and despised them for not hiding it more effectively from him. He folded the notes and slipped them into his pocket. As he turned to go, he looked down and saw reddish streaks and smears over many of the scattered clothes around his feet. For a moment he was terrified, because he thought it was blood, and that he was perhaps bleeding from some secret, painless wound. Then he realised that it was only the sand from the quarry which still clung to his shoes, and was reassured.

He went down the stairs in a series of flying leaps. When he got to the bottom, he stood still and looked round him for something to destroy. On the wall hung a large barometer. He gripped it firmly in both hands and gave a tentative pull. There was a grinding sound and some flakes of plaster fluttered down on to the brown linoleum. He braced his foot against the wall, bent his knee, and pulled with all his strength. It came away from the wall with a resounding crack, and he staggered back with it. Behind him hung a huge mirror, framed in mahogany and spotted with tarnish as if with some unpleasant disease. From its surface his own face, pale and unfamiliar, looked uncertainly back at him.

He retreated the length of the hall and hoisted the barometer high above his head. Then, gathering himself on to his toes, he ran at the mirror and smashed the barometer full into the glass with all his strength. Both mirror and barometer smashed under the impact. Glass splintered and cascaded on to the floor in hundreds of tiny splinters. The frame of the mirror swung askew on the wall, holding a few shattered pieces of broken glass in which he could see reflected an odd, broken image of himself – an eye here, half a mouth there, a strand of dark hair streaked across pale skin. He put the barometer down and surveyed the wreckage. Then he dusted himself down, sleeked his hair back with his cupped hands, and left the house.

He almost ran down the drive. He did not turn to look back at the house. He went out into the road and set off towards the town. The air was warm on his face and when he looked up at the sky it seemed to him much darker than usual. He could not see whether there were dark clouds above him, but no stars were visible, and the tops of the trees, usually discernible as a ragged black ridge, merged with the darkness. The road was absolutely silent. A faint droning was the only sound. After a while he recognised it as an aeroplane cruising somewhere above him to his left. It sounded soft and idle in the darkness.

He found the girl where he had often seen her, standing in the darkness of a small lane between two lighted shop fronts, and this time he went up and spoke to her. She came with him immediately and walked obediently beside him, a white blouse, a pale face occasionally turned up to him. When she was undressed and turned to him in the grass, smiling a little, he was amazed at the length of her spine, the smooth arch of her shoulders, and at the glimpse of her breast hanging heavy on her ribs. She took him by surprise, not with

247

her beauty, but with her strength and her compactness. He moved a little towards her, swallowing, hunched against her friendly, contemptuous acquiescence. But she put an arm up and jerked him down on top of her into the grass, and he felt her fingers undoing his clothes with the same deftness with which she had undone her own.

Riding her precariously as she bucked beneath him like a recalcitrant horse he saw, without realising that he saw, the huge slow drops of rain sliding down on to them through the leaves. He did not feel them for a long time, although they struck his bare back like drumsticks on a drum. When he became aware of them, and of the thunder rumbling in the distance, he lifted his head from her for a moment and saw the rain slanting down the shaft of light from the street lamp in the road and falling on to her scattered hair.

They lay together, curled like animals in the grass. The rain fell in a furry mist on to her shoulder and speckled its smoothness with minute droplets of drifting moisture. It looked like a cloud of tiny insects. Randy thought briefly of the quarry. He pulled her soft body against him, deliberately rough, so that she cried out because he was hurting her. He went on gripping her, enjoying the sensation of her flesh shrinking under his fingers as he tried to exorcise the hurt the boy had done to him.

Todd's mother looked like a child in her skimpy oatmeal coat. From where he stood at the far end of the platform Todd could see her waiting patiently in a sea of luggage. She was hatless, and her small head, dark against the light coat, gleamed like silk. Todd turned away, and hunched himself against the thin rain blowing in under the station roof. He looked down the length of gleaming rail which ran away out of sight as it rounded the corner. The trees, heavy with moisture, sagged against the grey sky. Their outlines were in constant sluggish motion as they were swayed by the gusts of wind. Todd turned the collar of his mackintosh up round his neck and began walking slowly away towards the end of the platform. A small boy, his brown hair sleeked and dark in the rain, squatted patiently by the railings. His navy mackintosh trailed round his legs into the mud. He looked up at Todd with bright brown eyes, then away again. Todd stood beside him and kicked idly at the ground.

'Train-spotting?'

'Yes. I've got quite a lot.' He held his notebook up for a moment and then thrust it away again into the recesses of his mackintosh.

'It's a bit wet, isn't it?'

'I don't mind.'

They looked away down the line. The rain, persistent and chilling, blew against them.

The boy said,

'Are you catching the train?'

'Yes.'

'Where are you going?'

'To Italy.'

The boy cocked his head up with interest.

'All the way by train?'

'No. We're going to London and staying overnight. Then flying.'

The boy said wistfully,

'I've never been in an aeroplane.'

'You haven't missed much.'

'What's it like?'

'Not half as interesting as a train. Most of the time you're above the clouds so that it's like looking down at a lot of cotton wool, and when you're not, it's just like looking down at a map.'

'Oh,' the boy said politely. He thought it over. 'All the same, I'd like to try it. To see for myself, you know.'

'Wouldn't you like to go to Italy?'

'Not really, thank you. I mean, I suppose it's jolly interesting and all that, but what I'd like most would be the bit in the plane.'

They went on looking down the track. Presently the boy turned to look behind them.

'I say,' he said, 'are those your people down there? They seem to be waving.'

Todd looked too.

'Yes, they are, aren't they. I'd better go. Good-bye.'

'Good-bye,' said the boy. 'I hope you have a good time,' he added kindly.

'Thank you. I expect I shall.'

Mrs Gascoigne stopped waving as he approached. When he came up to her she said crossly,

'Todd darling, I wish you wouldn't wander away like that. The train's due any minute, and Mark will want you to help him with the luggage.'

'Sorry. Where is he?'

'Getting a paper. He's been ages.'

Todd looked past her and saw Savory's tall figure approaching unhurriedly.

'It's all right, he's coming.'

Mrs Gascoigne shivered.

'It's so damn cold on this beastly station. Thank God we're getting away. At least Italy should be warm.'

'I thought you didn't like heat. Haven't you had enough of it recently?'

'I thought I had, but it's been raining for a fortnight, ever since the weather broke, and I've had enough of it. Oh Mark, darling – there you are. You've been ages.'

'I am so sorry, Clare. I was getting you these.'

He held out a large box of chocolates, wrapped in transparent paper and finished with a ribbon bow which was darkly spotted with rain.

She took them and began to say something, but the train, rumbling into the station, drowned her voice. They all began piling the cases into an empty compartment. A porter appeared to help, and had to be tipped. None of them had any change and in the end Savory leaned out of the window and thrust a ten-shilling note into his hand just as the train moved away from the platform.

Mrs Gascoigne sat down and began peeling off her gloves.

'What frightful extravagance – ten shillings! You needn't have given him anything. He only put one case in. You and Todd did all the rest.'

He stood in front of her with his legs straddled against the movement of the train. His narrow dark coat made him look immensely tall. He shrugged his shoulders and spread out his gloved hands in a gesture of mock submission.

'After all,' he beamed, 'tomorrow is our wedding day. We can afford to be generous, can we not?'

She shivered, huddling herself into her thin coat.

'Thank God we're off at last. All that rain was beginning to get on my nerves. Todd, can't you shut that window? The rain's blowing in.'

Todd was standing with his head and shoulders thrust far out of the window and did not seem to hear her.

'Oh dear,' she said anxiously. 'Surely he shouldn't lean so far out. Do tell him, Mark.'

Savory sat down beside her and spread out his long legs. He reached out for her hand and patted it soothingly before tucking it away under his arm.

'Don't worry about him, Clare. He's all right. You really must try not to worry so much about everything. Sit still and relax.'

'Dear Mark,' she said. She hesitated, then allowed her head to rest gently on his shoulder. 'I'm so glad we're off at last. Everything's going to be wonderful, I know it is.'

He looked down at her face, very pale against the dark cloth of his coat. She did not see the small proprietary smile which momentarily curled the corners of his long mouth.

Todd braced his shoulder against the edge of the window and let the gusts of wind and rain blow straight into his face.

As they slid out of the station he saw the boy standing with his arm raised to him as if in salute, and he threw his own arm up and out in a gesture of recognition and farewell. They looked at each other, unsmiling and grave, as they drew rapidly apart. A gust of rain blew between them, the train rounded the corner, and the figure was gone. The train began to gather speed as the track circled the town, skirting the meadows which surrounded the outlying houses, and then straightened away into a patch of comparatively open country. Todd shut his eyes and let the rain gather on his skin and trickle over his mouth and chin. The steady motion of the train, its very roar and rattle, seemed to be centred in his own body. He abandoned himself to it, and let it whirl him on and away.

The heavy sky drooped between the damp green trees. The rain beat rhythmically on his skin, and he kept his eyes tightly closed so that he should not see the irregular outline of the quarry flash up between the trees. It was a long way away, but still visible across the open ground.